CROSSED QUILLS

Also by Carola Dunn
in Large Print:

Miss Hartwell's Dilemma
Requiem for a Mezza
Two Corinthians
The Winter Garden Mystery

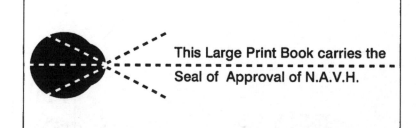

This Large Print Book carries the
Seal of Approval of N.A.V.H.

CROSSED QUILLS

Carola Dunn

G.K. Hall & Co. • Thorndike, Maine

Published in 1999 by arrangement with Zebra Books, an imprint of Kensington Publishing Corp.

G.K. Hall Large Print Romance Series.

The text of this Large Print edition is unabridged.
Other aspects of the book may vary from the original edition.

Set in 16 pt. Plantin.

Printed in the United States on permanent paper.

Library of Congress Cataloging-in-Publication Data

Dunn, Carola.
    Crossed quills / Carola Dunn.
      p.   cm.
    ISBN 0-7838-8770-1 (lg. print : hc : alk. paper)
    1. Large type books.   I. Title.
   [PR6054.U537C76   1999]
   823'.914—dc21
                                     99-41967

CROSSED QUILLS

1

"Brilliant!" sighed Wynn, tossing the *Political Register* onto the table at his elbow. He leaned back in his chair and reached for his glass of brandy, a superb pre-Revolution vintage. "I'd give my right arm to write like that."

"If you gave your right arm," pointed out the Honorable Gilbert Chubb, "you wouldn't be able to write at all."

Wynn grinned, shaking his head at Chubby's invincible literalism. "My left arm, then. Don't you agree that Prometheus is brilliant? His arguments are well-reasoned yet pithy, both incisive and persuasive. Whereas Cobbett's language is far too incendiary to be taken seriously by anyone but rabble-rousers and the starving masses. Just listen to this bit here."

Chubby groaned as Wynn picked up the *Register* again, the shilling edition. He no longer had to be satisfied with the twopenny pamphlet edition, reduced in size from the newspaper to avoid the stamp tax which put it beyond the reach of the poor.

"No, please!" Chubby begged. "I don't mind listening to your speeches, old chap, but I'll be damned if I'll sit still for any more Prometheus, however pithy."

"My efforts only make you laugh." Wynn kicked gloomily at the nearest of the sheets of close-written foolscap scattered on the hearth-rug.

"I didn't laugh."

"You sniggered. I heard you. I don't blame you, mind. There's no denying that the style I developed to write those wretched Gothic romances is as unsuitable for a maiden speech to the House of Lords as a nightshirt in a ballroom. Somehow I just can't seem to keep out the melodrama and bombast."

"Seems to me," said Chubby judiciously, "you were a devilish sight happier writing your romances than you have been since your great-uncle popped off and made you Viscount Selworth."

Wynn glanced around the cosy library, walled with calf-bound books; the solid, old-fashioned oak, beech, and cherry wood furniture gleaming in the light of a dozen wax candles; the fire blazing on the hearth. How could he regret inheriting Kymford? His books — exciting, amusing, and distinctly bawdy — though popular had never afforded more than a meagre supplement to his stepfather's meagre benefice.

Yet he and his family had never been without food or clothes or a roof over their heads. They had even scraped up enough to give his eldest sister a Season on the fringes of Society. In spite of gowns turned, made over, and re-trimmed, Albinia had married well, into an ancient if untitled family.

In fact, they had fared splendidly compared to a large proportion of Britain's people, workless and hungry since the end of the war. Now, having inherited a seat in Parliament along with the Selworth title and fortune, Wynn was eager to do his best for his fellow-countrymen.

"Happy or not," he said, "I shan't have a hope of a serious career in politics if anyone gets wind of my authorship of such lamentably unserious tales."

"*I* shan't tell," Chubby assured him.

"No one else knows — except my publisher, naturally — but I can't risk writing any more. The last romance by Valentine Dred will appear in a month or so. It was fun while it lasted, but it's speeches for me from now on."

Wearily, he bent down to gather up his latest literary effort. He crumpled the sheets together and tossed them on the fire. The words he had struggled over flared up. Black cinders floated up the chimney.

"Tell you what," said Chubby, looking pleased with himself, "you want to get Prometheus to help you with that speech. I daresay the fellow could turn it out in a trice, just the way you want it."

"Prometheus is dead."

"Dammit, he can't be!" Chubby protested. "The stuff you read me was all about the universal suffrage petitions and Prinny getting shot

9

at in the Mall. That happened only last week, the twenty-eighth of January, you said. A fine state of affairs when people make excuses for people firing at the Prince Regent!"

"You were listening?" Wynn said in mock surprise. "You're right, of course, but so am I."

"Now you're talking in riddles," his friend complained. "What the deuce do you mean? Either a chap's dead or he ain't."

"Not Prometheus. He's chained to a rock for eternity with an eagle eating his liver, as punishment for giving fire to mankind."

"A load of rot, those Greek stories. Stands to reason, he'd die."

"But he didn't."

"Cut line, Wynn, do. Maybe that Prometheus is still alive chained to a rock somewhere, but you're not telling me he writes articles for William Cobbett's 'twopenny trash'!"

Wynn laughed. "All right. 'Prometheus' was commonly known to be the pen-name of Benjamin Lisle, the Radical M. P. Lisle died last year, but Prometheus continues to write — as you pointed out — on current events. No one knows who has taken on the pseudonym. Therefore, I can't approach the gentleman in question to beg his assistance with this devilish speech."

The speech lay in abeyance for the following fortnight as Wynn set himself to entertain Chubby, his first guest at Kymford. New to the dignities and responsibilities of a noble land-owner, he enjoyed showing off his farms, orchards, woods, and coverts.

He was also glad of the opportunity to consult his friend. Mr. Chubb, heir to a baron, had been brought up to understand the management of a large estate. Though by no means the brightest star in the firmament, he had an almost instinctive grasp of such esoteric (to Wynn) subjects as drainage and crop rotation. He knew almost as much about sheep and cattle as about horses.

"M'father's more of a country squire, you know, than a member of the Ton," he said apologetically, as they halted their mounts by a gate, to gaze out over a field striped with green shoots of winter wheat. "He'd rather spend his blunt on a new breed of milch-cow than on Weston's tailoring — for himself or for me."

Wynn glanced from Chubby's neat but modest brown riding coat, buckskin breeches, and serviceable riding boots, to his own shabby version of the same. He laughed ruefully.

"I've been far too busy moving the family from the rectory to Kymford, exploring the place, and working on my speech to spare a thought for new clothes. I daresay I shall have to dress up to address the House of Lords, if I'm ever satisfied enough with the damn thing to present it."

"You'll have to fig yourself out decently anyway, if your sister's to make her curtsy to

11

Society this spring."

"Millicent won't need me to squire her about. Mama will stay here to look after my stepfather and the children, but Albinia's taking on the whole business, bless her. Debenham is all the escort they will need. My part is just to frank her, which I can afford to do in style now."

"Don't you believe it," Chubby warned. "Mrs. Debenham and Miss Warren will expect you to do the pretty, too, take my word for it. Thank heaven I haven't any sisters."

"If you had, you might not find yourself so tongue-tied around young females, old fellow. Though, Lord knows, Millicent seldom lets anyone get a word in edgewise. What a chatterbox!"

"That's all right. It means I don't have to try to come up with something to say to her."

"Well, I'll be damned if I'm going to dance attendance on the chit, though I'll keep an eye on her until she finds her feet. I'll be too busy with Parliament. Balls and routs and Venetian breakfasts — what a waste of time! Let's ride on. So the land looks to you to be in good heart? You think my bailiff is competent?"

They returned to topics more interesting than clothes and come-outs. Wynn's great-uncle had been an old-fashioned but conscientious landlord. Something of a recluse, long outliving the rest of his immediate family, he had plowed the profits from his rents back into the soil. The farms belonging to Kymford were prosperous, the lesser tenants well housed, and there were funds in Consols besides.

The late Viscount Selworth had kept the early Jacobean manor house in good condition, without attempting to turn it into a mansion. Not wasting his money on building fine porticos or changing casements to sash windows, he had instead installed modern conveniences such as water closets and a closed stove in the kitchen. Comfortable if not smart, to a large family from a small rectory the house seemed the height of luxury.

All in all it was an inheritance to be proud of. Wynn was duly proud, and grateful.

Gratitude to Providence for his good fortune made him all the more anxious to help those less fortunate. His tenants' lot might be improved by the cautious and gradual introduction of the up-to-date agricultural methods Chubby suggested, but they were not in dire need.

"But half the population is destitute," he explained to Albinia some two weeks later.

He had brought Millicent up to London to prepare for her first Season. Persuaded, somewhat against her will, that she was tired from the journey, she had been bundled off to bed for a rest before dinner, leaving her elders to a comfortable cose. George Debenham was out on business, so Wynn was closeted with his favorite sister.

Albinia was, in fact, his only full sister, the rest of his siblings being the offspring of his mother and the Reverend Ernest Warren. Six years Wynn's junior, Mrs. Debenham was a pretty, lively young matron of four-and-twenty summers, with fair hair, blue eyes, and a round, rosy-cheeked face. She had left her two little boys in the country, with their paternal grandparents, to come up to Town and present her half-sister to the Polite World.

Now she looked in dismay at her brother and said, "You are not going to make speeches at me, are you, Wynn dear? I know there is a great deal of poverty, and George and I do what we can to relieve the paupers in our part of the country, I assure you. George says, the need is too great for private charity to suffice."

"Exactly," Wynn exclaimed, jumping up and striding the length of the elegant drawing room. "Nothing will suffice as long as the laws remain unchanged. The Government must be persuaded to act, to lower taxes on necessities and —"

"Wynn, you are speechifying!"

He turned back towards her with a sheepish grin. "Sorry, Bina." Running his hand through hair as fair as hers, he dropped back onto the sofa beside her. "The thing is, I'm a member of the House of Lords now."

"Heavens, so you are! You mean to take your seat?"

"Of course. It's my duty to involve myself in

politics since I believe those in power are —"

"Speech!" Albinia protested yet again.

"Speech is the trouble. If I'm to have any influence at all, it's very important that my maiden speech should be well received. And I just can't seem to get the knack of it."

"Of making a speech? Pray do not practice on me."

"Of writing one, to start with. Dash it, if only Benjamin Lisle were still alive!"

"The Member of Parliament? Why?"

Wynn explained about Prometheus. "Lisle's articles used to be a trifle too inflammatory for my taste, but whoever is using his pen-name writes just the sort of thing I want to say, just the way I want to say it. Only no one knows who he is."

"Why not ask his family?" Albinia suggested. "They must surely have given permission for his pen-name to be used."

"I can't very well intrude upon his widow. She don't know me from the Sheik of Araby."

Albinia smiled. "Perhaps not, but she knows me, and her daughter is a friend of mine."

"Bina, you're gammoning me!"

"I am not. Pippa — Philippa — Lisle came out the same year I did, and in much the same circumstances, the difference being that I was lucky and found George. We were both older than most girls in their first Season, neither of us had *entrée* to the inner circles of the *beau monde,* and we both had to make do and mend.

15

We even used to exchange gowns with each other to enlarge our wardrobes."

"You must have been very good friends," Wynn remarked thoughtfully.

"We were, and we have kept in touch with regular letters ever since. You would have met her if you had deigned to put in an appearance at my aunt's house during my Season."

"Can you imagine how things would have gone at home if Papa had been left alone with the children? Besides, you may have had to make do and mend, my dear, but it was out of the question for me to squander the ready on togging myself out to make a decent appearance in Town."

"At a guess," said Albinia, looking him up and down with amusement, "clothes have not precisely been a priority with you since you *have* been able to afford the proper attire for your new station in life. You will have to acquire a new wardrobe before Millie is ready to go about."

"Oh no, I'm not escorting that little bagpipe to balls and such!"

"Oh yes, you are," Albinia calmly contradicted him, "and as a reward, I shall give you a letter to deliver to Pippa, as an excuse for calling."

"*Lord* Selworth and Mr. Chubb, madam." Sukey, the plump, middle-aged maid, beamed with delight. After a few visits of condolence on

16

the demise of Mr. Lisle, the nobility had ceased to call at Sweetbriar Cottage.

As conversation stilled in the small parlor, crowded with afternoon callers, Pippa looked round in surprise. Selworth? His lordship must be related to Albinia — which did not explain his presence here in this out-of-the-way Buckinghamshire village.

Yes, that flyaway flaxen hair was the image of Bina's. A close relative, then, perhaps the elder brother she used to talk about in such worshipful tones. She had mentioned a title in a distant part of the family. The two must have somehow come together.

Lord Selworth was slim, and not much above middling height, shorter than his companion, who was tall and lanky, with an incongruously round face. Both wore riding dress, with mud-splashed boots. Mr. Chubb, after a quick, nervous glance about the room, appeared to find a peculiar fascination in the toes of those boots.

Bashful, poor fellow, Pippa diagnosed. Prematurely thinning hair doubtless added to his diffidence.

While these thoughts sped through her mind, her mother had risen to greet the unexpected visitors with her usual placid friendliness.

"Forgive our intrusion, ma'am," Lord Selworth responded with an attractive smile, "and our dirt. We happened to be passing nearby and I was commissioned by my sister, Mrs. Debenham, to carry a letter to your

17

daughter. Miss Lisle is a friend of long-standing, I collect."

"Yes, indeed. Pippa, my love."

Passing nearby? Whence and whither, Pippa wondered as she rose to make her curtsy. The village was well off any beaten track, lost in beechwoods at the back of beyond. And she had received a letter from Bina only a fortnight since, she recalled.

"And this is our vicar, Mr. Postlethwaite, Lord Selworth," Mrs. Lisle continued, then turned away to say, "Mr. Chubb, do let me make you known to my younger daughter, Kitty."

Lord Selworth bowed to Pippa and exchanged bows with Mr. Postlethwaite. The vicar looked decidedly discomposed. A perennial suitor of Pippa's, he was a pleasant, worthy gentleman she occasionally considered accepting. Never for long, though. He would be shocked to the core should she ever dare reveal her unorthodox views on the Established Church.

However, he clearly looked upon Lord Selworth as a rival. Ridiculous, when Pippa had so far exchanged no more than a how-do-you-do with Bina's brother, who would doubtless be on his way after a polite five minutes, never to be seen again.

A pity, she thought wistfully. While he was not precisely handsome, at close quarters his lordship's smile was simply devastating. Pippa could not help returning it.

"You have a letter for me, Lord Selworth?"

"Oh, yes." He felt in the pocket of his dark brown riding coat — on the verge of fraying at the cuffs, she noted. His title must have descended to him without a fortune. "Dash it, where did I put the thing?" He felt in the opposite pocket, then in the inside breast pocket. "Ah, here it is."

Taking the folded missive, Pippa set it aside for later perusal. Odd that he should have had to fumble for it, when it was his sole reason for calling. "Mrs. Debenham is well, I trust, sir?" she said.

"In fine fettle, Miss Lisle. She is looking forward to the coming Season."

"She is to bring out your sister, is she not? She mentioned Miss Millicent Warren's come-out in her last letter. Has she gone up to London already?"

How awkward it was to make polite conversation standing up in the cramped parlor! Pippa's eyes were on a level with his chin — a strong, determined chin — and she was too close to glance up without appearing arch. On the other hand, not raising her gaze must make her look timidly demure, equally at odds with her character. She wished she might invite him to sit down, but the vicar clung tenaciously to her side and there were not seats enough for all.

Ah, the Misses Bradshaw were half-reluctantly taking their leave. The news of Lord Selworth's visit would be all over the village within the half hour.

"Excuse me, my lord, I must see Miss Bradshaw and Miss Dorothy out." Pippa did not want the old dears to feel slighted by her paying more attention to a nobleman, a fleeting acquaintance, than to her neighbors. Daughters of the previous vicar, they lived in greatly reduced circumstances.

Several minutes passed in the presentation of a jar of strawberry jam and effusive thanks therefor. Returning from the front door across the tiny hall, Pippa paused on the parlor's threshold.

His lordship and his friend had taken the Misses Bradshaws' chairs. The speechless Mr. Chubb sat next to Kitty. She was being kind to him in between making arrangements with her friend Mary, Squire Ruddock's daughter, to visit the Hall to play duets upon the new pianoforte.

Across from them, gazing fixedly at Kitty, Mary's brother John appeared to be suffering from an acute attack of indigestion. He had recently taken to attempting to ape Lord Byron's romantically brooding manner, without much success to date. Kitty was worth gazing upon, though, thought her partial sister. The amber shade of her high-waisted kerseymere gown complemented her dark curls beautifully, and her rosy cheeks never looked sallow.

Lord Selworth, seated next to Mrs. Lisle, conversed courteously with his hostess and Mrs. Stockton, the apothecary's stout wife. He smiled again at Pippa, who was hesitating in the doorway. Her heart did a most peculiar flip-flop.

Drat the man, did he realize how disturbing his smile was? Could he not keep a straight face? Still, he would be leaving any minute. He and Mr. Chubb had no doubt awaited her return to the parlor to make their farewells, to avoid adding to the crush in the minuscule entry. If Pippa returned to her seat beside the vicar, which she was most unwilling to do, she would only have to pop up again to say goodbye.

But, though the gentlemen rose politely when she failed to sit down at once, Lord Selworth showed no sign of departing. Rather than keep them on their feet, Pippa subsided perforce.

She was forced to listen to a low-voiced soliloquy from Mr. Postlethwaite, on the subject of Town Bucks and their extravagant, self-indulgent habits. Never had she had less patience with that good man.

Mary completed her business with Kitty and dragged her brother away to escort her home. Mrs. and Miss Welladay and Miss Jane Welladay, wife and daughters of a yeoman farmer, stopped by on their way home from market, to show off some French merino bought at a bargain. Leaving, they bore off

Mrs. Stockton with them. Lord Selworth and Mr. Chubb stayed and stayed. So, determinedly, did the vicar.

Conversation becoming general, the weather for the past three months was discussed in excruciating detail. Pippa was nearly ready to scream when the maidservant from the vicarage arrived with a message from Mrs. Postlethwaite, desiring her son's presence at home.

"I shall be glad to set you in the right way, my lord," said Mr. Postlethwaite in a last-ditch effort to outflank his enemy. "The lanes hereabouts are lamentably confusing to the uninitiated."

"I thank you, sir," Lord Selworth replied cordially, "but Chubb and I are in no hurry. That is, we don't object to going a little astray, seeing something more of the fine countryside in this part of the world."

The vicar left, disgruntled.

Pippa's suspicions redoubled. To be sure, the country was beautiful — in June. Now, at the end of February, it was a study in sodden, muddy sepias and duns. No flush of green yet tipped the beech trees' boughs; thorny hedgerows dripped, honeysuckle and dog-rose a distant dream; the bottoms were mired ankle-deep. Walking abroad was a penance, riding no pleasure. What was Lord Selworth up to?

She soon found out. He turned to her mother and said coaxingly, "Mrs. Lisle, I must confess to being here under false pretences. I have come to speak to you about Prometheus."

Her head whirling, Pippa gripped her hands tightly in her lap. Had the Government sent him? Surely William Cobbett had not given away Prometheus' true identity. However much trouble he was in, blamed for civil disorders all over the nation, the publisher, editor, and chief contributor to the *Political Register* would not betray his friends.

Cobbett was a true and generous friend, who paid liberally for Prometheus' articles despite his own financial woes. Without that income, the Lisles would be in sore straits — and the income would cease if the world discovered who had taken over Benjamin Lisle's pen-name.

Cobbett could not afford to go on publishing articles the world did not take seriously. How much influence would they exert if it became known that the author was a mere female?

And a youthful female, at that!

2

"Prometheus?" said Mrs. Lisle cautiously. Avoiding Lord Selworth's eye, she tucked a graying curl under her lilac-ribboned cap.

Pippa regarded her mother with affection. Mama's calm nature, especially in contrast to Papa's quicksilver intellect, led some to consider her slow-witted. Not so her elder daughter.

Mr. Lisle's political career had been founded on the bedrock of his wife's common sense and exceptional ability to hold household. Too principled to accept the perquisites of his seat in the House of Commons, the sinecures and outright bribes offered for his support, he had relied on her to contrive on their small income. She had succeeded to admiration. Their home was a modest but comfortable haven whither he retreated every weekend during the Parliamentary sessions.

She had taught their daughters herself, not only the housewifely arts, but such ladylike accomplishments as music, fine needlework, watercolors, and dancing. It was not Mama's fault that Pippa had not "taken" during her one scrimped and saved-for London Season.

Skinny and dark when the fashion was for

well-rounded blondes, more interested in politics and rhetoric than fashion and gossip, Pippa herself was to blame. For Mama's sake, she had done her best to conform, and Mama had never reproached her for failing to catch a husband. Papa was pleased, since, escaping with relief back to Sweetbriar Cottage, his daughter resumed the making of fair copies of his speeches and articles.

As his health deteriorated, Pippa had taken more and more responsibility for the content and phrasing of his work. When he went to his reward in the Afterlife in which he disbelieved, what more natural than that she should take on the mantle of Prometheus?

Mama would never give away the secret, neither on purpose nor inadvertently. Nor would Kitty, as practical and commonsensical as their mother in spite of being the prettiest girl in the entire neighborhood.

Pippa glanced at her young sister. Kitty's sparkling brown eyes met hers in a look brimming with merriment. At the same time, she continued to tell Mr. Chubb quite seriously about the poultry which were her especial care. The bashful young man seemed interested, and even ventured a question. Dear Kitty had quickly set him at his ease.

Lord Selworth, to the contrary, had lost his appearance of ease. Under Mama's questioning gaze, he ran his hand through his hair with an air of harassed uncertainty. He opened his mouth, but no words issued forth.

"Prometheus?" Mrs. Lisle asked again.

"Yes, ma'am. I know your late husband wrote under that name — I must offer my condolences, belated, I fear. A sad loss to the nation!"

"And to his family," the widow said with quietly sorrowful dignity.

"Of course. I . . . er . . . You are aware, I daresay, that someone else is now employing Mr. Lisle's pseudonym?"

"Certainly. The person concerned very properly requested my permission."

"Then you know who he is?" Lord Selworth enquired eagerly.

"I regret that I am not at liberty to divulge the name."

His lordship's face fell, but he rallied. "Perhaps I can change your mind, ma'am, when you hear why I wish to approach the gentleman."

Mrs. Lisle's mouth twitched, and she cast a quizzical glance at her elder daughter. For an anxious moment, Pippa feared her mother would be unable to repress the chuckle quivering on her lips.

However, with assumed gravity she replied, "I doubt it, Lord Selworth, but you are at liberty to try."

He smiled at her. "You are laughing at me, I see. I expect more persuasive men than I have badgered you in vain. But perhaps their reasons were less . . . altruistic. I hope you will consider my aims altruistic."

"Tell me."

Once more his lordship ran his hand through his hair, increasing its likeness to an ill-made hayrick. As if suddenly recalling its unfortunate tendency to go its own way, he then hastily smoothed it down, with a rueful sidelong peek at Pippa. It was her turn to try not to chuckle.

"May I enlist you on my side, Miss Lisle?" he begged.

"It is not my place to enlighten you as to Prometheus' identity, sir," she said, adding frankly, "I cannot imagine any circumstances which would change that, but I own I should be glad to hear what you have to say."

"Very well. First, I must tell you that I have unexpectedly and very recently inherited the viscountcy, from a distant relative with whom my immediate family had lost touch. I had no idea I was so close in line to the succession."

"Indeed!" said Mrs. Lisle skeptically.

"Albinia certainly never knew, Mama. Lord Selworth's father died many years ago, did he not, sir?"

"Near twenty, ma'am. My eldest half-sister is eighteen. My mother has too large a second family to keep track of her first husband's relatives, and my stepfather is a rather unworldly clergyman. I knew, of course, that my great-grandfather was titled, but the connection was too distant to be of pressing interest."

27

Mrs. Lisle was still disbelieving. "You never wondered?"

"Mama, pray do not catechise Lord Selworth!" said Pippa, laughing.

"No, no, Miss Lisle, I have no objection. Convincing you of my credentials must include explaining why I have no inbred sympathy with the landowning classes. To tell the truth, I had little time to fret over my noble relatives, and no inclination to apply to them for assistance." A flush stained his fair skin. "Since I attained years of discretion, I have been busy helping to support my family."

"Too proud to ask for help, yet ashamed of working for a living," Mrs. Lisle observed dryly.

"Not at all!" exclaimed Lord Selworth with considerable indignation, his color still further heightened.

Though her mother appeared satisfied, Pippa wondered if it was the kind of work the viscount had done which embarrassed him, rather than the fact of working. If he were a character in one of the Gothic romances that she found an agreeable change from polemics, he would have taken to the highways as a Gentleman of the Road.

With regret, she decided a career as a highwayman was sadly improbable. Perhaps he had been employed by one of those middlemen or jobbers whom Papa and Mr. Cobbett regarded as abominable parasites.

Maybe that was the only work he could find,

she thought charitably.

"Anyway, that is all in the past," his lordship said hurriedly. "Now I am a peer; I have a seat in the House of Lords. I want to do what I can to help the poor, but I cannot expect to wield any influence unless I make an impression with my maiden speech. I have tried to compose a suitable oration," he confessed, "but I made a mull of it."

"So you wish to consult Prometheus?" Pippa guessed.

"I have long admired his writings. I hope he will realize that, quite apart from the injury to my *pride*" — he gave Mrs. Lisle a wry look — "it will do the cause no good if I stand up and make a cake of myself."

"Speaking of cake," Kitty put in, "do you wish me to make tea, Mama?"

"Pray do, my love. You will drink tea, gentlemen?"

"Thank you, ma'am, we shall be delighted."

Mr. Chubb mumbled something indistinguishable, turned crimson, and muttered semi-audibly, "Give you a hand, Miss Catherine."

Kitty smiled at him and said, "How kind of you, sir."

A besotted look on his face, he followed her out. Pippa swallowed a sigh. Her sister had made another instant conquest.

Lord Selworth frowned after his friend, but quickly returned to business. "I am sorely in need of Prometheus' advice, Mrs. Lisle. Naturally I expect to pay for his assistance."

"No matter how much you are willing to pay, sir," Mrs. Lisle warned him, "Prometheus would never write or help to write anything not wholeheartedly in accord with my husband's principles."

"Nor would I ask it of him, ma'am. I fancy my aims agree with those of the late Mr. Lisle and the gentleman who has stepped into his shoes, or picked up his quill, I should say."

Mrs. Lisle nodded approvingly. "I am delighted to hear it. The poor and voteless have too few champions in the House of Lords."

"Mama!" Pippa exclaimed in alarm. "I think it most unlikely that Prometheus will be willing to unmask, even in so *noble* a cause." Drat, she should not have risked the pun. Being clever might arouse the viscount's suspicions. She must strive to seem feather-witted — yet she could not let Mama make unredeemable promises. "Did not Mr. Cobbett's letter say those horrid Tories are threatening him with imprisonment again?"

"I assure you, Miss Lisle, I should do nothing to endanger Prometheus. His secret would be safe with me. Besides, he is no vitriolic insurrectionist, as Cobbett frequently appears to be. Cobbett's prejudices too often get the better of his common sense, and even drive him to be careless with facts, whereas Prometheus is known for his brilliant use of reasoned argument."

Pippa felt herself blushing at this fervent compliment. "I beg your pardon, sir," she said hastily, hoping he would ascribe her pink face to embarrassment for having misjudged him. "I did not mean to suggest that you would betray Prometheus on purpose."

"Your concern for the gentleman's safety does you credit, Miss Lisle." The viscount's warm smile did nothing to cool her cheeks. "He is a close friend of the family, I collect, or a relative, perhaps?"

To Pippa's relief, her mother drew his lordship's attention. "I have no sons, Lord Selworth," she said, with severity belied by the twinkle in her eye, "nor brothers, nor nephews."

Perfectly true, and perfectly irrelevant.

"I did not intend to probe, ma'am. Or perhaps I did — my apologies. However, it is clear that you are personally acquainted with Prometheus. All I ask is that you set my proposal fairly before him."

"A reasonable request, is it not, Pippa? If you will leave your direction, sir, I shall see that you are notified of the outcome, one way or the other."

"If you think you might have an answer for me by tomorrow, we shall put up at the inn in the village."

"The Jolly Bodger is not known for its comfort, sir," Pippa advised him, trying to discourage him from remaining in the vicinity. "It is little more than a tavern."

"The Jolly Bodger?" Kitty asked cheerfully as she ushered in Mr. Chubb bearing a laden tea-tray. "Are you staying there tonight? Set it down here, if you please, sir. Shall I pour, Mama?"

On receiving an affirmative, she busied herself with cups and saucers, allotting the only two remaining matching sets to the gentlemen.

"Are we staying, Wynn?" Mr. Chubb enquired, passing tea and honey cake. Pippa thought he sounded hopeful.

"The inn is shockingly uncomfortable," she restressed, "and I have heard horrid tales of their dinners."

"You are welcome to dine with us, Lord Selworth, Mr. Chubb," Mrs. Lisle offered, "if you care to dare the other discomforts. We have not room to put you up, alas."

Pippa stared at her mother in dismay. She was positively encouraging the viscount! Surely she did not suppose Pippa was prepared to disclose her secret to him?

He would be incredulous at first. Once convinced of the truth, he would cease to admire and start to wonder at her. Like Dr. Samuel Johnson, he would say, doubtless to himself, being a courteous gentleman, "A woman preaching is like a dog's walking on his hind legs. It is not done well: but you are surprised to find it done at all."

Even if she could trust him to hold his

tongue, of which she was by no means certain, to have him regard her as a nine days' wonder would be painful, she acknowledged. Not that he showed any signs of admiring her for herself. She had no reason to expect it. Nor did she consider him anything out of the common way for a personable gentleman —

Until he smiled, and he was smiling at her now, the dastard!

"You are thoughtful, Miss Lisle," he said in an undertone. Mama was occupied in listening to Mr. Chubb's long, inarticulate utterance of gratitude for her invitation, which Pippa gathered had been accepted while she reflected. "I trust," Lord Selworth continued, "that the presence of two extra mouths at dinner will cause no difficulties?"

Pippa was about to inform him waspishly of her ignorance of such housekeeping details. Realizing he might well enquire as to how she occupied her time if not in womanly domestic tasks, she drowned the words in a gulp of tea.

Her face must have reflected her annoyance, however, for he suggested tentatively, "Shall we cry off? Be honest with me."

It was considerate of him to ask, she told herself sheepishly. Most men would not think twice about the awkwardness of feeding unexpected guests. "I am sure Mama would not have invited you were there any difficulty, sir," she said, her tone cool.

"I fear you are still not persuaded of my innocuous intentions towards your friend. I give you my word, Miss Lisle, no harm shall come to him through me. He has only to refuse my request and not another word shall be said — I shall cease to seek him out. But pray don't deny him the chance to decide for himself."

Pippa had already decided. She wished she could say so without further ado. Since that was impossible, she sighed and promised, "I shall not try to keep Mama from discussing your offer with Prometheus."

Standing at the parlor window, Pippa watched the gentlemen in their top hats and greatcoats tramping down the garden path in the dusk, on the way to take rooms at the Jolly Bodger. Their tethered horses' ears stuck up above the beech hedge, still thickly hung with dead brown leaves.

The dead leaves depressed her. So did the muddy flower beds on each side of the path, though snowdrops bravely strove to raise their heads, battered and splattered by the recent rains, among green spikes of daffodil and papery crocus buds. In spite of their promise of spring, she felt winter would go on forever.

Much as she loved Mama and Kitty, the spice had gone out of life when Papa died.

Her writing — the emotions aroused by the injustices she wrote about — were a palliative, not a remedy. When she laid down her quill and posted the result to Mr. Cobbett, the emptiness returned.

What frightened her was that she saw no end to the desert. Kitty would marry, whether John Ruddock or some other love-struck swain, and go away. Pippa might surrender her hand to Mr. Postlethwaite, but her heart was untouched. Worse, she would have to give up the work which, she sometimes fancied, was all that kept her from running mad.

Would children compensate? She found it impossible to imagine indulging with the vicar in those intimacies necessary to create a family.

The click of the gate latch returned her to the present. She swung back to the lamp-lit room.

"Mama, this is the outside of enough. You know I dare not reveal my authorship."

"It would have looked very singular, my love, had we declined to convey Lord Selworth's proposal. He might have attempted to approach Prometheus in some other way over which we had less control. At the very least his curiosity would be aroused, and by conjecture he might arrive at the truth. He struck me as an intelligent and determined young man."

"Pigheaded! As though a hundred others could not help him equally well — a dozen, at any rate. You are right, of course, but I wish you had insisted on writing with the answer instead of encouraging him to stay by inviting him to dinner!"

Her mother laughed. "I had no choice in the matter once you had abused the Bodger's fare."

"Perhaps that was a mistake," Pippa admitted with a wry grimace. "You will just have to tell him tomorrow that you have spoken to Prometheus, who desired you to convey a refusal."

Mrs. Lisle had opened her workbox as soon as the gentlemen left. She was darning a stocking heel, and her needle flashed back and forth twice before she responded, "Are you so sure you ought to refuse, Pippa?"

"Yes," Pippa said promptly. Lord Selworth had succeeded in shaking her composure without even trying. To work with him would be to endure a constant state of uncomfortable ferment. "Even if I agreed, I expect he would change his mind as soon as he discovered Prometheus is a female. And though he may be *willing* to keep the secret, who can guess whether he is capable of it? Should he let slip only to Mr. Chubb —"

"No fear of Mr. Chubb letting the cat out of the bag," said Kitty, giggling as she glanced up from her hemming. "It was a struggle to extract a single word from him. He is woefully shy."

"With ladies, certainly," Pippa said, "but I daresay he is on easier terms among gentlemen."

"Do you think so?" Kitty enquired with interest. "I hope you are right, for he is quite amiable. He was interested in my chickens, or at least kind enough to seem so, and he helped with the tea-tray, though I fancy he had never before set foot in a kitchen! I hate to picture him going through life with his tongue tied in knots."

"He had more to say for himself than John Ruddock," Mrs. Lisle pointed out tartly. "What a mooncalf the boy is!"

"A veritable nodcock," Pippa agreed, "but we are straying from the point, Mama. I cannot risk telling Lord Selworth that I write the articles, so I must refuse him."

"I suppose so, my love. It is a great pity, for if William Cobbett is imprisoned again and forced to stop publishing the *Register* for a while, the money from Lord Selworth would come in handy."

"I doubt he could pay much. Title and fortune do not always coincide. Did you not notice how shabby his clothes are?"

"Yes," said her mother thoughtfully, needle poised in midair. "It is the more admirable that he wishes to spend part of what he has to ensure a serious reception of his ideas for the relief of the truly poor."

"The viscount may indeed be all that is admirable. The situation remains unchanged. He will have to contrive without my assistance."

"Pippa," said Kitty, "I do not perfectly understand why you cannot help Lord Selworth without his knowing who you are. That you are Prometheus, I mean. He will be in London, after all, and you here, so you will have to write back and forth. You have only to tell him Prometheus chooses to communicate through you,

37

rather than directly."

"He might believe it," Pippa said doubtfully, "given the present threat to Mr. Cobbett." Her resistance began to crumble. With Lord Selworth at a distance, there was no danger to her peace of mind.

"I wonder." Mrs. Lisle's gaze was fixed on an invisible scene. A smile curved her lips. "Yes, it could work. A clever notion, Kitty love, and I see no reason why it should not work even if we were in London."

"Mama!" cried her daughters as one. Kitty's eyes sparkled with excited hope. "We are going to London?" she asked.

"Impossible," Pippa objected. "Lord Selworth would be bound to discover our whereabouts."

"We shall not try to keep it from him. What is important is to give him the impression that *Prometheus* remains in the country."

"Corresponding with his lordship, through me?" Pippa felt a peculiar twist of anticipation. Alarmed, she protested, "But, Mama, he might expect to deal with me in person if we were in Town."

"Very likely, my love."

"I cannot!"

"Mama," Kitty burst out, "can we truly go to London? Is it not horridly expensive?"

"I have been saving, thanks to your sister's contributions. Pippa had her Season, and I have always intended that you should, too. I had thought to wait until next spring — you will be nineteen by then, but better another twelvemonth and another few pounds put by. However . . ." Mrs. Lisle paused dramatically.

"With what Lord Selworth will pay Pippa, we shall have enough?"

"We do not know what he will pay," Pippa reminded her, "and it is not likely to be a great deal."

"I have a better notion." With the air of a fairground conjurer pulling a gold watch from a yokel's hatband, Mrs. Lisle continued. "We shall not ask Lord Selworth for money. We shall tell him Prometheus is so kind a friend of ours that he wishes to be paid with introductions for you girls into the best Society!"

Kitty's face was ecstatic. Pippa could not bear to disappoint her little sister.

Resigning herself to working with the disturbing Lord Selworth, she merely demurred, "Not for me, Mama. My first Season was a disaster, and I do not care to repeat the experience at my advanced age, especially before an audience as critical as the *haut ton*."

"My love, you are much improved in both looks and address since then, and hardly at your last prayers! Still, I do not mean to carp at you. It is for you decide."

Kitty protested, "But it will be horridly unfair, Pippa, if you must work to pay for my pleasure."

"I enjoy wrestling with ideas and words, dearest," Pippa assured her, with a smile, "much more than dancing. And *very* much more than sewing. If you will engage to spare me the wielding of a needle, I shall gladly wield the pen to enable you to take the Ton by storm."

3

"She is as kind as she is pretty," Chubby en-
thused as they turned their horses' heads back
towards the village.

"Kind!" Wynn exclaimed. "I hardly think so.
She was not at all pleased when her mama invited us to dinner, and her warnings about the
inn were obviously designed to drive us away.
But as for 'as kind as she is pretty,' I daresay
you are right, for no one could call Miss Lisle
pretty."

"Oh, Miss Lisle! It's Miss Kitty I mean.
Didn't you notice how she went on talking to
me even though I couldn't think of any clever
compliments? Not prattling on about hats and
gowns, either. She has some very sound ideas
on poultry management."

Wynn grinned. "Does she, indeed?"

"And she let me help her with the tea, too,
though most young ladies would be ashamed to
admit they hadn't enough servants."

"Is Miss Kitty to cook our dinner?" Wynn
demanded in mock alarm.

"I expect she is capable of it, but Sukey, their
maid, does that. They have just the one maid,
and her husband who is gardener and handy-
man, and a woman who comes in to do floors

41

and laundry and such."

"My dear fellow, you disappoint me," Wynn teased. "I was ready to allot the laundry to Mrs. Lisle and the digging and wood-chopping to Miss Lisle."

"Are Mrs. Lisle's hands rough and red?" Chubby asked seriously. "I did not notice that Miss Lisle's face is weathered at all. You say she is not pretty, but I did not think her ill-favored."

"Lord no, she is no antidote. When animated, her face is quite fetching if rather pale, and that simple style of knotting back her hair suits her, but she would not do as the heroine of a romance, you know."

"Oh, your heroines must all be diamonds of the first water, though clad in rags!"

"One must have rags. How is the hero to discern her beauty — or beauties — if not through the holes?"

"I think," said Chubby doggedly, "a neat, plain dress don't hide a girl's beauty. Miss Kitty looked very well in that yellow woollen thing she was wearing, without laces or furbelows *or* holes."

"I cry pax, old chap. Pax!" Wynn begged, laughing. "Let us stipulate that Miss Catherine Lisle is a very pretty chit, and have done. Here is our inn."

The Jolly Bodger was long and low, built of red brick mellowed by age to a rosy hue, criss-crossed by ancient, crooked beams. In the deepening dusk of the cloudy evening, lamp-light shone from small, diamond-paned casement windows. A lantern suspended above the inn sign illuminated a faded picture of a man with an axe over his shoulder. A foaming tankard in his other hand presumably represented jollity, as well as advertising the inn's wares. His expression was indistinguishable.

"What's a bodger?" Chubby asked, dismounting.

"I've not the least notion, except that his trade requires an axe. A headsman, no doubt."

"An executioner? Hang it all, Wynn, what a grim name for an inn!"

"As well call it the Happy Hangman or the Gay Gibbet," Wynn agreed, smothering a smile as he hitched his hired mount to a post. "By Miss Lisle's description, it sounds like a grim place. Still, I don't know that that's what a bodger is," he added, taking pity on his easily gulled friend. "No doubt Miss Lisle will know. I'll ask her this evening."

"I'll ask the landlord tonight," said Chubby, "before we take rooms. Be damned if I'll be able to sleep with an executioner hanging outside my window!"

He pushed open the creaking door, over which was written *Prop. Chas. Bucket.* Wynn followed him, stepping directly into the taproom.

It was a cosy place, despite walls and ceiling blackened by centuries of tobacco and wood-fire smoke. A cheerful fire burned in the grate, its ruddy gleam reflecting from the well-polished pewter tankards in the callused hands of the occupants. The tiny windows which would make the room gloomy in summer now kept out the chill February night.

"It doesn't look bad," Wynn observed, the more convinced that Miss Lisle had done her best to drive him away.

"Ho, landlord!" cried Chubby.

A small, spare man in an apron came through a door at the back of the room. "Chas Bucket at your service, sir," he said genially.

"What's a bodger?"

"A bodger, sir?" Mr. Bucket asked in surprise. "Why, bless your heart, sir, a bodger's a chap what goes out in the beech woods to shape the wood rough-hewn, afore it's took to the cabinetmakers for a-making of chairs and the like."

Listening, Wynn wondered why he had proposed to ask Miss Lisle, in particular, for the information. Unaware that it was a local term for a local craftsman, for some reason he had assumed she would know the answer. He could not recall anything she had said to make him suppose her to be both intelligent and well-informed, yet that was the impression he had of her.

A false impression, possibly. What he could be certain of was her antagonism. She did not want him to work with Prometheus. In fact, she

44

distrusted him and did not want him to discover the writer's identity.

She was downright protective of Prometheus. Could the fellow be a suitor she was in love with? Not the vicar, heaven forbid! Surely she could do better than that prosy bore, even if she was not a diamond of the first water.

With an odd sense of relief, Wynn realized that whatever Prometheus was, his writings proved him no prosy bore. He didn't like to think of her tied to Postlethwaite for life.

If Miss Lisle loved Prometheus, no wonder she was reluctant to entrust his safety to a stranger. Wynn had done his best to reassure her. Though she had surrendered, she had remained deucedly cool, not to say frosty. Best avoid the touchy topic at dinner. What he wanted was a nice, neutral subject.

Bodgers, for instance. Of course, in hindsight, that must be why he had offered to ask her rather than anyone else.

The landlord was waving at a settle in the inglenook. "Tom Bowyer, there, he's a bodger, sir. Mayhap he'll tell you more."

Chubby started towards the inglenook. Wynn reached out and hauled him back.

"All you need to know is that his trade isn't going to give you nightmares."

"I'm interested," Chubby said indignantly, "and my father will be too, if you let me find out. We don't have bodgers in our part of the world, though a fair bit of our timber goes to

45

the furniture workshops."

"My humble apologies! I didn't realize you were in pursuit of enlightenment. Off with you, then, and I'll sort out our accommodations."

"Accommodations, sir?" Chas Bucket sounded distinctly dubious.

"Yes, we'll need a couple of chambers for the night."

"Well, sir, being as how this here do be an inn, not a hedge tavern, I'm bound by law to offer accommodations to any as seeks 'em. But the fac' is, we've only got the one chamber, sir, and it ain't fitting for gentlemen. It's gen'rally carters and drovers what stops here, sir, and that's the truth."

So Miss Lisle had not been cozening him, though it did not mean she had not been anxious to be rid of him. "Let me see it," Wynn said cautiously.

"I'll call the missus."

Mrs. Bucket was a stout, red-faced woman beneath whom the narrow stairs squawked alarmingly. She panted to the top and flung open the nearest door, standing back to let Wynn see.

The chamber was just big enough to contain a vast bed, into which four or five drovers or carters might be fitted nose to toes, and a chest. The ceiling sloped down to a window even tinier than those below. Though not tall, Wynn could only stand upright just inside the door — not that it mattered, since that was the only unoccupied bit of floor.

"'Tis a good featherbed," wheezed Mrs. Bucket behind him, "and I s'll put on clean sheets for your worships."

Wynn had no desire to ride on several miles to find a better hostelry, then ride back and forth again for dinner, in the dark, on unfamiliar roads, and under a sky threatening rain. He could always send word to Mrs. Lisle that he and Chubby would be unable to accept her invitation after all. Yet he found he very much wanted to dine with the Lisles, to talk to Miss Lisle about matters which would not arouse her protective instincts.

At least the chamber looked reasonably clean, whatever the state of the sheets beneath the counterpane. But . . . "No washstand?"

"There do be the pump out back," the landlady advised him.

Wynn shivered. "Sixpence for a basin of hot water in the kitchen," he bargained. "And another sixpence to press our evening clothes."

"Lor' save you, your worship, you don't need to dress up for scrag end o' mutton and cold pease pudden fried up."

Wynn shuddered as a long-forgotten nursery rhyme returned to haunt him:

> Pease pudding hot,
> Pease pudding cold,
> Pease pudding in the pot
> Nine days old.

"Thank you, ma'am, but we are to dine with Mrs. Lisle," he said with relief; then another horrid thought struck him. "And we'll pay extra to have the bed to ourselves."

Mrs. Bucket chuckled, her vast bosom billowing. "Lor' save you, sir," she said again, "I knows better'n to put mucky workingmen in wi' gentry. We've had gentlemen stay afore, when poor Mr. Lisle was alive. 'Tis late in the day for carters or drovers, but any comes by, there's allus the hayloft."

Coming to an agreement on terms, Wynn followed his hostess down to see the horses stabled, and to retrieve the saddlebags and his friend.

Shivering in her shift, Pippa doubtfully regarded her reflection in the mirror. She had hoped the curls Kitty had labored over with a hot iron would make her look less intellectual than her usual severe coiffure. They just made her look like someone else, not herself at all.

"Very pretty, my love," said her mother, coming into the small chamber, already dressed in her Sunday-best gray silk.

"I am not trying to look pretty," Pippa said crossly. "I just want Lord Selworth to believe I am more concerned about my appearance than my mind. But the curl is already coming out."

"Perhaps just one more turn," said Kitty, reaching for the iron leaning on the grate, where glowing embers battled the draft from the ill-fitting window.

"No, my hair is incurably straight and that is all there is to it. Thank you for your efforts, Kitty dear. I should have known it was useless. I shall just pin it up, as usual."

"Thread a ribbon through the braid before you knot it," Mrs. Lisle suggested. "Which gown are you going to wear?"

"The green Circassian cloth, I suppose. I refuse to freeze for Lord Selworth's sake."

"Enough of this nonsense!" her mother said sharply. "That gown does very well when we are alone, but whatever your opinion of the viscount, you will dress nicely for guests, my girl. There is a good fire in the dining parlor, and you may wear a shawl. Let me see." She crossed to the old beechwood wardrobe.

"Oh, the apricot poplin." Pippa did not own so many dresses as to make the choice difficult. "I have a bit of ribbon to match. I beg your pardon, Mama, for being prickly. Lord Selworth's interest in Prometheus has ruffled me a trifle."

Mrs. Lisle gave her a loving smile. "I know, dearest, but truly I believe all will work out for the best. Lord Selworth seems to me too much the gentleman to give away your secret, should he guess it, and Papa would be very proud of your labor on behalf of the unfortunate. Kitty, go and dress now. I shall finish off your sister's hair, then come to help with your fastenings."

While Mama's nimble fingers braided the

49

satin ribbon into her hair and pinned the plait into her usual topknot, Pippa pondered what she had said.

Was Lord Selworth too gentlemanly to betray her? He was a gentleman by rank, though recently risen to the peerage — what *had* been his profession before? — but Papa had often pointed out the frequent gap between rank and behavior. His daughters were not to be taken in by a title. Still, the viscount's concern for the poor argued in his favor, and it was not just talk or he would not have sought out Prometheus.

Unless he was a Government spy.

Surely not! That smile which sent shivers down her spine had warmed his blue eyes in a way no spy could feign. Pippa dismissed the possibility with a shake of her head.

"Ouch!"

"Hold still, child, or I shall jab you again, and the whole will come down before I have pinned it securely."

"Yes, Mama," Pippa said meekly.

Her thoughts continued to wander. Assuming Lord Selworth's stated aims were genuine, Papa would wish her to help him. She had taken up the mantle of Prometheus chiefly in tribute to her dearly loved, much admired, and greatly missed parent. Also, she acknowledged, because she was proud of her ability and enjoyed the work.

It went without saying that she believed in Papa's ideals, but she was afraid the plight of the voteless masses had had less influence on her decision than it ought. Without the other spurs to write for Mr. Cobbett, she might have satisfied her charitable instincts with carrying soup to sick cottagers. *Not* sewing for the poor-basket.

"I fear I am sadly selfish, Mama," she said, chagrined.

"How can you say so, my love?" After pushing in a last hairpin, her mother enveloped her in a warm embrace. "Your concern about giving away the identity of Prometheus is perfectly understandable, though, I trust, unnecessary. There is perhaps some little risk, but I consider it justified in view of the opportunity for your sister. And the good you may do in helping Lord Selworth, of course."

Her disgust with herself lightened by Mama's order of priority, Pippa warned, "Lord Selworth may not be willing to pay with an introduction into Society."

"We can but ask," Mrs. Lisle said serenely.

"Not until tomorrow, remember. We have not had time to 'consult Prometheus.'"

"Darling," said Mrs. Lisle, a twinkle in her eye, "though you are the acknowledged intellectual of the family, I hope I am neither feather-witted nor in my dotage!"

With that she swept out, leaving her abashed daughter to dress.

The apricot poplin, a silk and worsted weave, was actually quite warm, as well as pretty enough to make up, almost, for the lack of curls and Pippa's pale complexion. Mama and Kitty were skillful dressmakers. The high neckline and the cuffs of the long sleeves were trimmed with Honiton lace. Another strip of lace circled the hem of the skirt, between two rows of satin ribbon a shade darker than the poplin, a leftover length of which was braided into Pippa's hair. The same ribbon circled the high waist, tying just below her bosom in a bow with long, fluttering ends.

Her bosom drew her scrutiny. All too aware of her scrawny figure, Pippa rarely bothered to use the looking glass except to make sure she was tidy — and that not as often as Mama would wish. She had been known to greet callers with a spot of ink on her chin or sleeve.

Now she discovered she *did* have a bosom! Mama was right: her looks had improved while she was not watching. Her clavicles no longer ridged the bodice, nor did her hipbones protrude when she smoothed down her skirt. Turning, she peered over her shoulder and saw no sign of jutting shoulder blades.

She swung back to study her face. Not only had her chin no inkspot, it was not pointed like an imp's, but gently rounded, as were her once sharp cheekbones. Even her nose was less like a beak.

Pippa realized she had not really noticed herself in years, merely seeing a fleeting image she vaguely recognized as herself. She would never be as pretty as Kitty, she thought, but neither was she woefully plain. Perhaps Mr. Postlethwaite was not so utterly lacking in taste as she had supposed!

Perhaps Lord Selworth might . . . She cut off the wistful thought before it completed itself in her mind, and started again. Perhaps she could make Lord Selworth believe she was a commonplace young lady too concerned with her appearance to have room in her head for politics. She opened a drawer and took out the carved ivory rose pendant and earrings Papa had given her for her eighteenth birthday.

"And do you share your father's political opinions, Miss Lisle?" Lord Selworth enquired politely, passing the bowl of leek soup Mama had ladled from the tureen.

"La, sir," Pippa trilled, with an attempt at a simper, "is it not a daughter's duty to embrace her father's principles, whether or not she understands them?"

Lord Selworth blinked. Had she laid it on rather too rare and thick?

Accepting his own bowl of soup, the viscount said, "I regret to see anyone espouse views she, or he, doesn't understand. Do you not agree, ma'am?" he asked Mrs. Lisle.

"In general," she said, "but where understanding fails, it is surely preferable for a daughter to be guided by a father she respects."

"Gentlemen know best," Pippa said inanely,

then immediately wished she had not voiced a dogma so at odds with her own beliefs, even for the sake of misleading Lord Selworth.

He took her to task at once. "Desolated as I am to contradict a lady, gentlemen as a class cannot possibly know best, or they would all agree, which is very far from the truth!"

Pippa had to laugh. "As my father's daughter, I cannot fail to be aware of that truth. Papa throve on controversy. I find it conceivable that some of his stated views, if not his principles, were founded upon a desire to contradict."

"Hardly an example one would wish to hold up to one's daughters," said Mrs. Lisle dryly, with a warning glance. "You have more than one younger sister, I collect, Lord Selworth, besides Mrs. Debenham?"

"Three half-sisters, ma'am, and four half-brothers. I own, the spirit of contradiction needs no reinforcement in them, boys or girls," he said with a rueful smile.

"Your mother has her hands full!"

"She has been too much occupied with the youngest, and with keeping house, to check them, and my stepfather is too gentle. Fortunately, I'm now able to provide a governess for the girls and to send the older boys to school."

"You do not care to have your brothers at home?" Pippa asked reproachfully.

"Oh, I shouldn't mind it now that I have a house and grounds extensive enough to contain their energies. You cannot imagine the turmoil created by a large and lively family in a small rectory. Nine children, remember, including Bina and me. Not two sedate young ladies like you and Miss Kitty."

Pippa was not sure she appreciated being called sedate, but she admitted, "I can imagine one might come to long for peace and quiet."

Lord Selworth grinned. "To say the least! Not that I would have you suppose my brothers and sisters are really mischievous. They are likeable enough, only in need of discipline."

"Can you not provide it? If the eldest Miss Warren is to make her début this spring, you must be much older than the others."

"A veritable graybeard, in fact!" He took pity on her confusion. "You are right. I'm ten years older than Millie. But while I have some influence over my siblings, it would be unconscionable of me to usurp my stepfather's place."

"Whatever your opinion of his tutelage, or lack thereof. Yes, I do see your difficulty."

"So I feel school is the best place for my brothers. I went to school," Lord Selworth said cheerfully. "It was my father's wish, and he left just funds enough for the purpose. Not Eton or Harrow or Winchester, but a respectable academy. I'm sending the boys there, and I doubt they'll suffer for it. Chubby, did attending Tuke House blight your life?"

Mr. Chubb had fallen silent, having, in response to Kitty's query about the inn, regaled her with every scrap of information he had gathered on the subject of bodgers. He looked up from his soup and said, "Blight? No. Dashed good soup, ma'am. Leeks from your own garden?"

"Yes. The receipt is one collected by Kitty. Whenever we eat anything particularly good at someone else's house, she makes a point of requesting the receipt."

"Dashed good notion. Don't suppose you'd let me have it for my mother's cook, Miss Kitty?" Mr. Chubb turned bright red. "The leek soup, not the whole collection," he clarified in a hurried mumble. "Don't want to impose."

"I shall be happy to copy it out for you, sir," Kitty said soothingly.

"Dashed kind. Leeks grow well at home. No blight."

"Are you interested in gardening, Mr. Chubb?" Kitty asked as Sukey removed the soup plates. "Sukey's husband takes care of the kitchen garden, but Pippa and I grow flowers."

Pippa seized upon the subject, which could not possibly lead Lord Selworth to see her as intellectual. Though Mr. Chubb was more conversant with edible crops than flowers, the three found common ground in a discussion of blights, insect pests, and weeds.

As they ate fricasseed chicken with carrots and parsnips, the talk moved on to the depredations of rabbits and wood pigeons.

"Shoot 'em," said Mr. Chubb.

"It is the only way to keep them down," Kitty agreed.

"Pigeon pie."

"Rabbit stew. I have an excellent receipt. It is a nuisance digging out the shot, though."

Pippa, while she enjoyed pigeon pie and rabbit stew, not only had no interest in cookery, but did not like to think of the poor creatures having to be shot first. She would have dropped out of the conversation, but Mama and Lord Selworth were discussing Papa's career. If she listened more closely to them, she would be tempted to put her oar in, at the risk of revealing her knowledge of politics.

Instead, she said to Mr. Chubb, "Do you marl your soil? Ours is so chalky, it is not necessary."

His response led to other soil amendments. Pippa sought a polite circumlocution — suitable for the dinner table — for manure, only to have Kitty and Mr. Chubb argue unabashedly over the relative merits of fowl droppings and cattle muck.

Conscious of Lord Selworth lending an amused ear, Pippa wished her mother would call Kitty to order. Trying to conceal her intellectual abilities was one thing; joining in a debate on the grosser aspects of rural economy was quite another. However, either Mrs. Lisle did not hear her younger daughter, or she chose not to reprove her for fear of embarrassing Mr. Chubb, who was guilty of the same fault.

Pippa had to acknowledge that the bashful gentleman might well be driven back into his shell, never to reemerge.

Mrs. Lisle started to reminisce about her husband's first election. Since Pippa had been an infant at the time, she felt safe in transferring her attention to the familiar story. Mr. Lisle had lost, but he had fought hard and his efforts had drawn the notice of the wealthy patrons who made future wins possible.

With a struggle, Pippa managed not to inveigh against the corrupt electoral system. Lord Selworth said it for her.

"Wealth ought not to be necessary. As long as the present system holds sway, the poor will never be properly represented in Parliament, their grievances will never be heard by —"

"Here, old chap," Mr. Chubb intervened, "spare us the speeches at the dinner table. There's a good fellow. Preaching to the converted, dash it. I say, ma'am, I've been telling Miss Kitty she ought to get a milch-cow."

Indulgently, Mrs. Lisle encouraged him to give his reasons.

Pippa turned to Lord Selworth. "Have you considered, sir, that as well as taking your own seat in the Lords, you might help a like-minded commoner into Parliament?"

"Why no, I hadn't."

His arrested look, surprised and interested,

made her flush. Wishing she had not spoken, she added hastily, "I don't wish to presume. Of course, I know nothing of your means, and you have a large family to support. Seven younger children, you said? What are their names?"

He followed her lead, and she dared to hope she had distracted him. It was a temporary reprieve, however. She had given her assent to Mama's plan, but how on earth was she to help Lord Selworth write his speech without giving herself away?

4

"Dashed pleasant evening!" said Chubby as they hurried back along the dark lane to the Jolly Bodger, through a chilly drizzle. "I don't know when I've enjoyed myself more."

"I don't know when I've heard you talk so much," Wynn teased, "at least not among womenfolk."

"Did I talk too much?" his friend asked anxiously.

"Lord, no! Two whole sentences would amount to more than usual."

"It's just that Miss Kitty is dashed easy to talk to. She's interested in the same sort of things I am."

Wynn wondered if Kitty Lisle was not more polite and kind than interested, but he would not dream of saying so. "It was a delightful evening," he agreed. "Singing glees is one free amusement my family often indulges in — with mixed results, I confess. I didn't know you sang."

"Used to sing in the church choir," Chubby confessed. "Miss Kitty has a capital voice, and she plays the spinet devilish neatly, don't she?"

"Miss Lisle sings well, too, even if she did refuse to play on the grounds that no criminal

60

can be forced to give evidence against himself! She puzzles me."

"Miss Lisle? Nice girl. No, nice young lady. Mrs. Debenham's age, ain't she? Practically on the shelf, poor thing."

"Hardly," said Wynn with some asperity. "Didn't you see the vicar casting sheep's eyes at her this afternoon?"

"Did he? Well, but a vicar, you know. I daresay he's looking for a housekeeper and someone to help with parish work. Nothing puzzling about that. Stands to reason, a girl wouldn't take a parson if she could catch anything better."

Amused as much by Chubby's tortuous thought process as by his conclusions, Wynn said lightly, "I can't agree with that, you know. My mother and my stepfather are quite devoted to each other."

The lantern over the inn sign illuminated Chubby's pink, horrified face. "I say, old chap, forgive me! Quite forgot Mr. Warren's in orders."

"My dear fellow, I shan't call you out. Don't give it another thought. I just wanted to set you straight." He pushed open the door. "Let's have a nightcap, and a game of piquet if Bucket can provide cards."

A greasy pack with no seven of diamonds amused them for an hour or so. Until they lay in bed, a scrawny feather bolster between them, and Chubby snuffed the candle, Wynn did not spare another thought for Miss Lisle. Then he reverted to his puzzlement.

Most of the time, she seemed much like any other young lady of his acquaintance. True, she had not set her cap at him, a practice he had grown used to in the few months since his accession to the viscountcy had made him a matrimonial prize. But though pursued by damsels from miles around Kymford, he was not so set up in his own conceit as to expect every female of marriageable — or near marriageable — age to swoon at his feet. It was possible, just barely possible, that Miss Lisle preferred Mr. Postlethwaite, though more likely that Prometheus was her beloved.

However, it was not her preference in suitors which puzzled Wynn. It was the surprisingly penetrating remarks she made from time to time. Coming from an otherwise unremarkable young woman, these flashes of erudition stood out like pearls of wisdom in a bucketful of oyster shells.

No doubt she was merely repeating parrot-fashion what she had learnt from her father, Wynn thought sleepily. Mrs. Lisle said Pippa used to copy out his scribbling in a fair hand, so she could have absorbed and repeated his ideas without truly understanding. That must be the answer.

She understood enough to make appropriate use of what she had learnt, though. And enough to be aware of the danger to Radical writers in the present political climate.

Wynn hoped he had convinced her he was to be trusted. Not through him would her lover come to harm, if he decided to help. Mrs. Lisle had told Wynn on parting that Prometheus had been informed of his request. A response should be forthcoming by midday tomorrow.

Satisfied with his efforts to ensure the success of his speech, Wynn drifted off to sleep, in spite of the unconscionably lumpy mattress. His last thought was that Miss Lisle, whatever her motives, had told the truth about the Jolly Bodger.

"Was thinking I might stroll up to the Hall this morning," said Chubby, unconvincingly casual, "and pay my respects to Miss Ruddock. You coming?"

Pushing aside his plate of rock-hard eggs and leathery bacon, Wynn regarded his friend with suspicion. "Miss Ruddock? Who the deuce is Miss Ruddock?"

"The squire's daughter. I made her acquaintance yesterday. That was her talking to Miss Kitty, and her great oaf of a brother gaping at her like a . . . like a . . ."

"Like the ravening maw of a sea monster?"

"Lord, no. Like a village idiot."

"Why on earth would he gape at his sister like a village idiot, unless he is one?"

"Gaping at Miss Kitty, old chap. Stands to reason even a jobbernowl like that wouldn't go around gaping at his sister, however pretty she was."

"Miss Ruddock's pretty?" Wynn could not remember noticing her in particular.

"Nothing out of the ordinary."

"Then why . . . ? Chubby, don't tell me you have come upon *two* young females you find conversable in the same village?"

Chubby shook his head. "There's only one Miss Kitty," he said simply.

"My dear fellow, you can't be head over ears on such a brief acquaintance!"

"Why not? Bedamned if your dashed heroes and heroines don't fall in love at first sight, every last one of 'em. Why shouldn't I?"

"But . . ." The only reason Wynn could think of was that his books were fiction and this was real life. It seemed inadequate. "All right, if you are so besotted with Kitty Lisle, why call upon Miss Ruddock? Are you hoping she will put in a good word for you with her friend?"

"I'm not besotted. I love her. And she's going to the Hall this morning to play duets on the pianoforte. Got a new one. The Ruddocks, that is. Heard 'em talking about it. I know a slowtop like me hasn't a chance with her, but I thought maybe she wouldn't mind if I went to listen."

"Why shouldn't you have a chance with her? You're heir to a barony, and plump in the pocket besides. She may not know it, and you can't very well puff off your own consequence, but I can easily drop a tactful mention in passing. You'd be a splendid match for a purse-pinched girl stuck here in the country with a village idiot for her only suitor."

"If Ruddock were the only one . . ." Chubby said gloomily. "But there are bound to be others about the place, and worse still, she told me her mama has saved up to give her a Season in London. She'll have all the eligibles on the Town flocking after her."

Wynn doubted it, but to say so not only might raise unwarranted hopes in Chubby's breast, but would cast aspersions on his beloved. While he wondered what to say, Mrs. Bucket heaved into sight.

"Off your grub, your worship?" she enquired sympathetically.

"I'm afraid I'm not very hungry," Wynn agreed.

" 'Spect Mistress Wynn set a good feed afore you yestre'en. Ah well, the pig'll eat it." Picking up his plate and Chubby's empty one, she waddled out.

The empty plate almost made Wynn take his friend's sentiments seriously. Gilbert Chubb was usually quite particular about what he ate. To consume his breakfast without noticing that it was virtually inedible was the equivalent in him of the traditional lovesick swain's loss of appetite.

On the other hand, Chubby had reached the advanced age of eight-and-twenty without ever suffering the pangs of calf love. Very likely that

65

was all that ailed him now, the more painful for being a belated case. If so, the more he saw of the object of his infatuation, the sooner he'd be cured. Miss Kitty could not possibly be the paragon he believed.

"I'll come up to the Hall with you," Wynn decided. "Mrs. Lisle isn't expecting me till noon. Let's hope she will invite us to eat a nuncheon!"

Miss Kitty and Miss Ruddock were nothing loath to have an audience of gentlemen for their duets. However, Mary Ruddock's pleasure in entertaining a lord clearly far outweighed Kitty Lisle's in Chubby's attendance. She greeted him with friendly equanimity and paid him no more attention than she did Wynn, or her friend Mary.

With Mary present, Chubby lapsed into taciturnity, his few utterances brief and incoherent. His manners were too good to allow him to sit and stare at Kitty like a booby, but he was incapable of doing anything to advance himself in her affections.

Just as well, Wynn thought. He did not want his best friend to marry and retire to the country to raise a family just when his own political ambitions were going to fix him in London for a good part of the year.

He was further reassured by Miss Kitty's tranquil farewells. She was to spend all day at the Hall. Wynn had to depart at midday to call upon her mother, and Chubby could not properly prolong his visit.

When they took their leave, Kitty smiled and said gaily, "I did not forget the leek soup, Mr. Chubb. I copied out the receipt, but I left it at home for you since I did not expect to see you again. Ask my sister. She knows where I put it." Brushing aside Chubby's stammered thanks, she turned to Wynn, a mischievous look in her eyes. "I do hope you come to an agreement with Prometheus, sir. I am excessively fond of Prometheus."

Chubby groaned as they walked down the carriage drive towards the village. "She's in love with that damned fellow Prometheus. I thought he was an old man."

"I fancy not," Wynn said hesitantly.

"You found out that much about him, did you?"

"Not exactly. I suspect he's a youngish man because I believe Miss Lisle's in love with him, too. Why else should she be so protective of him?"

"Good gad, the fellow's a regular Turk!"

"This is England. Console yourself. He can't have 'em both."

"Perhaps not," Chubby gloomed, his round, usually cheerful face set in lines of despondency, "but he'll choose Miss Kitty. Stands to reason. She's younger and ten times prettier."

"Not ten times," Wynn protested.

"To me she is," Chubby maintained stoutly. "Prettiest thing I ever saw. And the kindest heart in the kingdom."

"Spare me your raptures, old chap. I must collect my arguments in case this rural Lothario needs further persuasion."

As they walked on in silence, Chubby picked up a stick and cut viciously at the nettles in the ditch as if each one represented the rural Lothario's neck.

No persuasive arguments came to Wynn. Instead, he found himself considering what would happen if Prometheus agreed to help. Would he come up to London or, horrid thought, might he expect Wynn to stay on at the appalling Jolly Bodger while consulting him?

Miss Lisle would surely go to stay in Town with her mother and sister, if Chubby had correctly understood their plans. No doubt Prometheus would choose to go, too, to be near his sweetheart. Which of the young ladies did he prefer? Or was he making up to both, the blackguard?

Mrs. Lisle seemed utterly unsuspecting of the villain she regarded as an intimate friend of the family. *Intimate,* ha! Ought Wynn to warn her?

Suddenly recognizing his ruminations as the beginning of a Gothic plot, Wynn laughed aloud. However he started out, everything turned to melodrama, which was precisely why he needed Prometheus' assistance. Doubtless the fellow was perfectly inoffensive, and it made no difference to Wynn which of the Lisle sisters he preferred.

"All very well for you to laugh," Chubby said accusingly. "You ain't in love."

"Thank heaven!" said Wynn.

Sweetbriar Cottage came into sight just as a pale wash of sunlight slithered between the clouds. In the beech hedge, still hung with last year's sere leaves, glossy brown buds swelled with promise. A wren, already nest-building, chattered in noisy annoyance as the gentlemen approached. Pushing open the white gate, Wynn saw that several bright yellow crocuses had burst into bloom overnight.

"Cheer up," he said, "Spring is on its way. At least once Miss Kitty's in London, you'll be able to see her."

Chubby brightened. "That's right. I couldn't very well keep popping down here, could I? I'll make sure to get their direction in Town before we leave."

The maid ushered them into the small parlor. By daylight, without a crowd of people, Wynn saw how shabby it was. Polished wood gleamed, but the upholstery stuffs, once patterned, had faded to a nearly uniform murky rose. A colorful hooked rug on the floor all too obviously hid a worn spot in the threadbare carpet.

All in all, it reminded him of the rectory where he grew up. He himself had been quite a dab at hooking a rug.

Mrs. Lisle looked up from her needlework with a smile, a greeting, and an invitation to be seated. Bowing, Wynn looked questioningly at

Miss Lisle, who stood by the window as if she had been watching for their arrival.

Reluctance in every line of her slender figure, she came forward and sat down, thus allowing the gentlemen to take their seats.

"Has Prometheus reached a decision, ma'am?" Wynn asked Mrs. Lisle eagerly.

"Yes, I have a decision to pass on to you. I hope you will not take it amiss."

His spirits sinking, Wynn glanced around the room, though he knew quite well no stranger was there. "He is not here. It is a negative I suppose."

"On the contrary. Prometheus is willing to help you."

"He is coming?" Wynn started up. "Or does he wish me to go to him? How I look forward to meeting him!"

"I fear you will be disappointed. I am not permitted to introduce you. Prometheus wishes to remain incognito and to work with you, as with Mr. Cobbett, entirely through my daughter." Mrs. Lisle smiled slightly at Wynn's astonishment. "Pippa was used to help her papa, you know. She is quite competent to . . . to act as an intermediary, let us say."

Wynn turned to Pippa. "Miss Lisle, far be it from me to doubt your competence. I hate to be instrumental in placing such a burden on your shoulders. You must have better things to do with your time."

"No." She shook her head, a hint of irony in

the quirk of her lips. "What could be better than helping to forward Papa's favorite causes? But before you rejoice, wait until you have heard what further conditions Prometheus has set, what payment is to be exacted."

"I am willing to pay any reasonable sum, ma'am," Wynn assured Mrs. Lisle, "but . . . conditions?"

For the first time in their admittedly brief acquaintance, the widow looked a trifle discomposed. "The payment is not in money," she said with an air of dogged determination. "You must understand, Prometheus was my husband's pupil and intimate associate, and remains closely concerned with the family. The recompense required for assisting you is that you provide an entrée into the best Society for Kitty and Pippa."

If Wynn was startled, so was Miss Lisle, who cried in obvious dismay, "But, Mama —"

"For both my daughters," Mrs. Lisle cut her off firmly. "Pippa has already made her come-out, but that is no reason for her to miss the pleasures of the Season."

"No indeed, ma'am," Wynn agreed, with a glance of pitying sympathy for Pippa. If Prometheus wanted her introduced into the Marriage Mart that was the London Season, he certainly could have no urgent desire to make her his bride, poor girl. Nor Kitty neither, apparently. An Adonis, perhaps, rather than a Lothario — the pursued, not the pursuer.

Pippa was furious. She was annoyed with her mother, who had said she could decide for herself about venturing upon a second Season, and she bitterly resented Lord Selworth's condescending pity.

Who was he to make it obvious he expected her to repeat her failure? She and Mama must both be mistaken in believing her looks had improved. Mama was partial, but how could Pippa, with her vaunted intelligence, have so misled herself? She was as plain and as gauche as ever, and an ape-leader to boot, she thought miserably.

"You cannot do it, can you?" she said sharply to Lord Selworth, who had lapsed into a reflective silence. "I daresay your credit would not survive foisting such an unfashionable family upon the Ton."

He gave her a smile of such dazzling sweetness that her anger evaporated like dew in the sun. "Not at all, Miss Lisle. The sad fact is that I am too new come to the title to *have* any credit with the *haut ton*. I cannot suppose my sponsorship would do you any good."

"Need a lady anyway," Chubby blurted out. He crimsoned but plowed on gamely. "Gentleman can't sponsor ladies, old fellow, with the best credit and the best will in the world."

Lord Selworth turned his smile on his friend. "Just what I was thinking, my dear chap. Fortunately, there is a lady waiting in the wings, and one who already knows Miss Lisle. Please convey to Prometheus, ma'am, that I accede to his requests so far as is in my power. Now all depends on my sister. And, to tell the truth, I shall be mightily surprised if Bina refuses her aid."

Recalling Albinia's worship of her brother, and considering her steadfast friendship, Pippa rather doubted it, too.

5

"Of *course* I had Mrs. Debenham in mind, dearest," said Mrs. Lisle complacently, when the gentlemen, after a neat nuncheon, had departed for London. "Most implausible for Prometheus, however, so I could not mention her without making it apparent that I had a hand in the proposal, which would *not* serve."

"Gracious no!" Pippa shuddered. "I pray he never finds out. From Prometheus it is a generous notion; from us, the beneficiaries, both encroaching and shockingly self-serving."

"Far from it, my love! Your sister is the beneficiary, and it was not her notion. She is worth a little roundaboutation, is she not?"

"I agreed to do it, did I not? But talking of roundaboutation, Mama, you said I was to decide for myself whether to take part in the Season's entertainments. Now Lord Selworth expects me to go to balls and parties and I shall be the most d-dreadful f-failure again!" Ending on a wail, Pippa felt for her handkerchief.

"You will not!" her mother said adamantly. "Have a little faith in yourself, Pippa. Actually, what I meant was that it was your decision whether to agree to the whole scheme."

74

"That is not what it sounded like," Pippa sniffed.

"No, it was carefully worded."

"Mama, I do believe you grow quite hardened in deceit!"

"I trust you noticed," Mrs. Lisle said with pride, "I did not once refer to Prometheus as 'he' or 'him.'"

Pippa had to smile. "Yes, I noticed. But that does not change the fact that you told Lord Selworth I shall take part in the Season."

"Think, dearest! I had to. Mrs. Debenham is *your* friend. Even I have not the sheer effrontery to ask her to sponsor Kitty alone. I hope you will go to one or two dances at least, to see how you go on, but if you hate it, my love, you know I shall not force you to continue."

Dropping to the floor, Pippa rested her cheek against her mother's knee. "Oh Mama, I dread it so."

"I know, Pippa love, but give it a chance." Mrs. Lisle stroked her hair. "I cannot bear for you to wither away into an old maid, or worse, to become Mrs. Postlethwaite! Not that I mean to say the vicar is not a worthy man, and kind in his way."

"It was kind in Lord Selworth, was it not, to offer to find us a place to stay in London?"

"Yes indeed. I do not know how we should contrive without his assistance. Most houses will be taken already at this late date, and I cannot afford to pay enough to give us much choice at the best of times. I hope Kitty will not be disappointed to be living in an unfashionable district."

"She will learn to know her true friends by whether they consider themselves too grand to call," Pippa said tartly. "Dearest Mama, how can she, or I, be disappointed when we have the best mama in the world?"

Mrs. Lisle smiled. "I trust you will one day discover," she said softly, "that what a mother does for her children she does to please herself. Well then, I hope we shall not all be disappointed. It is by no means certain Mrs. Debenham will choose to support her brother. For all we know, she disapproves of his Radical views."

"Wynn, the most vexatious thing!" Millicent jumped up and ran to meet her brother at the drawing-room door. Hanging on his arm, she prattled on, "Some horrid busybody has persuaded Mama that Bina is too young to be a proper chaperon for me. Mama says she will come to lend us countenance, but Bina says we must not tear her away from the children and Papa, and the only other person who will do is George's horrid Aunt Prendergast. Wynn, I cannot bear —"

"Hush, chatterbox! And pray don't let me hear you speaking ill of George's relatives." Detaching her from his sleeve, over her blond head he gave his brother-in-law a wry nod. "Especially in his presence! Apologize, Millie."

"Well, I'm sorry, George, but it was you who told me —"

"It's all too true," George Debenham interrupted, having already learnt the necessity if one was to make oneself heard in his young sister-in-law's presence. A tall, dark, rather saturnine gentleman, he moved forward and shook Wynn's hand. "I wouldn't wish my aunt on anyone, and poor Bina is in despair."

"But there is no one else, Wynn," Millie moaned. "Neither George nor Mama and Papa have any relatives both suitable and available. I do think Mama could leave the children now that there are servants to take care of them and Papa, but Bina says —"

"Bina says," said that lady as Wynn bent to kiss her cheek, noting that she looked more determined than despairing, "Mama hates to be away from the young ones and Papa, and she hates London. I recall all too well how she pined when she brought me up for my Season. I will *not* be responsible for putting her through the misery again."

"Quite right," Wynn seconded her. Her unruffled firmness reminded him strongly of Mrs. Lisle. A splendid notion struck him. "Hush, infant," he ordered, raising his hand as Millie started to babble again. "If you will only let me think, I may have the answer."

In a pregnant silence, he sat down, absently accepting the glass of Madeira Debenham inserted into his hand.

Mrs. Lisle lacked connections in the *beau monde,* but she was perfectly respectable. Bina had the connections, through her husband, but lacked an older lady to lend her countenance as a chaperon. She was acquainted with Mrs. Lisle, and she was Pippa Lisle's friend.

On the other hand, Debenham had at most a fleeting acquaintance with the Lisles, several years ago. Was it too much to ask him to take into his house three females of whom he knew next to nothing? Was it too much to ask of Millie, to share her Season fully with Kitty Lisle rather than just having Bina invite the Lisles to a few parties?

He looked at Millicent, sitting on the edge of her chair with her eager gaze fixed on her brother. Her mouth opened, but closed again at his frown. Apart from the ever-wagging tongue, she was amiable enough, a pretty chit in her new, modish morning gown, with blue eyes and the fair hair inherited from their mother, but no conceited beauty. The contrast with Kitty's darkness would be a charming sight for connoisseurs of feminine pulchritude.

And Kitty's availability as a listener might do much to spare Albinia from the ever-wagging tongue.

"Wynn, what is it?" Millie's muteness had reached its outer limit. "What is the answer? Have you remembered another aunt? It does not matter if she is quite decrepit, for all she need do is live here and be respectably elderly while Bina takes me to parties and —"

"Not an aunt, and not in the least decrepit. But — forgive me, Millie, and you, too, Debenham — this is something I must discuss privately with Bina. If she mislikes the idea, it need go no further. Otherwise, nothing shall be done without the assent of both of you."

"I should hope not," Debenham growled with a mock ferocious glance at Albinia.

"Nothing shall be done without your consent, husband mine," she said tranquilly.

"And mine," Millie insisted. "Wynn said I have to agree as well, don't forget. Who is she, Wynn? Is it someone I shall like? Is she —"

"Come along, Millicent," said Debenham. "Come to my den and tell me all about your presentation gown. Again." With a martyred face, he swept her ruthlessly from the room.

"Deuced lucky you are, my dear," said Wynn, "to catch a capital fellow like George."

"Pray never tell him so, Wynn. He is under the impression he caught me. Now, what is all this mystification about?"

"The Lisles."

"You have been to see them already? How is my dear Pippa?"

"Very well," Wynn said impatiently. "At least, she seemed in the pink of health and no one mentioned any dread disease. She sent her best regards, or whatever it is females send each other."

"Thank you for conveying her greeting so elegantly! What of your mission? Were they able to introduce you to Proteus?"

"Prometheus, Bina, Prometheus. Yes and no."

Bina laughed. "My dear brother, this shilly-shallying will never do if you wish to make a good impression with your speech. Come, let us have a round tale."

"You started all that nonsense about Miss Lisle's health!" Wynn grumbled. "She, incidentally, was most reluctant even to put my case to Prometheus. Her mother persuaded her to allow the gentleman to make up his own mind."

"And he said 'yes and no'?"

"He said yes, but as payment he wishes me to introduce the younger Lisle girl to the Ton. Both girls, actually, only Miss Lisle was not merely reluctant but strongly averse to a second Season."

"Poor Pippa had a miserable time of her first, I fear. But, Wynn, a gentleman cannot sponsor ladies. Do I, by any chance, see where this is leading?"

"I expect so," Wynn admitted. "I would never make the mistake of regarding you as a widgeon just because you don't know Prometheus from Proteus. Will you do it, Bina?"

"Let me make sure I comprehend the full depths of your deviousness," Albinia said cautiously. "You wish me to sponsor Kitty Lisle.

80

No difficulty there. Invitations to a few parties, introductions to a few hostesses, easily done. Is she pretty?"

Wynn grinned. "Ask Chubby. He's heels over head for the chit."

"Mr. Chubb went with you?" She held up her hands. "No, no more red herrings, I beg of you! If I am not mistaken, you believe Mrs. Lisle would be an acceptable substitute for Aunt Prendergast."

"Would she not? I cannot imagine anyone disliking her, but no doubt you saw more of her during Miss Lisle's Season than I did in two short days."

"Oh, as to that, I liked her very well. She was very kind to me when Mama could not cope. But it is a question of whether the world, the starchiest part of the world, will regard her as a suitable . . . chaperon's chaperon!" Bina's smooth forehead wrinkled in thought. Her brother held his breath. "A respectable, well-bred widow of a certain age . . . Wynn, I cannot see why she should not be acceptable."

Wynn breathed again. "To you, to the world, what of George? He is not acquainted with the Lisles, is he? Mrs. Lisle would have to live in the house to be of any use to you."

"George will be only too delighted to welcome anyone who obviates the need to receive his aunt," Bina said dryly. "When I tell him she was kind to me, he will greet her with raptures. Or if he does not, I shall want to know why. But

81

Pippa and Miss Kitty will have to stay, too, of course. I hope Millie's nose will not be put out of joint. Is Kitty pretty? Your opinion, now, not Mr. Chubb's."

"Very pretty," said Wynn, pausing before he added, "and as dark as her sister."

"Aha! Millie will be glad to hear it. And is she as amiable as Pippa?"

"Much more so. I don't wish to malign your friend, Bina, but I should say she can be prickly upon occasion."

Bina smiled, a reminiscent smile. "Yes, Pippa was never a commonplace, compliant sort of girl. I shall have to make sure she has an agreeable experience this time. Pray invite them, Wynn, and leave George and Millicent to me. This is going to be such fun!"

This is going to be simply dreadful, Pippa thought, gazing unhappily out of the carriage window. As well as suffering through at least a few balls and routs for Mama's sake, she was going to have to struggle to keep her alter ego secret from Lord Selworth while helping him with his speech. If he resided with the Debenhams in Town, it would be a doomed struggle.

Even the pleasant prospect of seeing Albinia again was marred by a sense of obligation. However kindly she tried to convey her need of Mama's chaperonage, her offer of accommodation was the height of generosity. As for her husband, he must be very fond indeed to allow three strangers in his home for a stay of several months, and to go so far as to send this comfortable carriage to fetch them.

"Mama, I cannot believe we ought to have accepted the Debenhams' invitation," Pippa said for the dozenth time.

Mrs. Lisle shook her head, smiling. "I should not have dreamt of angling for such hospitality, still less of making it a part of Prometheus' conditions. However, as it was freely offered, I have no hesitation in accepting. With no rent to pay, there will be much more money to dress you two properly. Not to mention the advantages of having an address in the best part of Town."

"I think it is simply splendid of Mrs. Debenham," said Kitty, "but Miss Warren does seem to believe Mama's presence is necessary to them. And she is happy to share her Season with me, as far as I can make out!" She took from her reticule the crossed and recrossed letter Millicent Warren had sent along with her sister's invitation.

While Kitty and Mrs. Lisle pored again over the indecipherable scribble, Pippa reflected upon the disadvantages of living with two practical optimists. Mama and her sister simply did not understand Pippa's concerns. Though capable of dealing with adversity, both accepted good fortune without a second thought, never fretting about the dark cloud behind every silver lining.

Put thus, it sounded ridiculous, Pippa admonished herself. She really must learn to take the smooth with the rough, not to cross her bridges before she came to them — while continuing not to count her chickens before they hatched. And to avoid clichés like the plague.

Her chief worry, she realized, was lest she fail Lord Selworth. A speech was very different from an article, Papa had taught her, but he had always written his own. By the time she took over the greater part of the labor of writing his articles, he was too ill to make speeches. Suppose, after all Lord Selworth's and his sister's kindness, she proved incompetent to improve on his own efforts?

Cross that bridge if and when you come to it, she reminded herself.

"Mama," cried Kitty, "do look at those celandines. How they shine in the sun. I should like a ball gown that color."

"White and pastels, my love, for a girl making her début, though perhaps a satin underdress would be acceptable. Mrs. Debenham will know. But Pippa would look very well in a bright shade of yellow, I fancy. What do you think, Pippa?"

Pippa glanced out at the hedge bank, golden-yellow with the shiny little flowers. "Perhaps, Mama," she said cautiously, but a surge of hope took her by surprise.

She had forgotten she was no longer condemned to the pale colors which suited her so ill — made her look ill, in fact. In vivid shades, and without the need to skimp quite so much on fabrics, maybe she could show Lord Selworth she was not altogether an antidote.

Rouge? she pondered. If she was practically on the shelf, surely she was old enough to try rouge, just a little bit, carefully applied. She must consult Bina.

Kitty tapped her arm. "You are lost in a brown study again," she said with a smile. "I asked you what Mr. Debenham is like. Mama has no more than the haziest recollection of him, but you were Mrs. Debenham's best friend, so you must recall the gentleman she married."

"I did not see a great deal of him. For the most part he moved in circles we did not aspire to. The Debenhams are a very old and well-respected Kent family, I collect, connected to the nobility by marriage, though not titled. Once Bina had caught his eye, she was invited to the houses of the best hostesses."

"But what was he *like?*"

"Tall, dark, and handsome, like the hero of a romance."

"Oh, handsome! I do not care about his looks, only his character. He sent his carriage and is to let us stay at his house, so he is kind and generous, but so is Mr. Postlethwaite."

Pippa laughed. "As like as cheese and chalk — both can be cut and crumbled! Generous he may be, but I suspect his kindness has more in it of indulgence for his wife. As I recall, he impressed me as being decidedly high in the instep, frequently satirical, and not a little cynical."

"Then he must positively dote on Mrs. Debenham," Kitty marvelled. "He must have fallen *desperately* in love with her to marry her before her brother became a lord. And she has reformed his character. Oh, excessively romantic!"

"Such high flights," Mrs. Lisle reproved with a smile. "I daresay desperation had nothing to do with it, simply that they found they should suit, a far sounder basis for marriage."

"I expect Bina does suit him very well," Pippa concurred. "Like the two of you, she is calm and cheerful, and no doubt bears with his crotchets to admiration. However, I may be slandering him! Remember, I did not know him well."

"You are too prosaic, I vow," Kitty exclaimed. "I am sure it is a love match. Never fear, though, Mama, I shall not require a tall, dark, handsome gentleman who loves me desperately. I shall be quite satisfied to find someone who *suits.*"

"As long as he indulges your every whim?" Pippa teased.

"Kitty is by far too sensible to take odd whims into her head," said their mother. "Yet I would not have you suppose suitability precludes love. My dearest wish is for each of you to find a gentleman with whom you can be as happy as I was with your dear papa."

Pippa vowed to do everything within her power to make sure her sister found happiness. For herself she had no such hope.

She could never be contented with a husband who did not respect and appreciate her talents, nor with one who did not share her beliefs. Where was she to find another paragon like Papa?

Lord Selworth — no. Though his political philosophy was in harmony with hers, she had every reason to assume he shared the world's view of clever females. That one of the Lisle ladies might be Prometheus had not so much as crossed his mind, because the sole purpose for the existence of females was to look decorative.

And to bear children, whispered a small voice in Pippa's head. Feeling a warmth stealing up her cheeks, she turned her face to the window.

Country born and bred, Pippa was not entirely ignorant of the significance of the marriage bed. Would the intimacies which seemed so distasteful when considered in connection with Mr. Postlethwaite appear less so with respect to Lord Selworth?

Pippa put her hands to her hot cheeks. That was a subject she ought not — must not — did not wish to pursue.

Fortunately, her leisure for reflection was at an end, their journey nearly so. Kitty had a thousand questions as the carriage passed the Tyburn turnpike and continued along Oxford Street. She gazed all agog at the busy shops, their lamp-lit windows displaying china, silks, watches, fans, pyramids of fruit, or crystal flasks of different colored spirits. Pedestrians thronged the broad, flagged pavements; along the center of the street stood a row of carriages which yet left space enough for two coaches to pass on either side.

"Is it not splendid?" cried Kitty. "Shall we shop here, Mama?"

"Sometimes, I expect. It is less expensive than Bond Street or Pall Mall. The cheapest places are further east, however. We shall have no shillings to waste."

Kitty's face fell. "No, I know, but may I visit these shops, just to look?"

"Of course, my love. And you need not fear that lower cost necessarily means lower quality. Shops in fashionable districts charge more because their customers can afford it and do not mind paying for the convenience."

"And because their rents are higher," Pippa pointed out, to be fair. As the carriage turned right into Davies Street, she continued, "Now this is Mayfair, is it not, Mama?"

Kitty once more glued her nose to the window. "The houses are quite smart," she said doubtfully, "and tall, but so very narrow. I can-

88

not see how Mrs. Debenham will fit us all in."

"Let us hope the Debenhams' is one of the larger houses," Mrs. Lisle said, "though if we have to sleep in the garrets, I, for one, shall not complain."

"Nor I," said Pippa, "but the servants may if they are driven out to bed down on the kitchen floor."

The carriage rolled on down the southwest side of Berkley Square, where the houses were grand enough to impress Kitty. At the bottom of the square they turned right into Charles Street, and pulled up before the largest house on the north side.

Kitty breathed an ecstatic sigh and exclaimed, "Oh, splendid! I should not mind sleeping on the kitchen floor, I vow! Their kitchen must be grander than my bedchamber at home."

Pippa smiled, but absently. The elegance of pillars and pilasters, pediments and cornices, elaborate fanlight and ornate wrought iron, dismayed her. Though aware that her friend had married well, she had continued to think of her in the setting where she had known her.

Albinia's letters, full of the dry, yet gently tolerant humor which had attracted Pippa to her, had not reflected her altered circumstances. She had become a wealthy, fashionable wife and mother, whereas Pippa remained an impecunious, unimportant spinster, now verging on old-maidship.

Bina must surely have changed to suit her new position. The easy friendship between them was in the past, and Pippa could only resolve sadly not to presume upon it.

6

The starchy butler, pink and black marble-floored hall, and handsome staircase further increased Kitty's rapture, and Pippa's misgivings.

"I know I shall enjoy myself excessively," Kitty whispered as they followed the butler and their mother up the stairs. "Dearest Pippa, thank you again for consenting to —"

"Hush, not a word. Pray recollect, it is Mama and our good friend Prometheus who have provided this opportunity."

"I shall not say a word," Kitty promised, "even if Miss Warren and I become as close friends as you and Mrs. Debenham. You have not told her?"

Pippa shook her head, her finger to her lips. The butler opened a door and announced, "Mrs. Lisle, Miss Lisle, Miss Catherine Lisle, madam."

He stepped aside. Mrs. Lisle glanced back at her daughters with a smile, then moved forward into the room. Peering past her, Pippa held her breath. Would Albinia greet them with condescension, and make it plain that she had invited them for her brother's sake? Would she stare at their shabby clothes, forgetting she had once scraped and saved?

How Pippa wished she had not come! It was not being an object of disdain she minded, it was the loss of the precious friendship, nurtured in absence, withering in the harsh light of reality.

"Mrs. Lisle, how utterly delightful to see you again!" Albinia Debenham swept forward with a rustle of silks, and took both Mrs. Lisle's hands in hers. "And how very kind of you to agree to lend us countenance, my sister and me. Allow me to present Millicent."

As Miss Warren made her curtsy and enthusiastically seconded her sister's gratitude, Albinia turned to Pippa and without further ado enveloped her in a hug.

"Dear, dear Pippa, how I have longed for this moment. What times we shall have together, just wait and see." Blue eyes sparkling, holding Pippa's hand, she turned to Kitty. "And you are Miss Catherine, of course. Yes, I see the resemblance. Welcome, my dear."

Pippa did not hear Kitty's response. She was overwhelmed with shame for having misjudged Bina. If only she were like Mama and Kitty, always expecting the best of people. Though they might sometimes be disappointed, they suffered neither anxiety before, nor pangs of guilt afterwards.

"Struck dumb, Pippa?" Bina said. Glancing at Miss Warren, she raised her eyes to heaven with a look of comical despair. Her sister was still chattering away to Mrs. Lisle about someone called Aunt Prendergast. "I cannot blame you," Bina continued. "You will soon learn to interrupt. Millie, pray come and make the acquaintance of Miss Lisle and Miss Catherine."

"Kitty, please, Mrs. Debenham. How do you do, Miss Warren?" Kitty's eyes sparkled with amusement as the full force of Millicent's verbiage flooded over her.

"Do call me Millie. We are going to be the greatest friends. It is above anything that you are come to stay! Coming out with a friend will be much more fun, do you not agree? And so very lucky you are dark and I am fair. We shall make quite a sensation, I am sure, though we must be careful to coordinate our colors. My favorite color is blue, but Bina says we shall have to wear white for grand balls because —"

"My mother told me the same," Kitty interrupted firmly, "and pale colors in general."

"Come up to my chamber and I shall show you the gowns I already have. Bina says she and Miss Lisle used to —"

"Bina says, first show Miss Lisle and Miss Kitty to their chamber, if you please. They will want to put off their bonnets and pelisses. Pippa, Miss Kitty, I hope you will not mind sharing a chamber."

Pippa found her tongue at last. "Not in the least."

"When I first saw the size of London

houses," Kitty said gaily, "I quite expected we should have to sleep in the garrets, if not on the kitchen floor."

"Not quite so bad," Bina said with a smile, "though even the best Town houses are wretchedly small compared to the country. Mrs. Lisle, will you come with me?"

They all went up another pair of stairs, then Bina led Mrs. Lisle to the back of the house while Pippa and Kitty followed Millicent to the front. Millie chattered the whole way.

"At the rectory I shared a chamber with Bina until she grew up and married. Then my next sister moved in with me, but when Wynn's great-uncle died and we removed to Kymford, we each got a chamber of our own. I asked Bina if you might share with me now, only she thought you would like to be with your sister. She said I would never get a wink of sleep if I had someone to talk to all night, and nor would you. I know I talk a lot, and it is not the least use telling me to stop, because once I have started I cannot, but you must just interrupt when you feel like it. Everyone does. Miss Lisle, pray interrupt when you will. Here is your chamber and mine is next door, so as soon as you have put off your bonnet —"

"I shall come to see your new gowns, Miss Warren," Kitty promised.

"Oh, 'Miss Warren'! You really must call me Millie. Let me see, yes, here is hot water for you already, and this is my maid, Nan," she continued as a smiling, round-faced girl in a gray stuff dress and white apron bobbed a curtsy. "Imagine, an abigail of my own! Nan will unpack for you and you must tell her what else you wish her to do. Nan, this is Miss Lisle, and Miss Catherine. I shall wait for you in my chamber, Kitty. I have all the latest fashion magazines, too. Do not be too long!"

As Millicent whisked out, seemingly afraid she would be tempted to stay if she did not remove herself quickly, Pippa surveyed the room. It was decorated in white and pale rose pink, with curtains and counterpanes patterned with wild roses. Larger than her and Kitty's chambers at home combined, it was more than spacious enough for the two beds, two wash-stands, a dressing table, and a huge clothes press. Banked coals glowed in the tiled fire-place.

"What luxury," Kitty marvelled, untying her bonnet ribbons. "Which bed would you like, Pippa? I am glad we are together. I like Millie, but —" She paused as Pippa glanced warningly at the maid. "But you and I know each other's ways."

When Nan had carried off their pelisses to be brushed, Pippa said, "We shall have to grow accustomed to having servants about and taking care what we say."

"Yes, thank you for stopping me." Kitty giggled. "In any case I am quite certain you can guess exactly what I was going to say."

"I daresay Nan guessed, too," Pippa said dryly.

"The trouble is, some of what Millie says is worth hearing, so one must listen all the time so as not to miss anything."

"She seems good-natured and well-intentioned, so do try to bear with her prattle."

"I mean to, but how fortunate that she is not offended by interruptions, or I might lose my voice through disuse!"

They washed faces and hands in the rose-sprigged china basins. Kitty tidied her hair at the dressing-table mirror and went off happily to examine Millicent's gowns. Pippa sat down at the dressing table. Her hair needed little attention, the advantage of straight tresses and a severe style. She wondered what to do next.

Someone tapped on the chamber door. Servants bringing up their boxes, she thought. Nan would want to unpack, so she had best get out of the way.

"Come in."

Albinia appeared. "Pippa, are you comfortable? Is all as it should be? You will have to accustom yourself to asking the servants for whatever you need. All too easy, I promise you. It took me no time at all to grow spoiled."

"No doubt," Pippa said, laughing. It was impossible to feel awkward with Bina. "You are certainly doing your best to spoil us. This room is charming, and very comfortable."

"Good. Millicent's maid will help you two,

and my dresser will take care of your mama. She is shockingly toplofty — Bister, I mean, not Mrs. Lisle — and I was quite terrified of her when George's mother made me hire her, but your mama had her eating out of her hand in no time."

"Mama is equal to anything."

"As I know very well. I meant to stay only to make her comfortable, but we started to reminisce, or I should not have left you so long. She is lying down now, in preparation for a strenuous day reconnoitering the shops tomorrow. Come down to my sitting room where we shall have peace for a private cose, a rarity in this house, I fear!"

"Your sister is very friendly," Pippa said diplomatically, following her hostess from the room. "She has made Kitty feel quite at home already."

"But one does need an occasional respite. Before we go down, let me just show you . . ." Bina opened the door next to Mrs. Lisle's chamber. "I have fitted the nursery up as a sitting room for you and Mrs. Lisle and the girls. I thought you would like that better than a separate bedchamber."

"Oh yes, I truly do not mind sharing with Kitty."

"If you look down, you can see our garden, though you will scarcely think so tiny a plot worthy of the name."

"There is a garden in here." Pippa glanced

around the room, all flowered chintzes and green dimity, with vases of daffodils here and there. She noted the writing table between the windows. It would be perfect for her work. "Thank you, Bina. I cannot judge whether or not you have grown spoiled, but I see you have grown into a first-rate hostess."

"My mama-in-law taught me the way of it. We entertain a good deal in the country. I only wish you had been one of our guests, long since," Bina said seriously as they started down the stairs. "At first I was caught up in adjusting to my new life, and then when I was settled enough to invite you, you wrote about your father's illness."

"I could not have left Papa. Nor Mama afterwards."

"I know. And then, when you were out of mourning, Wynn asked me to present Millie — our mama is *not* equal to anything, as you are aware. I had not thought to expose you to my dearly loved but loquacious sister . . . Here is my sitting room, next to our bedchamber, with George's dressing room beyond, and the drawing room opposite, as you saw."

She opened a door and ushered Pippa into a cosy room, all blue and cream, which someone more pretentious might have dubbed a boudoir. It contained not only comfortable chairs, a small sofa, and a walnut rolltop bureau, but a wardrobe and dressing table. A branch of candles was already lit, for the room faced north and the March evening was already drawing in.

"As I was saying," Bina continued when she had rung for tea and they were seated on either side of a flickering fire, "I had intended to postpone your invitation until the summer. Then Wynn told me about Prometheus and his price, and at the same time I found the threat of George's Aunt Prendergast dangling overhead like the sword of Damascus."

"Damocles," Pippa murmured. "Mr. Debenham's Aunt Prendergast was to be your dragon, I take it."

Bina nodded ruefully. "Someone persuaded Mama I am not old enough to chaperon Millie on my own. Aunt P. is indeed a dragon." She giggled. "Privately George calls her Aunt Prenderghastly, deplorable . . ."

"But clever."

"And appropriate. So you can guess how delighted I was to be able to wave Mrs. Lisle in her face, so to speak. Also, there will be four of us to share Millie's chatter, though I fear Miss Kitty will likely bear the brunt," she said guiltily.

"Kitty is like Mama," Pippa told her, "equal to anything."

"So, you see, I am shockingly selfish and prodigious grateful to Prometheus. Who is this mysterious gentleman who is so solicitous of your family, Pippa? Do tell!"

Pippa was tempted. She trusted Albinia not to broadcast her secret to the world. However, she was certain her friend would be vastly diverted by Lord Selworth's ignorance of who was really helping him, and she was incapable of hiding her amusement. Laughing eyes and a half-concealed smile at the wrong moment could easily lead her brother to the truth.

"Forgive me, Bina, I must not."

"No, of course it is not your secret. I shall not press you, though I assure you I am very safe. Why, Wynn does not even know that I know . . . But that is *his* secret." Her eyes sparkled with glee, just as Pippa had imagined in her own case. "Ah, here is our tea."

While one footman set up a small table in front of the fireplace and the other unloaded his tray onto it, Pippa wondered about the skeleton in Lord Selworth's closet. Unless he had more than one, his sister must have found out how he helped support his family before he inherited the viscountcy.

Bina obviously did not regard it as disgraceful. No doubt it was something dull and unromantic in the way of trade, anathema to the Ton, but perfectly acceptable to ordinary people. Pippa felt slightly hurt that he had not trusted her family not to despise him for it.

"Do you still take your tea without milk?" Bina asked.

"Yes, please. Lemon! What a treat!"

"You see, I remember. And gingersnaps, but do not eat too many. I have ordered all your favorites for dinner, the things we only had at parties: salmon in aspic, escalopes of veal, apricot-almond tarts — do you recall how we sent our partners back for more?"

"Oh yes!" said Pippa, blinking back tears. How could she have doubted her welcome?

"And," said Bina triumphantly, "from George's father's succession houses — a pineapple!"

They looked at each other and burst out laughing.

Into this scene of merriment intruded Lord Selworth. He was wearing evening dress, and despite the tears of mirth in her eyes Pippa noticed the pristine newness of his black coat, fawn Inexpressibles, white marcella waistcoat, and neat cravat.

"Excuse me, ladies," he said with a grin, "I did knock but I daresay you didn't hear. May I share the joke?"

Bina dabbed at her eyes with a tiny lace-edged handkerchief. "You are early, Wynn. Come in, do, and ring for another cup if you would like tea. As for the joke, whether we share it is Pippa's choice."

Pippa hesitated, suddenly shy of this elegant stranger. She and Bina had laughed at the absurd figures they had cut on that evening four years ago. She was not at all sure she wanted Lord Selworth to see her in so ridiculous a light.

Then he smiled at her, and it was the same heart-stopping smile as when he had been a shabby stranger. "Have mercy, Miss Lisle," he said. "You must know the agonies suffered by those who hear laughter and are not permitted to know the cause."

After all, if he thought her a ninnyhammer, he would be the less likely to guess she was Prometheus. "Bina told me she has provided a pineapple for dinner, sir, which reminded us of an occasion on which we both made cakes of ourselves. Pineapple was served at a supper at a ball we both attended."

"Neither of us had ever eaten it before," Bina put in. "We were sitting together, and our partners each brought us a slice."

"I had been chewing away for some time at the little round piece in the middle," Pippa went on, "when I looked up and saw Bina sawing away at hers with her knife. Our escorts were too embarrassed to tell us the core was too tough to be edible."

"They never stood up with us again."

"At least you were able to abandon yours. I had to swallow mine whole!"

Lord Selworth chuckled. "That reminds me of the first time I was served an artichoke, and choked half to death trying to eat the whole leaf. No ladies present, fortunately, or I'd never have been able to face them again."

"No artichokes tonight," said Bina. "Wynn, dinner is at eight, as usual. You are much too early. Pippa and I have not changed yet, and George has not even come home. You will have to entertain yourself."

"I had hoped for a word with Miss Lisle. Can you spare me a few minutes, Miss Lisle, before you dress?"

Pippa consulted the pretty china clock on the mantelpiece. Not yet seven. She supposed some ladies might take over an hour to change their dress for dinner. However, twenty minutes would be more than enough for her, and his artichoke confession had made her feel quite at ease with him again.

"By all means, Lord Selworth."

"Shall we step across to the drawing room? Our business is of no interest to Bina. I don't want to deprive you of your tea, though. Let me pour you another cup, and I'll carry it for you."

Preceding him into the drawing room, Pippa looked around, as she had not had leisure to do on her arrival earlier. She did not know a great deal about furniture, but she thought the prevalent style was slightly old-fashioned. The house belonged to George Debenham's parents, she remembered. Clearly they had no interest in keeping up with the latest rage in decoration.

The walls were plain cream, the chairs covered with moss green brocade figured in saffron yellow, and the curtains cream brocade with a saffron design. The effect was at once gracious, soothing, and comfortable.

Pippa took a seat on a sofa by the fire and held out her hands to the flames, a little nervous at finding herself alone with Lord Selworth. He had left the door open, she noted, and reminded herself that this was a business meeting.

"Are you still chilled after your carriage ride?" he asked abruptly, standing over her. "Are you fatigued from the journey? There is no real need for such haste on my part."

She smiled up at him. "No, I am neither cold nor tired, sir. It was but half a day's journey and Mr. Debenham's carriage is quite the most luxurious I have ever been in."

"I'm glad I thought to suggest that he send it for you."

"It was your notion? Thank you!"

"Oh, don't thank me," he said wryly. "It was entirely for my own benefit. I have not my own travelling chaise with me — which is in any case an antiquated and dilapidated vehicle — and I feared Prometheus would dislike your travelling on the Mail or the common stage. You must know it is an object with me to keep that gentleman happy."

Though she murmured assent, Pippa still thought it was considerate of him, even if he had made use of his brother-in-law's carriage for the kind gesture! Few gentlemen would have troubled to spare them the discomfort and expense of a journey by public coach.

"Will you not be seated, Lord Selworth?"

"Just a moment." He went over to a small table in a corner and retrieved a sheaf of papers, then returned to sit opposite her, holding them on his knee. "Before I show you what I have here, I fear I bear bad news."

"Bad news?" With Mama and Kitty abovestairs and in good health, Pippa could not imagine what he meant.

"Bad news for Prometheus, I should say, though I expect you also will be sorry to hear it. I heard rumors that William Cobbett was to be arrested, so I went to see him."

"Oh no, has he been imprisoned at Newgate again?" Pippa asked in dismay.

"No, but he feels it necessary to flee the country. Friends are helping him to evade arrest and take ship for America. He is on his way already."

"I am so glad, but I hope he will be safe in America. Papa told me he was prosecuted there, too, for his writings when last he went into exile."

"I believe so." Lord Selworth shook his head with an air of amused disapproval not unmixed with admiration. "Perhaps he will go to a different state, since each has its own laws, I understand. Be that as it may, he entrusted me with what he owes to Prometheus, a foolish gesture, perhaps, since he is badly in debt."

"Mr. Cobbett is an honest man," Pippa flared up, "if sometimes foolish and prejudiced in his enthusiasm."

Lord Selworth gave her a curious look. "I did not intend to cast doubt upon his honesty."

"I beg your pardon, sir, only Papa used to grow quite heated when people failed to appreciate Mr. Cobbett's many excellent qualities." Which was quite true, but Pippa also hoped the viscount would assume she had been merely quoting her father rather than expressing her own view.

She *must* keep a closer guard on her tongue.

"Cobbett deserves respect for his dedication to principle even at risk of his own safety," Lord Selworth said pacifically, adding with a rueful smile, "I share many of his opinions, and those of your father and Prometheus, as you know, but I'm not sure I'm willing to go to prison to defend them. Let us hope it will not come to that! Nor do I wish to be jailed for embezzlement — here is the money for you to convey to Prometheus."

Standing, he took from his pocket a small cloth purse, which clinked as he placed it in Pippa's hand. He sat down again, at her side now, and riffled through the sheaf of papers.

"I have here two versions of my speech. One is the full text, my latest effort, and the other the same stripped of all the flowery stuff." He dropped them in his lap, leant back, and ran his hand through his hair, his expression frustrated and mortified. "You see, it's the figures of speech and illustrative examples and that sort of thing which defeat me, yet one needs something if one is not to put one's audience to sleep."

"Nothing so dull as undiluted facts and figures. As Papa was wont to say!" Pippa added hastily.

"Precisely. Since you were used to make fair copies for Mr. Lisle, perhaps you would not mind skimming through and deciding which will be most useful for Prometheus to work on?"

Pippa could scarcely believe her luck. He had handed her the perfect excuse for knowing the contents of his speech. Moreover, without seeming to suspect the truth, he trusted her judgment as his go-between with Prometheus, making it much easier to pretend to interpret that mythical figure's pronouncements.

Besides being flattering.

"I shall be happy to read them," she said primly. "Do you wish me to inform you which I have picked before I send it to Prometheus? You are staying here?"

"Just send your choice, or both, if you think it best. I shall refund the postal charges, naturally. No, I'm not putting up here."

"Oh dear, have we driven you out?" Pippa asked in dismay. "I am so sorry!"

He smiled. "Come now, Miss Lisle, you must recollect that you are doing me a favor, not the reverse. I have perfectly comfortable lodgings, I promise you. A friend of Chubb's and mine has sublet his rooms in Albany to us for the Season, as neither of us has a family house in Town. Chubb's parents are as averse to London as was my great-uncle."

"Does Mr. Chubb mean to do the Season? How brave!" Pippa said without thinking, then clapped a horrified hand to her mouth.

To her relief, Lord Selworth's blue eyes twinkled. "Brave indeed. Perhaps I should warn you that he is rather taken with your sister. I hope she will continue forbearing."

"As long as he does not start to *brood* at her like John Ruddock," said Pippa tartly. "Heavens, look at the time. I must change for dinner."

On her way upstairs, she reflected with consternation on how easy she found it to talk to Lord Selworth. She was indeed fortunate that he was not residing with his sister! So much propinquity would certainly have led her into indiscretion.

Yet she could not deny that it would have been pleasant to spend some time with him other than over the Prometheus business. Pippa sighed.

7

Pippa giggled, then hastily glanced around the sitting room to make certain she was still alone.

The original image was striking: the Government as a castle on a hill, impressively dominant from a distance, a dangerous ruin close to. What had possessed Lord Selworth to elaborate his metaphor?

The common people figured as ghosts rattling their chains in the castle's dank dungeons, while their rulers held a ghostly banquet among tottering towers above. The noble peers would die of laughter. How fortunate that the viscount recognized his own limitations and had turned to Prometheus.

Lord Selworth must read the same Gothic romances Pippa borrowed from the subscription library in High Wycombe, she thought.

She read on, approving the sentiments and a few of the minor embellishments, chuckling over the wilder flights of fancy. The style reminded her of one particular author. She liked Valentine Dred's novels because there was always an undertone of amusement beneath the horrors of headless horsemen and mad monks. One smiled even as one shuddered. They must be Lord Selworth's favorites, too, to have so influenced him.

It was something else she and his lordship had in common. Something else she must take care not to reveal, for Mr. Dred's stories were not only thrilling and funny, they were distinctly bawdy. Not at all proper reading for an unmarried young lady!

Besides, a serious aspiring politician was bound to be distressed if informed that his style resembled that of a writer of racy fiction.

"Pippa!" Kitty came in, a spring in her step. Pippa quickly covered the manuscript with a large blotter, before she realized her sister was alone. "Still poring over those moldy old papers?"

"Neither old nor moldy," Pippa said with a smile, "and I find them interesting. And come to think of it, I don't need to hide them yet, since Lord Selworth asked me to read them. It is an automatic reaction! You are back early."

"Not at all. It is nearly one o'clock."

"Heavens, is it really?"

The speech was taking longer to read than she had supposed. How long ought a maiden speech in the House of Lords to last? According to Papa, for maximum impact a speech should be neither long enough to send listeners to sleep, nor so short it was easily overlooked among scores of others.

But at first reading Pippa was not sure whether Lord Selworth's was actually too long. She had paused to ponder phrases and paragraphs. It had taken a while to learn to decipher his large, sprawling hand, so different from Papa's and her own neat, small writing — which also made the number of pages misleading.

"You have not heard a word I've said!" Kitty protested.

"You have been to hundreds of shops, each one more splendid than the one before. Yet somehow you are still full of energy!"

"It was such fun. Dozens, not hundreds — at least a score — and all much larger and finer than anything at home. Mama has decided which we are to patronize, so this afternoon you are not excused. You must come to choose which materials you like so that Mama and I can begin to make up our gowns."

"I am perfectly willing to trust your judgment, Kitty. Well, yours and Mama's! I must finish reading this. Lord Selworth wishes me to decide which version to 'send to Prometheus.' "

"But you don't have to send it anywhere," Kitty pointed out, "so there is no hurry."

"Sshh!" Pippa glanced at the door. "Remember we are not at home. Anyone might come in."

"There is no hurry," Kitty repeated in an exaggerated whisper.

Pippa frowned. "I forgot to ask Lord Selworth when he expects to give the speech. I wonder whether the date is set?"

"It cannot be soon, or he would have asked

Prometheus to make haste. Darling Pippa, Mama says you must come, and I am sure Lord Selworth would not encourage you to disobey her for his sake."

Outside the sitting-room door, Wynn paused with his hand raised to knock. Miss Lisle to disobey her mother for his sake? What on earth was the girl talking about? Anyone would think he had tried to persuade her to elope!

He knocked. A pause ensued before Miss Lisle called, "Come in."

"Good morning, Miss Lisle, Miss Kitty."

"Oh, it is you," said Miss Lisle with relief. "I just shoved your papers into the drawer in case —" She stopped, her cheeks tinged with pink, and fished the manuscript out of the desk drawer.

Wynn pulled a face. "Is it so awful that I shall be utterly mortified should anyone else read it?"

"Not at all!" she disclaimed, then bit her lip, her changeable hazel eyes dancing.

She had most expressive eyes, Wynn noted, even as he said with a rueful shake of his head, "I see my *rough* draft amuses you."

"I am sorry," she said guiltily.

"Don't apologize! Chubb's reaction was exactly the same."

"I beg your pardon," Miss Kitty put in, "but if you two mean to discuss the speech, I shall leave you to it. Remember, Pippa, Mama expects you to go with us this afternoon." She tripped out, closing the door behind her.

Wynn hesitated, undecided whether to open the door again for propriety's sake. Everyone knew he and Miss Lisle had business together; everyone knew there was no more intimate association between them; and it would look so pointed. He left the door closed, pulled up a chair, and sat down beside the writing table.

"I'm afraid I have kept you from some outing this morning."

"One I gladly missed, but I must go with Mama and Kitty to the shops after luncheon, to buy dress materials. It will not delay things much, though I have not quite finished reading."

"My dear Miss Lisle, I realize the Season is far more important to you than my affairs can possibly be." He paused, with an enquiring look, as she opened her mouth. However, she closed it again firmly, rather tight-lipped. "Believe me, I intend no irony. I am eternally grateful for your help."

Sensitive lips relaxed in a quirk. "You too! Bina tries to make me believe we are doing her a favor, when it must be plain to the meanest intelligence how deeply indebted to her we are."

"I'm sure she will be as relieved as I if you will agree to cry quits! My bargain with Prometheus requires that you enjoy a Season, and believe me I don't wish to deprive you of any of its pleasures, shopping included. Besides, there's no knowing when I may be able to give the speech," he added with a smile.

She looked down, long, dark lashes veiling her eyes in apparent discomposure, to Wynn's puzzlement. In another female he might suspect coyness, but Miss Lisle seemed a stranger to the art of coquetry.

"No date has been set?" she said. "I forgot to ask."

"I haven't yet approached Lord Eldon, the Lord Chancellor, not being sure when I shall be prepared. So you may tell Prometheus I am in no great haste, though I hope this session of Parliament will be possible."

"With Mr. Cobbett gone to America, there will be no articles to write. Though other matters may intervene," she added hurriedly. "There should be plenty of time before the end of this session, but I can give you no assurances as to how long it will take."

"It depends upon how busy Prometheus is, of course, and upon how much work there is to do." Wynn gestured at the pile of papers and made a show of bracing himself. "Be honest, is it truly dreadful?"

"By no means. Your points are well ordered and well argued — insofar as I may presume to judge."

"It's the embellishments, isn't it? Meretricious metaphors and fanciful figures of speech, that's where my troubles lie. So you will send Prometheus the unadorned version, to be ornamented with genuine pearls in place of my artificial roses."

Deliberately sought, her laugh delighted him. "Your roses are not all artificial. Rather, they are rosebushes, sadly in need of pruning. I am sure Prometheus will agree. It will be much better to take your bushes as a starting point and keep what blooms can be saved."

"Watered with my tears! I own I should be glad to preserve a few."

"I daresay you will deliver the speech with more conviction if at least some of the imagery is your own. Papa said he could always tell in the House when a man had had his words written for him. The spark of enthusiasm would be missing."

"A fate I wish to avoid! Pray use your influence with Prometheus." Wynn observed her closely as he spoke, hoping for a hint as to how much influence she expected to have.

Again she lowered her lashes, and her porcelain-pale skin flooded with a rosy blush as she nodded.

Damn! he thought. She does love him. But as to whether she fancied Prometheus returned her love, Wynn was none the wiser.

"Prometheus has had a first consultation with Lord Selworth, I hear," said Mrs. Lisle, as the Debenhams' landau rolled along Charles Street. "How did it go?"

The landau's hoods were up against a fine

rain, so the Lisles were able to talk freely without fear of the coachman overhearing. Mrs. Lisle had refused to take a footman, who would draw too much attention in the districts they were bound for.

"I rubbed through unscathed," Pippa said doubtfully, "I think."

"Was he troublesome? I should not have expected it of him. Still, gentlemen become amazingly defensive when their competence is called into question, even when they have already admitted to being in difficulties."

"No, he took criticism like a lamb. And I trust he still has no notion that I am Prometheus."

Yet he had studied her face when he mentioned her influence with Prometheus, and she had felt her face grow stupidly hot. With luck he would put the blush down to his scrutiny — especially as she had still more stupidly flushed when he smiled. But no doubt he was accustomed to young ladies swooning when he smiled, she told herself tartly. She must hope to grow sufficiently accustomed to his smile for it to cease to ruffle her.

"Pippa, he did not attempt any familiarities? It was unwise of Kitty to leave you alone together!"

"He did not even try to flirt, Mama. I am quite sure my only attraction for him is as his conduit to Prometheus. At my age, I have no need of a chaperon when we are discussing

116

business in his sister's house." Nor at any other time or place, she thought, a trifle wistful.

"Let us have no more of this nonsense about your age, my love. No man of sense thinks the worse of a woman for being beyond the first foolishness of youth."

"Do you mean that I am foolish, Mama," Kitty cried, laughing, "and must marry a fool? I shall defy you and marry a man of genius."

Mrs. Lisle smiled. "You are a sensible girl for your age, Kitty, but remember that a fool is sometimes easier to deal with than a man of genius. Not that I wish you to choose your husband by his intellectual attainments. However, when you fall in love, as no doubt you will, ask yourself whether you can imagine the gentleman in question as a friend as well as a lover."

Pippa recalled receiving the same advice before her first Season. It had undoubtedly prevented her making a cake of herself over more than one beau of handsome face or insinuating charm. She had been quite unable to picture them taking a vigorous country walk with her, or talking politics at the breakfast table.

The longest, most vigorous of country walks would have exhausted her less than their afternoon of shopping. Muslins and shawls from Waithman's at Ludgate Hill; Irish linen from Newton's in Leicester Square; poplins from Layton and Shear at Bedford House; all these and the silk merchants and haberdashers of Cheapside blurred in Pippa's mind.

"Thank heaven for Bina's carriage," she said, leaving the shelter of a shop assistant's umbrella to climb into the landau for what she hoped was the last time today. "If we had had to traipse about in hackneys, I doubt I should have survived."

"Cranbourne Alley next, for bonnets," Kitty proposed, lively as ever, "now that we have the colors to be matched."

Pippa groaned.

"Not now," said her mother, to her relief. "Ladies do not frequent Cranbourne Alley so late in the day, and after we inspect our purchases this evening we shall have a better idea of what we need. As much as possible we must make one bonnet do for several gowns."

"I like trimming hats," said Kitty. "One or two plain bonnets and a variety of trimmings will be plenty."

"But consider, my love, when you change your dress you will not have time to be altering the trimmings of your bonnets."

They continued to discuss hats, while Pippa's mind drifted. Why did ladies only frequent Cranbourne Alley in the morning? Since Mama gave no reason, it was probably not a proper subject for young ladies. Unmarried young ladies, at least. Bina might know. Why were unmarried young ladies supposed to be kept in ignorance of so much that was going on in the world? Surely the more they knew the better they could deal with life.

If women were properly educated, they would want to run their own lives. Men would have to give up their authority — which was the answer to her question. They set the rules, and in their determination to keep hold of the reins, they dictated what respectable young ladies should or should not know.

Hence the need to keep the identity of Prometheus secret. However much men admired "his" articles, if they discovered a woman wrote them they would somehow convince themselves they were unworthy of serious consideration.

If Lord Selworth found out, he might believe himself justified in reneging on his agreement with Prometheus. The secret *must* be kept, or Kitty's Season would be ruined.

"It is a great pity styles have become so elaborate," Mrs. Lisle bemoaned. "Silks are more expensive than muslins, to start with. Then the wider skirts take more material, and there is endless trimming to be done."

A trifle enviously, Kitty asked, "Have you seen Millie's Presentation gown, Mama? The train alone uses yards and yards of lace, and the bodice is embroidered with seed pearls. And hoops are still *de rigueur* at Court, just like in the old days, so the skirt is enormous, and the petticoat also." She giggled. "I should feel such a figure of fun wearing hoops!"

"I am glad, dearest, because I cannot manage such an expense, though if it were possible I daresay Mrs. Debenham would be kind enough to present you."

"In any case," Pippa flared up, "it would go against all Papa's principles to make obeisance to the monarchy."

"In any case," Kitty pointed out pacifically, "the poor Queen is not well and Millie's Court dress may very well go to waste!"

"In any case," said Mrs. Lisle, "we shall be hard-pressed to make all the gowns we really need. I hope you will have time to help with the sewing, Pippa."

Pippa groaned again. "Pray do not expect me to cut out, Mama. You know I am terrified of making expensive mistakes. Give me the simplest seams and hems, and I shall contrive to do my part."

"We shall see. I do not wish you to tire your eyes with stitchery if you have a great deal of reading and writing to do."

"Think how tired the eyes of seamstresses must get."

"And they have not even the pleasure of sewing for themselves," Kitty agreed.

"They are paid for their labor," Mrs. Lisle said, "when many would be glad of any work."

"How lucky I am," cried Kitty, "not to have to work for my living, thanks to my dear family."

"And how lucky I am," said Pippa, "to be paid to do what I should very likely choose to do even without pay! It is a pity, though, that Mr. Cobbett has gone abroad. We shall have less money than you expected, Mama, and I have less excuse to avoid sewing."

The landau turned into Charles Street, passed the Running Footman public house at the corner of Hay's Mews, and stopped in front of the Debenhams' house. A boy ran up to hold the horses' heads while the coachman clambered down from his perch to come and let down the step.

Kitty glanced around and said, "We shall have to make several trips to carry in all these parcels."

"The footmen will fetch them," Mrs. Lisle told her. "It will never do for the Debenhams' guests to be seen trotting up the front steps laden with packages. We have done very nicely, girls, and there is more yet to be sent round by the shops." With satisfaction she shook her purse, which jingled. "Stuffed full when we started out but not empty yet — very nicely indeed!"

Pippa was shocked to realize how much they had bought. Why, Mama must have spent enough to keep a poor family for years! Papa's principles had fallen by the wayside without a word of protest from his elder daughter.

Yet she had had her Season, for all the good it did her, and it was not for her to spoil Kitty's. She said nothing now, but resolved to ask Mama later how Papa had felt about the expenditure on the earlier foray into the marriage market.

As they entered the hall, the butler informed them stiffly that Mrs. Debenham and Miss Warren were entertaining callers in the drawing room.

"We shall not disturb them," said Mrs. Lisle, smiling slightly at the butler's involuntary look of relief. "Have our purchases taken up to the little sitting room, if you please."

"At once, madam."

On the way upstairs, Mrs. Lisle observed complacently, "We are most fortunate that Mr. and Mrs. Debenham senior entertain a good deal at their country home. Although Mrs. George Debenham has only visited Town briefly since her marriage, she is already acquainted with a great many people, I collect."

"I believe so," Pippa agreed.

"For the present we shall concentrate on making up morning gowns and walking dresses so as to be able to join in morning calls. Time enough for evening gowns when we have met hostesses who are likely to invite us to evening parties."

"The primrose and white cloud muslin first," Kitty decided, bouncing up the second flight of stairs, "then the green sprig. Which do you want for your first gown, Pippa?"

After a moment's thought, Pippa confessed, "I fear I cannot for the life of me remember what I chose."

Her mother and sister laughingly scolded her. Kitty went on to remind her of deep rose mull muslin and violet jaconet muslin, willow green Circassian cloth, and celestial blue lustring.

"You will have to tell me which is suitable for which kind of dress," Pippa told her as they doffed bonnets and pelisses in their chamber. "I bought at your direction."

They hurried to the sitting room, where Mrs. Lisle joined them a moment later.

"This table is perfect for laying out and cutting patterns," she said, going over to a large table Pippa had scarcely noticed. "I daresay that is why Mrs. Debenham had it put in here. She attends to our needs with the greatest delicacy, never commenting on the difference in our situations. You could not have made a better friend, Pippa."

"I know it." Pippa drifted towards the little writing table. "Mama, pray excuse me for the moment. I should like to finish reading this speech while Bina and Millicent are otherwise occupied. Kitty may choose which dress I am to have first, and once it is cut out and pinned, I shall struggle with the seams."

Even as she spoke, she sat down at the desk. One of the drawers had had a key in it, and in this she had locked the manuscript, putting the key on a ribbon around her neck. She unlocked the drawer. Soon she was so absorbed she scarcely noticed the arrival of two laden footmen, the rustle of paper, Mama and Kitty's soft chatter, the snick of scissors. When a cup of tea miraculously appeared in front of her, she drank thirstily without sparing a thought for its provenance.

Coming to the end of Lord Selworth's speech, Pippa pondered the necessary alterations. She was almost sure it was going to be too long, even with the overfanciful passages cut down to size. He wanted to solve all the world's evils at once.

"Pippa," Kitty said gaily, "unless you wish this gown to be merely *nearly* the right size, you must come now and have pins stuck into you."

"Is it not enough that I shall soon be sticking needles into myself?" Pippa grumbled, but she locked away the speech and mustered her patience for the fitting.

Altogether weary of clothes, Pippa changed quickly for dinner. Leaving Kitty to share Nan's ministrations with Millicent, she went to her mother's chamber.

"May I come in, Mama? I want to talk to you."

"Of course, my love. Bister has done everything but put my cap on for me, so we shall not be disturbed." Mrs. Lisle, sitting at her dressing table, picked up her best cap and set it on her head. Tying the ribbons, she went on, "You are a little dismayed, are you not, by the number of gowns I propose to make for you? I have promised not to force you to go to parties if you attend a few and find you still dislike such affairs excessively."

"It is not so much that, Mama, as the cost."

"Are you afraid I shall fall into debt? You may be easy, dearest. You know your papa's opinion of those who buy luxuries upon credit and then deprive honest shopkeepers of their due."

"Papa held no high opinion of those who waste good money on luxuries when others want for necessities," Pippa pointed out. "I never wondered before, but seeing all we purchased today — Was he not distressed by the expenditure on my Season?"

"He realized the need. When I pointed out to him that in the circumscribed society at home you had little chance of meeting a man you could love, he had no objection to our repairing to Town. Or rather, his only objection was that he did not wish to lose you. He loved you dearly."

"I miss him dreadfully, still."

"And I, my love. But Papa knew you would one day want a home of your own. He was a sensible man, as well as an idealist, and he recognized his duty to his family as well as to humanity."

"Lord Selworth is the same, I think," Pippa said slowly. "Eager as he is to change the world, his first consideration upon attaining the viscountcy was to provide for his family."

"Very true."

"I believe he is very fond of them, but the sad truth is, if he gave away all his worldly wealth except enough to keep them from poverty, his influence would be greatly lessened." Becoming aware of her mother's intent scrutiny, Pippa grimaced. "He confuses me."

"My darling, I hope I have not imperilled your heart with my clever scheme! I should never forgive myself. You have had little contact with personable gentlemen; it is not surprising that his attentiveness should disturb you. Remind yourself that he seeks your company because of Prometheus."

"As *I* told *you*," Pippa concurred. "I know it well." She gave her anxious mother a reassuring smile, yet she could not have sworn that her heart was not in peril.

8

George Debenham dined at his club that evening. "He knows I shall require his escort once we begin to go about in company," Bina explained as the ladies went in to dinner. "He is making the most of a brief freedom before he is expected to dance attendance upon us."

"Shepherding five females about will keep him busy," Mrs. Lisle agreed with a smile.

A rooster with a flock of hens, Pippa thought. Or, as Lord Selworth would doubtless dramatically have it, a Turkish sultan with his harem. She wondered whether the viscount would occasionally condescend to escort his sisters. His presence would do much to reconcile her to frequenting the entertainments of the Season.

"So we shall have a comfortable domestic evening," Bina said. "Millicent and I request permission to display our needlework skills. Dare I hope you will trust us not to spoil your new gowns?"

"Oh no," said Mrs. Lisle, for once visibly flustered. "That is, of course we should trust you, but you cannot wish —"

"Indeed we do," Millicent burst out "For until you have fashionable gowns, Kitty cannot go about with me and that is what I want above anything, and we are both quite good at sewing. At least, Bina has done nothing but fine work for years and years, ever since she married, but I helped to make all the family clothes, shirts and chemises and trousers and aprons and —"

"A complete catalogue is unnecessary," Bina cut her off with a smile.

"And everything else right up until Wynn became suddenly rich, which was just a few months ago, so you see we can certainly be of assistance. And I am simply dying to see what you have bought and to learn where you found bargains, because the prices in the Bond Street shops are outrageous and those in Oxford Street not much lower, and when you have been accustomed all your life to counting pennies, it goes against the grain to see them squandered, I assure you," Millicent said earnestly, "though what grain has to do with anything, I cannot guess."

Here Kitty interrupted to explain to her that the grain concerned was wood, not corn. Mrs. Lisle seized the opportunity to gratefully accept Bina's offer of assistance, so the ladies spent a cosy evening with their needles.

At least, Pippa spent part of the evening with a needle. The third time she pricked her finger, she spotted a delicate India muslin. After the bustle attendant upon swift removal of the bloodstain, she was invited to read to the workers from one of Mr. Scott's novels.

This had the added advantage of curbing Millie's tongue. Somehow she managed to confine herself to comments upon the story and necessary questions about the sewing.

All in all, it was a pleasant and productive evening, ending with a gown for each of the Lisles finished to the last knot of ribbon.

"We shall do it again," Bina vowed, "for, you know, Mrs. Lisle, in this I am as self-interested as Millie. Until *you* are able to go about, I must not accept invitations to evening parties, and until *Pippa* can, I shall not wish to."

Pippa marked the place in the book and set it aside, and the others folded their work. As Mrs. Lisle, Kitty, and Millicent left the room, Bina held Pippa back, closing the door behind the others.

"Stay a moment. Pippa, the last thing I wish is to offend, but I see no reason why you and I should not share gowns again, as we used to."

"Oh Bina, how can you call yourself selfish or self-interested? You are quite the most generous of friends, but it will not do."

"Why not? Just because I had the good fortune to meet George four years ago, and you were not lucky enough to meet the right gentleman? It would save both labor and your mother's purse. Change a few ribbons and no one will recognize the dresses. You are as dark as ever, and I as fair, and we were always much of a size."

"I skinny and you slender," Pippa reminded

her. "The fact is, I shall need few gowns, as I do not mean to go about much. Just one or two parties to satisfy Mama."

"What nonsense, my dear! If you were skinny and I slender, now you are slender while my figure, I fear, is rapidly tending towards the matronly. With proper clothes and the wisdom of four more years — indeed, I cannot think why girls are thrown so young and ignorant into the world! — there is no reason why you should not enjoy yourself thoroughly this time."

"But I —"

Bina ruthlessly interrupted. "Besides, I shall not let you disappoint my brother."

"Lord Selworth?" Had he told his sister he looked forward to escorting Pippa to parties, perhaps even to dancing with her at balls? For a heart-stopping moment Pippa wondered, before the brief dream was swept away by the chilly wind of reality.

"Wynn promised Prometheus to introduce you to Society," Bina reminded her unnecessarily. "He will not feel he has carried out his end of the bargain if you merely attend a ball or two. So that is settled. We shall go through my wardrobe tomorrow and see what will suit you best."

Pippa surrendered, at least temporarily. Kissing Bina, she said, "How can I thank you, my dearest friend?"

"Pray do not! So tedious," Bina said with a smile, opening the door. "George gives me a simply enormous dress allowance, you must know. Now, let us set a time. What are your mama's plans for tomorrow morning?"

"We are to go to Cranbourne Alley to choose hats. That reminds me, why do ladies shop in Cranbourne Alley only in the mornings?" Pippa asked, following Bina out into the passage.

"Because it is an insalubrious district with a great many bawdy houses, and —" At the sound of a gasp behind them, she stopped and turned. "Yes, Reuben?"

One of the footmen had come out from the backstairs in time to hear his mistress's remark. Crimson to the ears, he stammered, "Was you wanting me to snuff the candles and bank the fire, madam?"

"Yes, thank you, we are finished in there." As the footman disappeared into the sitting room, Bina continued in a lower tone but without much concern, "Oh dear, I trust the Running Footman will not be all abuzz with tales of how we were caught discussing houses of ill repute! As I was saying, in the afternoon and evening, caps and bonnets are not the only wares displayed in Cranbourne Alley. Or so I have heard."

"I did not suppose you had gone to see for yourself!" Pippa assured her, laughing.

They parted, to retire for the night. In bed, Pippa and Kitty talked for a little while about the experiences of the day, but Kitty soon fell asleep in the middle of a sentence. Pippa lay wakeful, her thoughts returning to Lord Selworth's speech.

Perhaps she should suggest he stuck to one topic rather than trying to cram in all the ills he wished to combat. The talk of bawdy houses reminded her of Papa's descriptions of the dreadful lives of women, some no more than young girls, forced into prostitution by pimps and abbesses, or by simple poverty. Pippa had laughed at Bina's comment, but their plight was no laughing matter. Lord Selworth might be willing to take up their cause.

But Pippa could never bring herself to broach the subject with him, even if he believed the notion came from Prometheus. She had best just work with what he had given her.

She slept. In her dreams, she was back in the sitting room, trying on half-made clothes. As she stood in her shift, Lord Selworth came in without knocking. Failing to notice her deshabille, he swept her into a dance, but everyone else in the ballroom started to point at her and whisper to each other. Angrily, Lord Selworth accused her of displaying her wares.

Half-waking, Pippa muttered, "At least you have realized at last that I have wares to display!" She turned over and went back to sleep.

"I thought I might drop in to see Miss Lisle this morning," Wynn said casually, picking up

132

knife and fork to tackle a rather meagre beef-steak.

Chubby looked at him in surprise over the rim of his coffee cup. "Gurgle?" he said.

"Don't speak with your mouth full," Wynn reproved him. "Just to find out if she's forwarded my speech to Prometheus yet."

"Wouldn't plague her about it, if I was you. Don't want to vex her."

"I shouldn't dream of plaguing her," Wynn said with dignity. "A man may call on his sister, may he not? And being there, it's only polite to exchange a word or two with her guests. And if Miss Lisle has sent it off, what more likely than that she'll mention it?"

"Ah." Chubby chewed on this proposal and a mouthful of beef, swallowed both, and brightened. "In that case, I could come, too. I've met Mrs. Debenham. Met Miss Lisle, come to that, and Mrs. Lisle."

"Not to mention Miss Kitty."

Chubby pinkened. "Not the thing for a single gentleman to call on an unmarried young lady uninvited, but I can go with you to visit your sister."

"And being there," Wynn teasingly quoted himself, "it's only polite to exchange a word or two with her guests."

"If I can think of anything to say," Chubby fretted.

"Come now, you and Miss Kitty got on swimmingly."

"That was in the country. We're in Town now," said Chubby inarguably. "It's different. Not the thing to talk about cows and chickens in Town."

"I shouldn't worry, if I were you, old fellow," Wynn advised him. "The chances are, with Millicent there, neither of us will need or have the opportunity to open our mouths." He opened his newspaper to the political news.

As usual, the doings of Lord Liverpool and his myrmidons infuriated Wynn. The Prime Minister was still fighting the introduction of a sliding scale to the Corn Law to allow more grain imports. As well as his Tories, many Whig landowners of an otherwise Reformist bent supported him. Wynn itched to discuss this betrayal of the hungry poor with Miss Lisle.

Whoa! He was confusing Pippa Lisle with her father and Prometheus. Just because she seemed quite a clever young woman, he must not forget that she was a woman. Though she had clearly learnt from Benjamin Lisle something of the art of politics, Wynn would have to be careful not to discomfit her by stretching the limits of her understanding.

Tempted, he told himself severely that it would be most ungentlemanly to put her deliberately to the blush only because she was dashed pretty with roses in her cheeks.

"Do put that damn newspaper away and eat your breakfast," Chubby said impatiently. "If we don't get on, the ladies will have gone out."

Solely for his friend's sake, Wynn obliged. He, after all, was in no particular hurry to see Miss Lisle. Whether she had already sent off the manuscript or not, she would be unable to tell him what Prometheus thought of it for at least several days.

Breakfast dispatched, the gentlemen abandoned dressing gowns and carpet slippers in favor of morning coats and Hussar boots. Donning hats and gloves, they sallied forth untopcoated, for the sun shone and spring was in the air.

Had he been striding across the fields at home, Wynn would have whistled. In Piccadilly, he managed to restrain himself insofar as the whistle was concerned, though his gait had nothing in common with the saunter of a Bond Street Beau. As he walked, he looked about him with interest at the shops, the passersby, the vehicles in the street. He ought to have a carriage of his own. Curricle, phaeton, or gig, he pondered. Not a phaeton; one type was too impractical, the other too staid.

At his side Chubby, also country born and bred, kept pace. Not for several minutes did Wynn notice that his silent companion's gaze was fixed on his feet.

"It won't do," said Chubby at that moment, shaking his head.

"The boots? Dammit, I know we decided not to pay Hoby's exorbitant prices, but the fellow we patronized did a perfectly good job."

"Nothing wrong with the boots themselves — it's the polish. They ain't got the shine they had two days ago."

"We've been wearing 'em," Wynn pointed out as they turned up Berkley Street. "You can't expect them to look new forever."

"Not forever," Chubby admitted, "but for a while yet. If I had a proper valet . . . No, m' father would think I'd run mad."

"Miss Kitty won't care if your boots look two days old. The Lisles aren't so finical."

"Maybe not, but I wouldn't want Miss Kitty to think I don't hold her in high enough esteem to take the trouble. Besides," Chubby said doggedly, "whatever you say, Mrs. Debenham's going to expect you to do the pretty. Can't leave it all to Debenham, five females to squire about. Daresay he won't mind if I lend a hand, too."

To his surprise, Wynn discovered balls and routs and breakfasts no longer sounded like an utter waste of time, though he would not admit it aloud. His mother would expect him to accompany his sisters now and then, and he did not want to disgrace them.

Glancing down at his boots, he could not help but note the dullness of the blacking. "Come to think of it, I shan't make much of an impression in the Lords if I'm not turned out bang up to the mark. And you're right. The fellow who does for us hasn't time for a thorough job with half a dozen others to take care

136

of. I'll hire us a valet, or better, a chap who don't hold himself too high to cook us a decent breakfast, too."

"I say, didn't mean to hint —"

"You can pay what you're paying now, so that Lord Chubb won't know the difference. Look, there's the Sign of the Pot and Pineapple. Do you suppose Miss Lisle . . . the ladies would like some of Gunter's kickshaws?"

"You're the one with sisters."

"So I am. Come along, then."

They cut across the corner of Berkley Square to Number Seven, the premises of Gunter's, Confectioner, Pastrycook, and Caterer. Outside, a notice board announced the receipt of a cargo of ice from the Greenland seas; patrons were advised that cream fruit ices were once again available.

Wynn and Chubby were in pursuit of more durable prey. They emerged from the shop a few minutes later, each bearing a pasteboard box full of vanilla, apricot, cinnamon and orange flower pastilles; candied ginger; and Gunter's famous cedrati and bergamot chips.

"Shall we treat them to an ice this afternoon?" suggested Chubby.

"Not today. With all these bonbons as well, they'd make themselves sick," said Wynn with the ruthless practicality of the possessor of many small siblings.

"Miss Kitty wouldn't!"

"She might. Don't suppose she's used to a lot

of sweets. Miss Lisle wouldn't, nor her mother or my sister," Wynn conceded, "but I wouldn't put it past Millicent, and it would ruin the party."

Chubby blenched. "Yes, rather. I'll just dash back in and see how long they expect the ice to hold out."

He returned to report that Gunter's expected, barring shipwreck, to be able to serve ices well into the summer months. "So that's all right. Bring 'em round any time. You know what, old chap, I'm almost looking forward to the Season!"

"Your father doesn't object to your frittering away your time in Town?" Wynn asked as they turned the corner into Charles Street.

"Been at me for years to get a bit of Town bronze before I settle down. He and my mother hope I'll find a wife, of course, but I never expected I'd find a girl I'd really want to marry."

"Hold hard, Chubby, you can't be serious about the chit! You hardly know her."

"I know what I want," Chubby said stubbornly. "And I know I haven't much chance with such a wonderful girl."

Wynn still suspected calf love, in which case time would cure his friend if allowed to do its business. Whereas, should Kitty be offered and grasp an immediate opportunity to wed a future title and comfortable fortune, Chubby might find himself repenting at leisure.

"You don't mean to throw the handkerchief

right away, I hope," he said, stopping on his sister's doorstep.

"Lord no. It wouldn't be fair. She's bound to have dozens of offers. If she hasn't accepted someone better by the end of the Season, I'll try my luck."

Satisfied, Wynn gave a brisk *rat-tat* with the brass lion's-head knocker on the green front door.

The first footman opened the door. The butler would have been on hand to usher callers up to the drawing room if Mrs. Debenham were receiving, but after all Wynn was her brother.

"M'sisters in, Reuben?" he asked.

"Mrs. Debenham and Miss Warren are not at home, my lord."

"You mean they have gone out, or they're just 'not at home'?"

"Gone out, my lord," the footman clarified apologetically.

"What about the Lisles?"

"Not at home, my lord."

"Dash it all, man, are they in or not?" Wynn bethought himself too late that he had no right to intrude upon the Lisles — as opposed to his sister — if they were euphemistically "out" rather than really out.

Looking a trifle bemused, Reuben said, "Mrs. Lisle, Miss Lisle, and Miss Catherine *left the house* with Mrs. Debenham and Miss Warren."

"Blast. Where did they go, do you know?"

"To pay calls, I understand, my lord."

"No hope of catching up with them, then," said Wynn, disappointed.

"Miss Lisle did express the hope of stopping at Hookham's Library in Bond Street."

"Hookham's, eh? Splendid. I'll leave a note for Miss . . . for Mrs. Debenham."

"Mr. Debenham is at home, my lord. That is, he is in the house. Whether he is 'at home' —"

Wynn held up his hand. "Enough! We don't want to see Debenham."

"Always happy to see Debenham," Chubby corrected with punctilious politeness.

The gentleman in question burst out of his den at that moment. "What the deuce . . . ? Oh, it's you, Selworth. Good morning, Chubb. Is something amiss, Selworth?"

"Only the inability of the English upper classes and their servants to say what they mean. Not Reuben's fault," Wynn added quickly as Debenham cocked an eyebrow at his footman. "A minor misunderstanding. Sorry to disturb you. I just dropped in to see Albinia."

"All the ladies have gone out to pay morning calls on prospective hostesses and Almack's patronesses."

"So I gather. I'll leave Bina a note."

"Come into my den," said Debenham resignedly, ushering them into a pleasant, book-lined room. "May I offer you a glass of Madeira?"

"Thanks, but we've just breakfasted and we

140

don't want to keep you from your business." Wynn waved at the papers on the desk. "I've been meaning to say, Debenham, it's dashed good of you to put up the Lisles, especially as I know you disagree with my political opinions."

"My dear Selworth, you must know by now your sister can twist me around her little finger. As it turns out, they are a charming family and I'm happy to have them. Moreover, it leaves you with no excuse to avoid your share of escorting the ladies about."

"Naturally I'll do my share," said Wynn, his tone as hurt as if he had never contemplated leaving the whole affair to his brother-in-law. "In fact, I was going to offer our services, mine and Chubb's, to squire the ladies to the Park this afternoon."

Debenham pushed a sheet of paper, pen, and inkstand across the desk to him. "I'm sure they will be delighted to accept. I'm much obliged to you, Chubb, for lending your support."

"Not at all, not at all," Chubby muttered, blushing. "Do what I can. A pleasure."

"Allow me to include you in the standing invitation to my brother-in-law to take your mutton with us whenever it won't upset my wife's numbers for a dinner party."

"I say, dashed kind!"

Wynn blotted and folded his note, and he and Chubby took their leave, entrusting the sweetmeats to the footman. On reaching the street, Wynn turned left towards Bond Street.

"Where are we going?" Chubby asked.

"To Hookham's Library."

Chubby stopped dead. "I wondered why you were so pleased to hear Miss Lisle wanted to go to Hookham's."

"It's a good place to wait until they turn up."

"They may have gone there first. It strikes me you're even wilder to see Miss Lisle than I am to see Miss Kitty."

"Not at all," Wynn said defensively. "I simply want to find out about my speech."

"Well, you may not mind spending hours and hours in a library on the off chance, but I can think of better things to do with my time." He turned and started in the opposite direction, saying over his shoulder, "I'm off to Tattersall's to look for a carriage horse or pair. My father said I should buy myself a gig that's useful both in Town and in the country. I'll be able to take up Miss Kitty — or any of the ladies."

Wynn caught up with him. "All right, Tatt's it is. I was thinking of a tilbury gig."

As they strolled on, arguing the relative merits of various light carriages, Wynn wondered whether Chubby could possibly be right. Was he wilder — as wild — almost as wild to see Miss Lisle as his friend was to see Miss Kitty?

Impossible!

9

"The Misses Pendrell?" exclaimed Lord Selworth and Mr. Chubb with identical looks of horror. Pippa was hard put to it not to laugh aloud.

"We made their acquaintance at Lady Castlereagh's," Millicent rattled on, "and they asked us to walk with them in St. James's Park this afternoon and we —"

"Who are the Misses Pendrell?" Lord Selworth demanded with an ominous frown.

"They are some sort of relatives of Lady Castlereagh, Wynn, so we could not say no without offending her and she is one of the patronesses of Almack's, and besides, they are nice girls, are they not, Kitty? How were we to know you wished to go to Hyde Park with us? You need not come to St. James's Park if you do not —"

"I didn't bargain for swarms of unknown females. I'm happy to escort Miss Lisle and Miss Kitty, and I don't mind squiring you, Millie, but I draw the line at wholesale husband-hunting misses, however nice."

"I'll come," Mr. Chubb put in with a stoic air, then blushed and said pleadingly to Kitty, "if you don't mind."

"Of course not, but you must not feel obliged, sir. Lieutenant Pendrell promised to accompany his sisters, so we shall not be without male protection."

"I'll come," Mr. Chubb repeated, this time with determination.

Lord Selworth sighed. "I daresay I had best go, too, in case you need protection against this lieutenant chap. Females tend to fall for a dashing scarlet coat without considering what sort of scoundrel is wearing it."

"Lieutenant Pendrell wears Rifle green," Pippa informed him, "and he seems an inoffensive gentleman, not especially dashing."

"Ha! the better to humbug you," Lord Selworth said with a grin. "Do you go, Mrs. Lisle, Bina?"

"Not if you will be there to guard the lambs against the wolf in rifleman's clothing," said Bina. "Mrs. Lisle and I have plans to make."

The Pendrells arrived shortly, the young ladies in a smart barouche, their brother riding. On horseback, though his uniform was green, not scarlet, the lieutenant had a dashing air absent in the drawing room.

His sisters were delighted to find two more gentlemen were to join their party, especially when they heard one was a lord. They fluttered their eyelashes at Lord Selworth, but accepted his utter lack of interest philosophically.

As Millicent said, the Misses Pendrell were nice girls. There was not a great deal more to say about them, Pippa reflected, greeting them as Lord Selworth handed her into the carriage to join them. At least on first acquaintance, she corrected herself charitably.

Respectively eighteen and seventeen years of age, Miss Pendrell and Miss Vanessa both had light brown hair, with rather vapid but not unattractive faces. Their clothes were smart, though with a tendency towards overadornment. They had an inexhaustible fund of chatter on clothes, the weather, entertainments, and the latest *on-dit*, without in any way rivalling Millicent. Millie, in her good-natured way, had already assured them that they might interrupt her without offence. Of this permission they availed themselves unstintingly.

As the barouche rolled towards St. James's Park, Pippa, feeling ancient, was free to marvel at the dullness of the conversation without needing to join in. Miss Pendrell, seated beside her facing forward, occasionally turned to her politely as if to solicit her opinion. Luckily she was satisfied with an "Indeed," or a "Good gracious."

Kitty appeared to be enjoying herself. When she glanced across at Pippa, it was with a sort of conspiratorial amusement. She could chatter away with the best of them, her eyes said, but was it not absurd?

At first the narrow streets, and then the busy traffic of Piccadilly, prevented the gentlemen's riding alongside. When the barouche turned down Constitution Hill, between Green Park and the tree-hidden gardens of Buckingham House, Lord Selworth and the lieutenant at once moved forward on either side.

"I hope the talk of walking was not a fudge," Pippa said to the viscount in a low voice, though there was little fear of being overheard over Millicent's prattle. "I am sorely in need of exercise after sitting in carriages and drawing rooms all day."

"Do you ride?" he asked, ignoring Miss Vanessa Pendrell's attempts to catch his attention. "What a great deal I don't know about you!"

"How should you? No, I have never had a chance to learn to ride. I should have liked to learn, but I suppose I am too old now."

"Old! Don't let Bina hear you saying such a thing. I'd be glad to teach you — but London is no place to learn," he added hastily. "I'm thinking of buying a tilbury. I shall be able to take you driving, then. Chubb's set on a stanhope gig — says it's more practical."

"Why?"

"It has a larger boot. Some tilburies don't have a boot at all."

"The stanhope does sound more useful," Pippa said, looking around for Mr. Chubb.

"But a tilbury is more sporting," Lord Selworth argued.

"If you want to be sporting, why not get a curricle? If you ever wish to use it for longer journeys, two horses are more practical than one. Oh, poor Mr. Chubb!"

On the other side of the barouche, Lieutenant Pendrell had positioned his mount so as to monopolize Kitty. Mr. Chubb lurked beyond, scarcely able to see her, far less to exchange a word. He looked downcast but resigned, as if the situation was just what he had expected.

Kitty was laughing merrily at something the officer had said to her. Pippa hoped her sister was too sensible to be swept off her feet by the glamor of a uniform.

"Chubby's no dashing blade, just a thoroughly good sort," said Lord Selworth.

"I do think you ought not to call him Chubby," Pippa suggested tentatively. "I realize it comes from his name, but it cannot be comfortable having such a nickname. Whether it would be worse if he were actually chubby rather than thin as a rake, I cannot guess."

He stared down at her, eyebrows raised, a thoughtful look in his eyes. "You have a point there, Miss Lisle. It dates from our schooldays, of course. Boys are not the most sensitive of creatures, I fear, and the habit stuck without ever being consciously considered."

"It is really none of my business," Pippa said in some confusion. "I beg your pardon."

"No, no, I'm glad you mentioned it. You have not only a kind heart, but a perceptive mind."

Though pleased he should think her kind,

Pippa did not at all wish him to see her as perceptive. To her relief, they came to the beginning of the Mall and Miss Pendrell called to the coachman to stop. They all got down to walk, the gentlemen leaving their horses with the coachman.

Lieutenant Pendrell at once offered Kitty his arm and strolled off towards the lake. Mr. Chubb turned towards Pippa, but Lord Selworth had already determinedly appropriated her, positively seizing her hand and laying it on his arm.

"I'm sorry to throw Chubb to the wolves," he whispered, "but I'll be dashed if I'll sacrifice myself for him."

"You are far better able to hold your own," she reproved him, though she could not but be flattered by his preference for her company.

With an apprehensive glance at the three remaining young ladies, Mr. Chubb decided to choose the devil he knew. "M-miss Warren," he stammered with an uncertain gesture of his right hand.

Without a pause in the flow of words, Millicent smiled at him and took his arm. The Misses Pendrell cast hopeful looks at Lord Selworth, but he promptly adopted a Napoleonic pose with his free hand thrust between his coat buttons, and bent his head to speak to Pippa.

"Tell me when it's safe to look up," he hissed.

"You are a coxcomb, sir," she responded,

trying hard not to laugh.

Miss Pendrell hastened to take possession of Mr. Chubb's left arm, leaving Miss Vanessa to walk beside her. Bringing up the rear, Pippa saw Miss Pendrell address several questions to Mr. Chubb. After a series of incoherent monosyllables in answer, she gave up and followed Millicent's lead in talking past him as if he were not there.

"As long as he's not expected to speak, he'll live through it," said the callous viscount. "Speaking of speech, I don't suppose you have had a chance to finish reading mine. Bina said you were all sewing away last night to finish your new gowns. Which are very becoming!" he added quickly, with a sidelong inspection which swept Pippa from yellow-ribboned bonnet past shawl of Norwich silk to the frill round the hem of her buttercup muslin gown.

"I am persuaded, sir, that in spite of your sister's mention of the sewing, you have not until this very moment spared the product so much as a glance."

"Untrue, ma'am! At least," he said with a rueful grin, "even if I failed to pin down the cause, I was — am — aware of your being in particularly good looks today."

"Fine feathers make fine birds," Pippa said tartly, but she was pleased with the compliment — only because the more he believed her concerned with her looks, the less he would suspect her secret. "Bina kindly did *not* mention that I was dismissed as a seamstress for bleeding onto my work."

"Bleeding! You were hurt?"

"I did not mean to alarm you. I merely pricked my finger. Repeatedly. When it comes to needles I am all thumbs, I fear. However, my incompetence did allow me to finish reading your speech. Prometheus will soon be studying it."

"You have sent it off to him already? Thank you. Can you tell me how much I owe him for postage? I don't wish to leave him out of pocket for longer than need be."

His request put Pippa in something of a quandary. She could not charge him for what had not been spent.

"I was not sure whether Prometheus would have sufficient funds at hand to pay postage for so many sheets," she said. "Sending a packet by the stage, paying half in advance, is much cheaper, and you did say there was no real need for haste. It will be easier to reckon up the total at the end, when the work is all finished." And she would have time to think up a reason not to accept any money.

He nodded. "As you wish. But you must promise to let me know at once if the delay in payment causes any difficulties. Tell me, when you said you are in need of exercise, is this what you had in mind?"

"Heavens no. I would not call this a walk, scarcely even a saunter."

"A mere dawdle," Lord Selworth agreed. "Let us see which way the others turn to circle the lake, and we shall go the opposite way."

"I ought to chaperon the girls," Pippa said reluctantly.

"Chaperon? My dear Miss Lisle, if Albinia, married with two children, is too young to assume that weighty mantle without aid, you are unquestionably ineligible. Besides, I believe Millicent, Chubb, and two sisters are watch-dogs enough for the lieutenant. You don't mean to hint that Chubb is a threat to Millie and the Misses Pendrell, I take it?"

Laughing, Pippa shook her head. Reaching the lake, Kitty and Lieutenant Pendrell turned south, so Pippa and the viscount took the path along the north bank, walking at a brisk pace. Not until then did it dawn on her to ask herself whether it was quite proper for her to be alone with Lord Selworth.

He seemed to see nothing amiss, and his conduct was not remotely loverlike — not that she had for a moment expected it. Their relationship was not of that sort. Chiding herself for missishness, she nonetheless removed her hand from his arm to point to the flock of white pelicans on the lake, and failed to replace it.

Lord Selworth was interested in the pelicans and the other waterbirds swimming or resting on the grass under the willows and plane trees. Pippa knew no more than he about the rarer varieties, but they both vowed to look for an illustrated book and try to identify them. The spring flowers were easier: crocuses, daffodils, narcissus, cheeky-faced pansies, and bright-hued polyanthus.

Though Pippa had spent only a few months in London, Lord Selworth had spent less. She was able to point out to him, through gaps in the trees, the backs of St. James' Palace and Carlton House.

Unfortunately, the sight of Carlton House brought to the viscount's mind the Prince Regent's debts and the rest of his iniquities. Pippa forced herself to murmur agreement to his strictures without adding her own ideas on the subject. Before temptation grew too great to be resisted, they came to the end of the lake.

Before them the wide open space of the Parade Ground spread to the impressive buildings of the Horse Guards and the Admiralty. A crowd was gathering as a military band in scarlet, white and gold uttered a few preliminary toots on their gleaming brass instruments.

"Oh, may we stay and listen?" Pippa cried.

"Why not?" Lord Selworth turned to gaze back along the lake. "For a while, at least. The others will not catch up with us for a good five or ten minutes, and then we shall have as long again to catch up with them on the way back if they don't wish to listen."

"Yes, much better than to dawdle back or to have to wait at the barouche for them. This sounds familiar," Pippa said as the band struck up a rousing tune.

"A march."

"By Handel, I fancy. Kitty plays it upon the spinet, and I have been known to attempt it. How splendid it sounds with trumpets and horns and drums!"

"Perhaps you would have more success with a trumpet than a spinet," Lord Selworth proposed when the march ended.

"What a sensation that would create," Pippa exclaimed, smiling up at him, "a female playing the trumpet! However, I think I should prefer the clarinet. I once heard a concerto for clarinet by Mozart. Is there not something wonderfully mellow about the clarinet?"

Lord Selworth, it turned out, was unfamiliar with the clarinet, had, indeed, never attended a concert of the Philharmonic Society. Pippa, who had delighted in her one experience of orchestral music, advised him to purchase a ticket for the next performance.

"I am sure you will find it agreeable," she said.

"If you will go with me and explain which parts I must particularly admire. We shall make up a party, of course," he added hastily. "Your sister is musical; she will like to go, too."

The others came up then. "You are prodigious energetic, I vow, Miss Lisle!" said Miss Pendrell languidly. "We saw you striding along at a great rate. I am quite fatigued after walking so far."

153

"Yet I wager you think nothing of dancing all night," Lord Selworth drawled with a touch of sarcasm.

Lieutenant Pendrell laughed heartily. "He has you there, Lyddy. If you are so tired, you had best wait here while the rest of us go back and bring the barouche to fetch you. You are not tired, are you, Miss Catherine?"

"After so short a stroll?" said Kitty. "Heavens, no, though I do believe walking slowly is more tiring than walking fast. But there was such a great deal to admire. Pippa, did you ever see such a variety of fowl? And some of them very pretty. I wish we had brought bread crusts to feed them."

The Misses Pendrell stared, and even their brother, though clearly much prepossessed with Kitty, looked taken aback. Miss Vanessa murmured something to her sister; Pippa thought she caught the word "hoydens."

Mr. Chubb sprang to the rescue. "Splendid notion, Miss Kitty. We'll come back with bread, a loaf, two loaves. Drive you myself, soon as I've bought my carriage."

"I shall look forward to it, sir," Kitty said with a serene smile, not at all distressed by the Pendrells' disdain. "Do you suppose it might be possible to obtain eggs or ducklings of the rarer birds for my poultry yard?"

Pippa envied her sister's equable temperament. The jibe about her "striding" had hurt, though Lord Selworth's prompt retort soothed the wound. She resolved not to let petty snubs daunt her as they had in her first Season, not to allow others to dictate her behavior. This time she came without any expectation of attracting a husband, so what did it matter what people thought of her?

Lieutenant Pendrell did not long permit Mr. Chubb to enjoy Kitty's attention, Pippa saw. He won her back with an outrageous plan to enlist his fellow officers in a plot to ducknap her chosen waterfowl from the park one dark night. His sisters, too, abandoned their supercilious airs to join in the laughter.

Mr. Chubb was left to listen in philosophical silence to Millicent's monologue, which began with the misdeeds of a rooster at the Rectory and drifted into uncharted byways.

"Millie, Chubb," Lord Selworth interrupted, "Miss Lisle and I will listen to the band for a while, then catch you up."

"Come back to fetch you," Mr. Chubb suggested, "and Miss Pendrell."

"I fancy Miss Pendrell has forgotten her exhaustion," said Pippa dryly, waving at the others, who had already set out around the north side of the lake. "And I have not yet had as much exercise as I would wish."

"We shall stay and listen, too," said Millicent. "I do not mind walking fast, and I shall like to hear the music. I like a military band of all things, such a splendid sight in their scarlet —"

"Oh no," said Lord Selworth, "we shan't hear

155

a note if you stay. Take her away, Chubb, there's a good fellow."

Millie pulled a face at her brother, but obediently went off. She and Mr. Chubb might suit each other very well, Pippa decided. The lady would never be interrupted, and the gentleman would never have to struggle in vain for words to fill a silence.

Pippa and Lord Selworth stayed a few more minutes, then walked back along the southern path, talking of music. They joined the others at the barouche all too soon for Pippa. She was sure she had never passed a pleasanter afternoon, in spite of an odd contretemps or two, minor in retrospect.

It was wonderful to find a variety of subjects she could discuss sensibly with Lord Selworth. As long as they avoided politics, she felt no need to guard her tongue.

The trouble was, they both found politics so absorbing it was an excessively difficult subject to avoid.

10

"If skirts get any wider," grumbled George Debenham, seated between his wife and Mrs. Lisle, "we shall have to take two carriages."

"I hardly think it likely, dear," Albinia said placidly, tucking a white kid-gloved hand beneath his arm. "No one would choose to return to those ridiculous hooped skirts of the last century. It is bad enough having to wear them at Court."

"I am glad I never had to manage a hoop," said Pippa, sitting opposite her. She smoothed her ball gown with nervous fingers.

The claret red crepe, trimmed with full-blown white satin roses and worn over a white satin slip of Bina's, was quite the most beautiful dress she had ever owned. It was wasted on her. Even Bina's superior dresser had given up trying to put a fashionable curl in Pippa's hair, and pinned it up into a topknot as severe as her usual style. Her cheeks were so pale with trepidation, the least touch of rouge made her look like an actress, so that, too, had to be abandoned.

"I found the train of an evening dress difficult enough, remember, Bina?" she continued.

157

"I recall one or two stumbles," Bina admitted.

"Thank heaven they are no longer worn. As for a hoop, I would surely have made a shocking mull of it and disgraced myself."

"Must I be presented, Bina?" Millicent asked plaintively. "Everyone says it is a dreadful ordeal. You were not until you married, and Kitty does not have to. I should prefer just to go to balls without having to worry about it. I am sure we could alter my Presentation gown to make it into another ball gown. I wish I had thought of it sooner; then I could have worn it tonight, for our first ball."

"You are the sister of a peer now," said Bina, "which I was not then. It is proper for you to make your curtsy to the Queen, if she is well enough."

"She is *excessively* old," said Millicent, with a note of hope which drew instant censure from her elder sister.

Unrepressed, Millie chattered on. Pippa ceased to listen, concentrating on trying to still the flutters in her stomach. At her age, she ought to have outgrown such foolish apprehensions, yet she felt just as she had four years earlier on the way to a ball. Worse, even, since tonight she would be thrust into the heart of the *beau monde* instead of flitting about on the outskirts.

It was some comfort that Lord Selworth would be there. Indeed, he had already re-

158

quested a country dance of each of the ladies, as had Mr. Chubb, so Pippa would not be a wallflower the entire evening.

After dining at the Debenhams', the two of them were coming together in Lord Selworth's brand-new curricle. The viscount had confessed to Pippa that he was in not much less of a quake than his friend when it came to their first venture into Polite Society.

"Far more frightening than speaking before the entire House of Lords," he had said. "From all I hear, the ladies of the *haut ton* are a thousand times more critical."

Though she had not said so, Pippa thought she, too, had rather face the House of Lords, speech in hand.

Lord Selworth had promised Bina to be there. He would not break his promise, nor fail to attend his younger sister at her first ball, would he? Surely he and Mr. Chubb would not sheer off at the last minute!

Pippa longed to let down the window and peer out into the lamp-lit night at the row of carriages they had just joined. Millicent, with the same notion, nearly put it into practice.

"I wonder if Wynn is in front of us or close behind?" As she jumped up and reached for the strap, Mrs. Lisle caught her hand just in time.

"We shall get there no faster for fidgeting," she pointed out.

"May we not get down and walk, ma'am?" Millie begged. "I cannot sit still while we crawl along like this. We should arrive much sooner walking, and I daresay —"

"I fear etiquette requires us to arrive by carriage, my dear," Mrs. Lisle said sympathetically.

"What a goosecap you are, Millie," said Kitty. "You cannot wish to soil your slippers in the dirty street!"

"No indeed, I did not think. Miss Vanessa Pendrell says there is generally a carpet laid across the pavement to the front door to keep the ladies' feet clean, and if it looks like rain the first-rate hostesses have an awning set up over the carpet. Would it not be dreadful to arrive soaked to the skin at one's first ball? Silk spots so shockingly and — Oh, look, there is Wynn!" She pointed at the window on Pippa's side.

About to knock, Lord Selworth lowered his hand as Bina reached across to let down the window.

"We were held up," he said, raising his top hat in salute. "We're a long way back in the line. We didn't want you to think we had abandoned you, so we left the curricle with my groom and walked on."

"What!" Pippa exclaimed. "You entrusted your new carriage to a mere groom?"

He grinned at her, walking alongside as the Debenham carriage moved up a place. "I'd be happier standing guard over it all night, but then I might as well not have come at all. The fellow knows his head is on the block if there is a single scratch or nick in the paintwork."

"You settled on black picked out in gold?"

"Yes, or yellow, rather. Gold seemed unnecessarily extravagant. The seat is black leather."

"It sounds prodigious smart, Wynn," said Millicent. "You will be quite one of the swells. Will you take me for a drive in it? I should like it above anything. Only think —"

"If you promise not to frighten the horses with your prattle. I decided against maroon — your choice, Bina — in case I find myself driving a lady dressed in a conflicting color."

By the dim light within the carriage, Pippa saw Bina raise her eyebrows. "Did you indeed, brother mine! Are we all to be honored with invitations, then?"

"Certainly, starting with Miss Lisle, since it is on her advice I purchased a curricle instead of a tilbury."

"I only said two horses were better than one for longer journeys," Pippa protested.

"A very material point, Miss Lisle. I shall be able to leave the chaise for my mother's use while I gad about the countryside. Will you drive with me in the Park tomorrow afternoon?"

"I am honored, sir, and I shall be delighted to accept if my mother has no need of me. And if the weather continues fine. I should hate to be the cause of rain spots on your paintwork and the seat leather!"

"Your true concern is for your best bonnet,

confess! For the weather I cannot answer. I shall beg Mrs. Lisle on bended knee to spare you — as soon as we are inside, for here we are at the door at last."

He opened the door, and would have let down the step but that their host's footman forestalled him. However, the servant then stood back and permitted Lord Selworth to hand down first his sister and then Pippa.

George Debenham emerged next and turned to assist Mrs. Lisle. Mr. Chubb, who had been lurking behind Lord Selworth, moved forward to hand out Kitty, and Millicent, exclaiming over the red carpet, also accepted his help.

The footman signalled to the coachman to drive on. Another carriage pulled up as Mr. Debenham offered one arm to Mrs. Lisle and the other to his wife. By then, Pippa and Lord Selworth had moved as far as the doorstep to make room. The press of people behind forced them to continue into the house together.

Once they were inside the hall, the crush was much worse. Pippa gave up her shawl reluctantly, for between décolleté neckline and high waist, the bodice of her gown was alarmingly brief.

Lord Selworth did not appear to see anything amiss. "Dash it," he whispered in Pippa's ear, though he might as well have shouted for the babble of voices, "I don't want to go first. It's for Debenham to lead the way."

"I am sure Bina intended you to take in

Millicent," Pippa hissed back.

"In that case, by all means let us forge ahead. I had ten thousand times rather face the lions with you at my side than my sister! I trust you are acquainted with our hostess, for I certainly am not."

"I have been presented to her, but she will not remember me." Pippa glanced back at Bina, who gave her an encouraging smile. Hemmed in as they were, and constantly inching forward, they could not exchange a word, far less places.

Thus Pippa made a grand entry into the Fashionable World on the arm of one of its most eligible bachelors. That Viscount Selworth was little known to Society only increased the general interest in the young lady accompanying him. To this as much as to the Debenhams' sponsorship Pippa attributed her success.

For it was a success. She was not the Belle of the Ball. There were diamonds of the first water present, eligible maidens with large fortunes and blue bloodlines and fathomless funds of inconsequential chatter. Even Kitty and Millicent gathered larger crowds of would-be partners. Yet to one accustomed and expecting to sit out a great many dances, simply to stand up for nearly every set was triumph beyond her wildest dreams.

Mama was right. Pippa had gained in address in the past few years, if address was the ability to make small talk — and listen to it without obvious impatience. She found herself more tolerant of other people's foibles.

It helped that she no longer felt the pressure to catch a husband, experienced by every girl in her first Season. She did not study every gentleman she met wondering whether she could bear to be his wife, if ever he happened to show the slightest interest in her.

It helped also that she was one of hundreds in a huge ballroom, not one of a couple of dozen in two rooms thrown together with the carpet rolled back. She did not feel her looks, her clothes, her every move under constant scrutiny.

It helped to have three sets taken in advance, by Lord Selworth, Mr. Debenham, and Mr. Chubb. Knowing one would not be an utterly unredeemed wallflower gave one self-confidence. Pippa recalled entire evenings spent examining her toes. Tonight she looked about her, admiring the glitter of the chandeliers' lustres in the light of a thousand wax candles, and the scarcely less glittering throng swirling and spinning beneath.

She expressed some of these thoughts to her mother, when a partner delivered her back to Mrs. Lisle, where she sat at the side of the room chatting to the other chaperons.

"As I expected, my love," said Mrs. Lisle. "I am prodigious glad you are enjoying yourself. Dear Albinia would be most disappointed if all her efforts to that end were in vain, and she has been so kind I should hate to disappoint her."

"She is a darling. And Lord Selworth —" Pippa stopped in some confusion as that gentleman appeared at her elbow.

Eyebrows raised, he grinned. "Do go on, Miss Lisle. Dare I hope I am to receive the supreme accolade of being named a darling?"

"Certainly not," Pippa said crossly.

"They do say eavesdroppers seldom hear good of themselves," he acknowledged with a mournful sigh.

Goaded, Pippa told him, "I was going to say you have been *almost* as kind as your sister, but you are by far too great a tease for me to risk setting you up in your own conceit."

"Alas! I was about to beg you to be kind to me. You see, Bina has just warned me that whoever I take in to supper is bound to arouse a good deal of speculation." He glanced over his shoulder and continued in an exaggerated whisper, "And there is a young lady throwing out strong hints."

"Millicent —"

"Millie, I'm delighted to report, is already bespoken. By a gentleman of the strong, silent, saturnine sort who appears to find her amusing. Dare I hope, Miss Lisle, that you are still free for the supper dance?" He scanned her dance card. "Will you not come to the rescue? Persuade her, ma'am," he begged Mrs. Lisle.

"Lord Selworth has done his duty, I fancy,

Pippa. I have not seen him sit out a single dance. He is not to blame for any young ladies left partnerless."

"There, you see, I deserve your kindness. Have pity on me."

"If you wish, just to save you from speculation. Everyone will believe you are simply being kind to your sister's guest, not realizing it is I who am doing you the favor."

Writing his name on the card, he laughed and was about to retort when a large matron clad in plum-colored satin and superb rubies swooped upon Mrs. Lisle.

"Anna Burdick, as I live!"

"Eva Gore?" said Mrs. Lisle, a note of doubt in her voice as she stood up.

The matron chuckled merrily and patted her plump cheeks. "Yes, inside this is Eva Gore, now Marchioness of Stanborough, believe it or not. And you?"

"Mrs. Lisle. How delightful to see you again after so many years, Lady Stanborough. May I present my daughter, Philippa?"

Pippa made her curtsy, and Mrs. Lisle introduced Lord Selworth to the marchioness. "And here comes my younger daughter, Catherine," she added as the viscount bowed.

"Two out at once? I have a boy around here somewhere, my second son, Edward." Lady Stanborough craned her double-chinned neck and made an imperious summoning gesture. "A young man, I should say. He would be furious to hear me calling him a boy."

Kitty arrived on the arm of her partner, unknown to Pippa, and was presented to the friend of her mother's youth. Then Lord Edward came up. He was a plain young man, already running to plumpness. His high shirtpoints, waistcoat embroidered with pink and blue butterflies, and multitude of fobs suggested a fondness for foppery. His air of self-consequence might charitably be ascribed to the golden-haired beauty of the young lady at his side.

Once the introductions were completed, Lord Edward turned back to Lady Stanborough and said, "I am glad to see you have both your earrings, Mother. I've heard a ruby earring was found on the floor somewhere."

The marchioness felt the drops at her ears. "Yes, both there, thank heaven. The rubies are a family heirloom," she explained. "Stanborough would have been most distressed if I had lost one."

"They are very beautiful, ma'am," said Kitty, "just like enormous red currants."

Lady Stanborough looked decidedly taken aback by this rural metaphor. Her son, his partner, and Kitty's partner all looked shocked. Pippa racked her brains for something to say in support of her sister, but Mr. Chubb, arriving unnoticed in his silent way, beat her to it.

"Very true, Miss Kitty," he said resolutely. "The rubies glow just like red currants in the sun. Nothing prettier. And what's more, you can eat currants."

The shock was transferred to him. As he blushed, Lord Selworth hastily presented him to Lady Stanborough.

"My good friend, the *Honorable* Gilbert Chubb."

"Lord Chubb's heir?" asked Lady Stanborough with interest. "I knew your father once, but he never comes up to Town now."

Mr. Chubb, his flash in the pan extinguished, mumbled something about life in the country. He missed Kitty's grateful look since by then — Pippa noted with sympathy — he was examining his toes.

"I have not been up to Town in years," said Mrs. Lisle. "We are staying with the Debenhams."

"The Kent Debenhams?" Lady Stanborough enquired, clearly impressed.

"Philippa is a particular friend of Mrs. George Debenham."

Lord Edward turned to Pippa, claiming acquaintance with George Debenham. To her surprise, he solicited the honor of a dance and inscribed his name on her card for one of the sets after supper. Pippa's next partner came to fetch her just then, so she heard no more. However, as she danced, she saw her mother and the marchioness with their heads together, so she assumed Kitty's *faux pas* had been smoothed over.

Poor Kitty! Of course red currants looked like rubies, and vice versa. Why should she be considered gauche for mentioning the resemblance? Not that she appeared to be repining. Pippa saw her in the next set, smiling up at a startlingly handsome gentleman as they turned arm in arm.

Lord Selworth, promenading in another set with a sadly bran-faced young lady, caught Pippa's eye. He nodded towards Kitty, smiled, and winked.

The next country dance was the one preceding supper. When Lord Selworth came to lead Pippa onto the floor, she said to him innocently, "What were those extraordinary grimaces you directed at me a few minutes ago, sir?"

"Why, did you not guess . . . ? Ah, Miss Lisle, you are quizzing me, and you call *me* a tease! If you wish to be taken seriously, you must strive to suppress the gleam in your eyes."

"Do they glow like red currants?"

"They may tomorrow, if you dance until dawn and then rise too early!" He gazed down into her eyes, and shook his head. "No, like opals, always changing."

Lowering her gaze, Pippa hoped her cheeks were not glowing like red currants. "You are gallant, Lord Selworth. I do believe that is the prettiest thing anyone has ever said to me." Thoughtfully she cooled her hot cheeks with her fan, then looked up at him through her lashes. "Tonight, at least."

He burst out laughing. "Minx! Is it permissible to address a lady of your mature years as 'minx'?"

"No mature lady objects to being regarded as younger than she is. Though why anyone should wish to return to the agonizing awkwardness of extreme youth, I cannot conceive," she added candidly. "Still, not all girls are as easily mortified as I was. Kitty scarcely turned a hair just now."

"As I was attempting to draw to your attention with my 'extraordinary grimaces,' ma'am!"

"So I guessed," said Pippa, laughing.

She thoroughly enjoyed their dance, and the supper that followed. Lord Selworth set himself to entertain her, succeeding with such charm that she was sure every young lady he had danced with must be at least half in love with him.

Including herself?

She had been half in love with Wynn Selworth before the evening started. She must not allow herself to fall any deeper. He was kind, charming, amusing, attentive, and she knew him to be a man of principle. But that final quality nullified the one before: he was attentive because he had promised Prometheus to smooth the Lisles' path in Society.

To Lord Selworth, Pippa was a means to an end — a noble end, to be sure, but that did not change the basic fact. She *must* not forget it.

In the early hours of the morning, Wynn drove back to Albany through the dark streets. He could feel Chubby — no, Gil — at his side bursting to talk about the ball, but the presence of the groom on his perch behind them inhibited any but the most impersonal comment.

Clark, their shared gentleman's gentleman, was waiting up for them, determined to do his duty despite their instructions to the contrary. Unused to Town hours as they were, by the time he had stripped them of their evening finery they were both half-asleep, fit only to pull on nightshirts and tumble into their respective beds. Confidences had to wait until the morning.

The habit of early rising was not easily abridged by a single night's gallivanting. By half-past eight, Wynn and Gil were seated at the breakfast table in the sunny window of their parlor. The table also served Wynn as a desk — the friend who had sublet the rooms was never known to pick up a pen if he could help it, so needed no bureau.

Clark served them with fine rashers of gammon topped with sizzling eggs, and hot muffins with lashings of butter and honey. Pouring coffee, he left the pot to keep hot over a spirit lamp and went off to put a final polish on their boots.

Wynn swallowed a tender bite of gammon and said, "How did we manage without him?

The fellow's a treasure."

"Deuced lucky to get him," Gil Chubb agreed. "I must say I'd never have thought of looking for an ex-Navy man."

"A captain's servant has to do a bit of everything, from making salt beef and biscuit edible to keeping a dress uniform smart, and few half-pay captains can afford to keep servants. The way the Navy has been reduced since the war, I was sure there must be some in need of work. It's disgraceful the way the soldiers and sailors who beat Boney are neglected now."

Gil waved a fork at him. "No speeches! I say, Wynn, are you taking Miss Lisle for a drive in the Park today?"

"Yes," said Wynn contentedly, "but not till this afternoon, at the fashionable hour. No hurry."

"I know that. Do you think Miss Kitty might drive with me?"

"Ask her. You should have invited her last night. They are bound to have dozens of callers this morning, and she had swarms of beaux flocking around at the ball."

"I know." Gil heaved a dispirited sigh. "It's no more than I expected, but it's enough to drive a fellow to drink. D'you think she minded what I said about red currants and rubies?"

"Minded? Gad no! I'm sure she was devilish grateful for your gallant defence against those toplofty prigs. I didn't know you had it in you, old chap."

"You'll understand if you ever fall in love," said Gil with dignity.

Wynn's heart did an odd sort of flip-flop. He set down his knife and fork and said in a peculiar voice, "I think I am. I do believe I must be."

"Good Lord, you, too? With one of the girls you met last night?"

"Those featherheads? Not an ounce of brain between the lot of them!"

"Not Miss Lisle?"

"Philippa," said Wynn dreamily. "Pippa. Do you feel you really wouldn't object to spending the rest of your life with Kitty? Even seeing her at breakfast every morning? No, that's not right. It's more that you can't imagine waking up every morning and her not being there. It wouldn't be worth waking up."

Gil nodded. "That's it all right; only the chances are I'll have to," he moped. "All very well for you, but I haven't much hope of winning Kitty. Are you going to pop the question this afternoon?"

"N-no. It's too soon," Wynn declared in a sudden excess of panic. Suppose he was mistaken? Suppose this was the calf love he suspected in his friend's case? He had never imagined himself seriously in love before, nothing beyond an infatuation with an apple-cheeked dairymaid three years his senior and unreal fantasies about the squire's coquettish daughter. "No," he repeated. "What if she refused

173

me? She wouldn't wish to go on working with me, and I'd lose Prometheus' help."

"Of course she won't refuse you. You're a viscount, full of juice, not bad-looking, clever, and conversable. No girl in her right mind would refuse you."

"Miss Lisle might. She wouldn't marry for title or money. It'd be against her father's principles. And what's more, though she pays lip service to her father's opinions, it's my belief she's got ideas of her own. I can't count on her behaving like any other husband-hungry damsel, even if she doesn't love Prometheus. No," Wynn repeated, "I can't risk an offer until I've finished with Prometheus. A political career will be the only thing to make life worth living if she turns me down."

11

"Almack's!" squealed Millie, bursting into the ladies' sitting room. "Pippa, we have vouchers for Almack's! All of us."

Hastily slipping Lord Selworth's papers into the desk drawer, Pippa swung round as Kitty followed Millicent. Bina and Mrs. Lisle came in after them.

"It is quite true," Bina confirmed. "Maria Sefton, Emily Cowper, and Silence managed to overcome the scruples of the high-in-the-instep set."

"Silence?" Pippa asked vaguely, striving to disentangle her mind from the starving children of out-of-work weavers in the Midlands.

"Sally Jersey," Bina explained, "whose tongue runs on almost as much as Millicent's."

"Fortunately Lord Jersey is a Whig," said Mrs. Lisle, "and, though hardly a Radical, he was quite well acquainted with your father."

"Pippa, did you know Lord and Lady Jersey were married at Gretna Green?" Millicent asked. "Is it not romantic? And only think, her mama eloped to Scotland, too! She was a banker's daughter, and she ran off with the Earl of Westmorland, though he wasn't the earl yet, which is —"

"Millie!" protested her sister. "Pippa is not at all interested in such vulgar gossip, and I trust you do not mean to rattle on about Lady Jersey in company. She is one of the most important hostesses, besides being a patroness of Almack's. Her history is no secret, but if she were to learn you had been raking up the past, I daresay we should find our Almack's vouchers withdrawn."

"I shan't say another word," cried Millicent, horrified. "Miss Pendrell told me, so I did not —"

"Come and take off your bonnet, Millie," said Kitty, pulling on her friend's hand. "At the musicale last night, at least five gentlemen begged permission to call today."

"You sang charmingly," said Bina, "and the sort of songs gentlemen appreciate, not Italian arias like the rest."

"It is fortunate that they like country airs," Kitty said frankly, "for I do not know any Italian arias."

"Only two of the gentlemen left cards while we were out," Millicent reminded her, "so the other three may turn up at any moment. Let us hurry."

The girls went off. Bina sank into a chair.

"What energy the young have!" she sighed. "Do sit down, ma'am. They can manage without a chaperon for a few minutes, however many gallants arrive. Kitty is vastly popular, and Millicent profits from her friendship."

"Kitty does seem to have a great many admirers," said Mrs. Lisle with quiet satisfaction, "though how many are willing to take a wife without a portion remains to be seen. But there are those who prefer Millicent."

"One or two of those who have nothing to say for themselves," Bina agreed with a laugh, "though the most silent of all, Mr. Chubb, languishes after Kitty. I wonder if it is his doing that Wynn is so assiduous at doing his duty. I must confess I doubted he would attend more than the bare minimum of parties to launch Millie, but he goes with us everywhere." She gave Pippa a sly glance.

Pretending not to notice, Pippa reminded her, "Lord Selworth is anxious to turn us up sweet — us Lisles, that is — for fear of giving offence to Prometheus."

"He has done all Prometheus required," said Mrs. Lisle, "and more. I am sure Lord Selworth's chief aim is to promote the comfort of his sisters."

"He has always accepted responsibility for the family's well-being," Bina conceded. "I do believe, though, that he has not found the Season the ordeal he expected. It will be interesting to see if he fights shy of Almack's, which is, in its way, the distilled essence of the Season. Today being Thursday, he has a whole week to screw his courage to the sticking place."

"I had much rather not go," said Pippa. "Its

only purpose appears to be to exclude half of those who wish to go so that the rest may regard themselves as superior."

"The exclusivity is precisely why young ladies may be certain of meeting unexceptionable gentlemen," Bina argued, "many of them with marriage in mind."

"But I am not on the catch for a husband."

"Even so, I hope you will go with us, my love," Mrs. Lisle said. "Obtaining vouchers is more of a triumph than I ever expected. You are at liberty not to regard yourself as superior, but it cannot hurt for others to think you so."

Bina and Pippa both laughed; then Bina heaved herself to her feet with an exaggerated effort, saying, "I shall leave you to persuade her, ma'am. I had best go and see what the girls are doing."

Mrs. Lisle eyed her elder daughter consideringly. "I thought you had been enjoying yourself, dearest," she said. "If not, you have put on a brilliant show. Was it just so as not to appear ungrateful to Albinia?"

"Oh no, Mama, I have enjoyed myself much more than I supposed possible, much more than I ought when people all over the country are in desperate straits."

"I fear your absence from Almack's will not help to feed the hungry, my love. Indeed, who knows but what you will make some acquaintance there whom you may later influence for the general good."

"Now there is an original reason for attending an assembly!" Pippa teased. "I should do better to spend the time working on Lord Selworth's speech."

"How do you go on?"

"I can no longer postpone the evil day. When we meet at the theatre this evening, I shall tell him I have his manuscript and Prometheus wishes me to discuss the suggested alterations with him."

"Evil day?" asked Mrs. Lisle with raised eyebrows. "I have never known you reluctant to express your views!"

"On the contrary, I am constantly at great pains to hold back."

"Do you dislike the prospect of consulting with Lord Selworth? I was under the impression you took pleasure in his company."

"I do," Pippa confessed, turning away and hiding her face in her hands, "too much. Oh Mama, I know his only interest is in the connection to Prometheus, but I dread his finding out who Prometheus really is and turning from me in disgust."

Her mother came over and put an arm about her shoulders. "My poor darling, have you conceived a *tendre* for the viscount? It is my fault. I ought to have foreseen the possibility."

"It is only a slight attachment." Pippa strove to convince herself as much as Mama. "I shall be quite content to be his friend, truly. But I should hate to lose his friendship, and I doubt my ability to conceal the truth once I cannot avoid the subject of politics altogether."

"I suppose there is no chance . . . No, your papa was one in a million, and you being his daughter he had cause for pride in your intellectual achievements. You will just have to do your best to keep Lord Selworth in the dark, my love."

Pippa summoned up a smile. "So it is fortunate that I am not wildly enamored," she said wryly. "To be forced to withhold one's complete confidence from one's beloved cannot be considered desirable."

"The quality of mercy is not strain'd," quoth Portia. "It droppeth as the gentle rain from heaven upon the place beneath. It is twice blest: it blesseth him that gives and him that receives."

Lord Selworth leant forward to whisper in Pippa's ear, "Would that I might lift this speech entire!"

"Hush!" Pippa was entranced by *The Merchant of Venice*, often read, never before seen on the stage. Edmund Kean made Shylock come alive, no bogle but a tormented man struggling for his rights in an unsympathetic society.

Jews ought to have the vote, she thought, as well as Catholics, Nonconformists, and the property-less masses. Not to mention women. Had not Portia faced a court full of men and outargued them all? Three hundred years ago, with the example of his accomplished queen before him, Shakespeare had recognized the talents of women. Pippa was not unique in her abilities, merely rare in being encouraged to develop them.

Music brought her attention back to the stage. She had always found the final scene clever and amusing; now, with Lord Selworth close behind her, its bawdy innuendos made her blush. She fanned her face, glad that the heat of a thousand bodies and as many candles in the theatre was reason enough for pink cheeks.

The curtain descended for the last time. In the noise and bustle of departure, Pippa found it no easier than before or during the play to speak privately with Lord Selworth.

As he handed her into the Debenhams' carriage, she said, "I must talk to you. Are you free tomorrow morning?"

His face lit up. "You have heard from —" Glancing over his shoulder at the crush of play-goers close behind him, waiting for their carriages, he lowered his voice. "News from my mentor? Splendid! Will eleven be too early?"

"No, I shall expect you then." Sadly Pippa took her seat in the carriage. His delight at the conclusion he had so quickly jumped to, when she asked him to call, confirmed that his only interest in her was the connection to Prometheus.

As the carriage rolled towards Charles Street,

Bina interrupted Millicent's interminable review of the play. "Poor Shylock, losing his only daughter. It has made me realize how much I miss my boys. Mrs. Lisle, I have a great favor to beg of you. Now that you have met a great many people, would you mind chaperoning Pippa and the girls alone for a few days while I go down to Kent?"

"Not a bit, my dear," said Mrs. Lisle cheerfully. "You will return in good time for Almack's on Wednesday, no doubt, and we do not entertain formally before then, do we? For the rest, just make sure I know what invitations we have accepted each day, and I shall make your excuses to our hostesses."

"No dinner parties, as I recall, so my absence will not upset anyone's numbers."

"May I hope you can spare me also, ma'am?" George Debenham asked Mrs. Lisle. "There are one or two matters of business on which I should like to consult my father in person. If you don't care to be without male protection, I daresay Selworth will agree to stand in for me."

"I cannot think we shall need protection," Pippa protested. If Lord Selworth were to move into the house, she would be unable to work on his speech without fear of his catching her at it.

"We have had large numbers of gentlemen callers recently," Bina pointed out, "though I hardly fancy any of them are likely to trouble you."

"There is safety in numbers." Pippa did *not*

want Wynn Selworth constantly at hand, disturbing her peace of mind.

"Besides," said Kitty, a laugh in her voice, "I have noticed that Mr. Debenham takes great care to leave for his club well before our swarms of beaux begin to arrive. Whereas Lord Selworth or Mr. Chubb or both almost always turn up. I am sure we can rely upon Mr. Chubb as much as Lord Selworth if Lieutenant Pendrell starts to wave his sword or Lord Fenimore's invitations to a masked ball at the Pantheon become too pressing."

"Oh dear," said Mrs. Lisle, "has he asked you again, Kitty? Still, a butler and three stout footmen are surely sufficient to eject him should it become advisable!"

"I shall direct my butler to station two footmen within earshot whenever Lord Fenimore is admitted," George Debenham promised dryly.

Next morning, the Debenhams departed for Kent shortly before Lord Selworth arrived. Pippa had advised her mother of her appointment with the viscount. Mrs. Lisle and Kitty had no difficulty enticing Millicent out to the shops to look for matching ribbons and buttons and such fal-lals. Nor was Millie surprised that Pippa stayed at home. Her lack of interest in fashions and fripperies had long since ceased to arouse comment.

Millicent had been told originally that her brother had business with a friend of the Lisles.

The nature of the business was kept from her, in view of her lack of discretion, and she appeared to have forgotten all about it. Everyone agreed that the longer she could be kept in ignorance, the better.

So Pippa awaited Lord Selworth alone in the ladies' sitting room. She ruffled through the sheets of manuscript, noting with dismay the proliferation of red ink.

Had she made too many changes? He might be offended by such lavish criticism, or so discouraged he decided to give up.

Through the open window came the chime of church clocks striking eleven. Though she expected him and had left the door ajar, Lord Selworth's knock made Pippa start.

"I beg your pardon, Miss Lisle." He stood on the threshold, a trim figure in a blue morning coat, fawn Unmentionables, blue and gray striped waistcoat, and neatly tied cravat. Only the unmanageable flyaway hair had not been spruced up since their first meeting. Pippa was glad he had not taken to pomading it into submission. "I did not mean to startle you," he continued. "I ought to have sent a footman to announce me, perhaps. I have grown accustomed to treating my sister's house as my own, but she has gone off to Kent, I am told, and in her absence —"

"Oh no, Lord Selworth, I am sure Mama would not wish you to feel less at home because Bina is away. Do come in and be seated. It was idiotish of me to be taken by surprise when you arrived exactly on time."

He moved a chair alongside the desk and sat down. "Your thoughts were far away. I fear you were wondering how to convey Prometheus' verdict without driving me to despair."

His guess was too close to the truth. Mutely Pippa pushed the pile of papers across to him.

Ruffling through the sheets as she had just done, Lord Selworth groaned. "A sea of red ink! I daresay I ought to be grateful it isn't the red ink of debts. Have you read his comments, Miss Lisle? Can you tell me if it is salvageable, or shall I take up agriculture instead of politics? Has Prometheus pruned, as you suggested, or has he uprooted my roses and consigned them to the bonfire?"

"By no means. Your rootstock is sound. That is, Prometheus has no quarrel with what you wish to say, only it might be put more persuasively. At least . . ." Pippa hesitated.

"Pray let me know the worst."

"I . . . Prometheus is inclined to believe you are attempting to cover too many disparate subjects in a single speech. It might be more effective if you concentrate on a few closely related topics rather than putting all your convictions in one basket."

Lord Selworth looked much struck. "That is precisely what I was doing," he admitted with a rueful grimace. "Now I come to think of it, I suppose I tried to include the whole batch for fear of never having the opportunity to make a second speech!"

"But if the first is good enough, you will make many more," Pippa encouraged him. "I am not sure how long a maiden speech in the House of Lords is expected to last, but Papa used to say if your listeners are bored by the end, they will forget the beginning."

"And everything in between, no doubt. So Prometheus says it is too long, as well as too complex and too verbose?"

"It is hard to tell without reading it aloud."

"Which would be a waste of time until it is whipped roughly into shape. I had best take this home to study." He tapped the manuscript on the writing table to straighten the sheets. "Then, when I comprehend what Prometheus approves and what he condemns, I shall make a fresh start. Miss Lisle, may I ask a very great favor of you?"

"Of course," Pippa said cautiously.

"It is perfectly clear to me that you understand and agree with the criticisms Prometheus has written here. Will you be so good as to advise me as I go along, so that I shall not humiliate myself by sending him another thoroughly bungled effort?"

With what she hoped was a becoming degree of hesitant modesty, Pippa acquiesced. In fact she was delighted. She would be able to express her own opinions openly, without having to constantly filter them through "Prometheus suggests . . ." and "I believe Prometheus means . . ."

She must be careful not to venture far afield from the comments already attributed to her alter ego. Fortunately, she had dissected Lord Selworth's first effort with ruthless thoroughness. His second was unlikely to present new difficulties unsolvable by the same methods. On the whole, Pippa was inclined to believe she had a good chance of scraping through with her secret preserved.

Wynn spent the afternoon poring over his annotated speech. On the whole he had to agree with the extensive deletions. What remained was more forceful for being leaner, though it hurt to lose the intricate embellishments he had labored over so lovingly.

Perhaps some of the purple prose could be used in his next Gothic novel, he thought. Then he recalled that he must write no more romances. The risk of his authorship coming to light was too great.

Sighing, he returned to the manuscript. At least the germs of his metaphors had been preserved, thanks to Miss Lisle, no doubt. Here and there, Prometheus had even written in praise of a particularly strong image. There were one or two comments Wynn did not quite understand. Perhaps Miss Lisle would be able to elucidate, so that he did not have to trouble Prometheus about minor details. He did not wish to look more of a sapskull than he need.

Somehow he didn't mind Pippa Lisle seeing his blunders. He knew he had her sympathy and her approval of his aims.

That his speech had too many aims was obvious, now that she — or rather Prometheus — had pointed it out. Like a scatter of birdshot compared to a rifle bullet, his speech might hit with every ball, yet to little effect. Though he had succeeded in weaving his plethora of opinions into a coherent sequence of ideas, the central theme was weak.

Reading through again, he could not make up his mind where to concentrate his efforts. Prometheus had made no suggestions. Wynn decided to consult Pippa.

He set about abstracting from his manuscript a list of topics ranging from the Seditious Meetings Bill to the use of spring guns and mantraps against poachers: a regular stew, all excellent ingredients but losing their individual flavours in the mixture.

What he wanted was roast beef with a few complementary side dishes. In fact, he was deucedly hungry. Glancing at the clock on the mantel, he saw he had missed tea with the Lisles and escorting them to the Park. It was nearly time to change for dinner.

He and Gil Chubb had arranged to dine with friends at Boodle's Club, he remembered with annoyance. They were to meet the Lisles and

Millicent at some party afterwards, but that was no time or place to present his list to Miss Lisle and request her advice.

Was it too much to ask of her? She had not wanted to come to London for the Season, but Wynn had noticed that she seemed to be enjoying herself. It didn't seem quite fair to expect her to spend her time on politics, a subject she usually tried to avoid, in common with the majority of females. Of course she could have refused to help directly, to air her own opinions as opposed to conveying messages from Prometheus. However, Wynn suspected a sense of duty to her father's ideals had driven her to give her hesitant consent.

He was not really sure why he believed she was competent to advise him. Copying Benjamin Lisle's work was a far cry from producing original work. Still, if consulting her proved profitless, he could always take his minor difficulties directly to Prometheus.

And meanwhile he had a perfect excuse for spending a great deal of time with Miss Philippa Lisle.

"I have a confession to make," Wynn told Miss Lisle on Tuesday morning, laying down his pen and leaning back in his chair. "Promise you won't take snuff?"

"How can I?" she retorted. "Until I know what your offense is, I cannot guess whether it will offend me. However, I hope I can safely promise not to hit you on the head with the poker."

"You have my permission to haul me over the coals." He went over to the grate, where flickering sea-coals strove to disperse the chill of the drizzling day, and poked up the fire. "Come and warm your hands, Miss Lisle."

"Procrastinating, Lord Selworth?" With a smile, she came over and held out her hands to the flames he had stirred up.

"Not at all. It isn't the sort of confession which must be made for fear of being found out. My fingers are cold and cramped from writing, and you have done just as much writing as I have, if not more."

"Not this morning. I have been dictating to you. I trust you do not mean to confess to finding me shockingly dictatorial when all you wished for was a few gentle hints?" she asked anxiously.

"You are the gentlest of dictators. And you *have* been writing — if I had not watched, I should have guessed by the smudge of ink on your forehead." Such a broad, clear, intelligent forehead, with beautifully curved brows, set off by two wings of dark, smooth, glossy hair. "Have I ever told you how much I like the way you wear your hair?"

Blood tinting her pellucid cheeks, Pippa raised a hand to touch the hair at her temple. "Thank you, but I must say I should like to be able to coax it into curls in the evenings."

"Oh no, then it would be just like every other young lady's. You look distinguished, and elegant, and . . . intelligent. Which brings me back to my confession. When I asked you to help me, I had the gravest doubts of your ability to do so. There, it is said." Wynn laughed as her expression changed. "May I offer you the poker?"

"I have done very little." She bit her lip. "No more than . . . than giving a few suggestions as to how to set your ideas in order."

"You have done quite as much as I ever expected of Prometheus."

The color fled from her cheeks, and she shook her head violently. "Impossible!"

"I mean it. I wager he comes to you for — Good gad!" Wynn struck himself on the forehead with the heel of his hand. "How can I have been so blind? You *are* Prometheus!"

Miss Lisle swooned.

12

As the room ceased to whirl about Pippa's head, she became aware of a frantic voice.

"Miss Lisle! Pippa! Oh Lord!"

Through clearing mists, she saw Lord Selworth's appalled face. She was lying on the floor with her head in his lap. "I am . . ." She faltered and tried to sit up. Nausea rose in her throat.

"No, you aren't. You're pale as rice pudding. Lie still, or you will go off again. Good gad, Miss Lisle, you gave me a frightful shock!"

"Nothing to the . . . shock I gave myself. Did I . . . faint?" she asked, eyes closed.

"Went down like an elm in a gale. I just caught you before you whacked your head on the fender. No," he mused, "more like a wilting lily."

"You are too kind!"

"At any rate, I'd say it must have been a swoon, a faint if you prefer. I've no experience."

"Nor have I," Pippa said indignantly, opening her eyes, then hastily shutting them again as she met his blue gaze mere inches above her. "I have never fainted before in my life."

"I'm afraid it was my fault." Lord Selworth

squeezed her hand, which she had not realized he was clasping. She was still far too weak to withdraw it, she told herself, as he went on, "I gave you the first shock. I should not have accused you so abruptly."

Now she recalled in dismay why she had fainted. "It is not true," she cried, suddenly finding the strength to pull her hand from his and once more trying to sit up.

"Be still," he commanded, pressing her back with a hand to her shoulder. "Doing it rather too brown, my girl. Of course it's true. Why else should you have crumpled like an unstarched neckcloth?"

"You grow more and more complimentary, I vow! I want to get up."

He frowned down at her. "You are still awfully pale."

"I am naturally pale."

"True, but pearly pale, not pasty. Still, the floor cannot be comfortable."

Refusing to admit she was perfectly comfortable, Pippa said, "And suppose someone comes in?"

Lord Selworth cast an alarmed glance at the door, left ajar as propriety demanded. Without warning, he swept her up in strong arms, and before she had time for more than a gasp of surprise, he deposited her full-length on the nearest sofa.

She started to swing her feet to the floor.

"Please, lie still! If you collapse again, I shall

have to call your maid, since Mrs. Lisle is out. We cannot explain what happened, and what she'll guess doesn't bear imagining."

Pippa blushed, imagining all too clearly that Nan would assume Lord Selworth had attempted improper familiarities. Then, though she had briefly suppressed the awareness, she once again remembered what had in fact caused her to swoon.

"You know," she said faintly.

"That you are Prometheus?" He pulled up a chair. "Now I look back, it's quite obvious the family friend was a fiction, but then, everything is always clear in hindsight."

"It was Mama's notion to ask for a Season in payment, not mine."

"You would have refused me outright, would you not? To safeguard your secret. You are afraid of being sent to prison?"

"A little." Pippa shuddered. "You know how easy it is to be condemned for sedition now that *Habeas corpus* is suspended. Have you read of the appalling conditions of women in Newgate Gaol?"

"No, as you might guess since I'd have tried to fit it into my speech," he said ruefully.

Pippa managed to smile. "No doubt. I was less concerned about prison, though, than about not being taken seriously. Who will pay the least heed to my articles if they know them to be written by a woman?"

"I will!"

"You are kind to say so. However, you cannot persuade me you would have asked Prometheus to assist you if you had known then."

Lord Selworth frowned. "You may be right," he admitted. "So is it not fortunate that I remained in the dark until I had discovered your abilities for myself?"

"But now you will wish to find another mentor," Pippa said sadly. "No gentleman wishes to take advice from a female, especially one younger than himself."

"Come now, I am no Methuselah, Miss Lisle! And speaking of mythical figures — your wide acquaintance with Greek and Latin myth was one thing which gave you away — do you know who the original Mentor was?"

"Something to do with Odysseus." She was a trifle impatient with the irrelevant question when her future was at stake. "Adviser to his wife and son, Penelope and Telemachus, was he not? A man."

"Ah, but at some point in the story his place was taken by Athena in disguise. A female!" he said triumphantly.

"A goddess!"

His blue eyes gleamed. "If it weren't the sort of flummery tossed about by honey-tongued coxcombs, I might call you a goddess. Be that as it may, I most certainly wish you to continue to play the part of Athena, Mentor, or Prometheus. All three if you will! Surely you cannot find it in your heart to abandon me in the middle of this thicket of half-pruned rose-bushes?"

"If you truly wish me to continue, I shall." Pippa sighed. "But once everyone finds out that I am Prometheus . . ."

"Everyone finds out? Why the dev— deuce should anyone find out?" Lord Selworth drew himself up and addressed her sternly. "Miss Lisle, do you mean to insinuate that *I* might give you away?"

"Not on purpose!"

"Then you must be confusing me with Millicent."

"Oh no!" Relieved to see a twinkle in his eye, Pippa giggled. "Impossible."

"I am delighted to hear it. I shan't confide in her, believe me."

"Nor anyone else."

"Nor anyone else, I give you my word. Perhaps it will set your mind at ease if I give you a means of retaliation as well. I, too, have a secret I should hate to see bandied about the world."

"Tell me," Pippa breathed, burning with curiosity.

Lord Selworth turned rather pink. "You may recall I told your mama I worked to help support my family?"

"Yes, and you were so reticent about it I immediately thought the worst."

"Did you, indeed! Well, I don't know what your worst is, and I don't want to know, but it was nothing so very dreadful. I was neither pirate nor slaver, I assure you. The trouble is, public exposure would blight my political career, if not wither it entirely. Like you, I should not be taken seriously."

"Exposure of your consulting *me* would very likely be as bad for you," Pippa felt bound to point out. "I shall consider that surety enough, if you like. You need not tell me."

"Generously spoken, when I can see you are all agog. I would not be so cruel." Lord Selworth took a deep breath. "The fact of the matter is, I used to write quite successful Gothic romances. Like you, under a pseudonym."

"Valentine Dred!" cried Pippa.

"How did you know?" he asked, startled.

"I recognized your style, turns of phrase, in your speech."

"Oh Lord, is it so evident?"

"I never dreamt you had written the books, only that you had read and enjoyed them."

"Dare I hope you enjoyed them?"

Pippa was about to assure him that she loved his books, when she recalled the ribaldry which went with the tongue-in-cheek adventures. Lord Selworth had written those bawdy tales? Shocked, her face aflame, she looked away — and saw her ankles exposed to his view. Swinging her limbs down from the sofa, she primly smoothed her apricot mull muslin skirt over her knees, her gaze fixed on her fingers.

"Sir, your books are not at all proper for

young ladies to read."

Lord Selworth roared with laughter, the wretch! "My dear girl, if you have read enough of them to recognize my style, you have no possible excuse for denouncing them."

Bowing her head, Pippa wished she could sink through the floor. "I . . . I have read them all," she confessed in a constricted voice, "and I like them very much. *Not* because of the . . . the improper bits, but because you seem not to take your characters and their exploits and misadventures very seriously. I hope I am not mistaken?" she asked, looking up as interest overcame embarrassment.

"No indeed. I'm glad you realized it. Not all my reviewers have been equally perceptive!" he told her wryly. "But you understand why I fear I shall not be taken any more seriously than I take my stories if I'm discovered to be the author."

"Yes. I suppose you will not write any more now? What a pity!"

"There is one more due to come out shortly, *The Masked Marauder.*"

"A splendid title," Pippa exclaimed.

"Perhaps I ought to have stopped publication when my great-uncle died, but the bookseller pleaded with me to let it go forward. To tell the truth, having written the dashed thing, I should be sorry not to see it in print."

"I can imagine. I feel much the same about my articles, and a novel is a far greater undertaking. How did you come to begin writing them?"

"I started by scribbling down the scary stories I used to tell Albinia, when she was still in the nursery."

"Oh, that must be why she guessed."

Lord Selworth looked stunned and alarmed. "Bina guessed?"

"So I would assume. She told me she knew a secret of yours and had kept it so well even you were unaware that she knew. It is safe with her. She refused to tell me. Does no one else know?"

"The bookseller, of course, and Gil Chubb. Who knows about Prometheus?"

"Mr. Cobbett, Mama, and Kitty. And now you."

"Don't faint again, I beg of you!"

"I cannot think how I came to do anything so totty-headed," Pippa said candidly. "It must have been because you took me by surprise. I am perfectly well now. Shall we go back to work?" She started to rise.

He put out a hand to stop her. "No, we have done enough for today."

"Do you know yet when you will be able to speak?"

"No, but these last few days I have grown confident enough of having a speech worth giving to have a word with Lord Grey and Lord Holland. They promise to approach Lord Eldon in my behalf. The Chancellor is an intransigent Tory, however, who will be in no hurry to fit a Reformist speech into the agenda, far less one they suspect of being Radical. We have time enough."

"Nonetheless, I should like to —"

"Not now," he said commandingly, his gaze searching. "You must not overtire yourself with poring over my papers."

"I am not tired," Pippa protested. "We are already agreed that my complexion is naturally pale."

Lord Selworth grinned. "Then let us put roses in your cheeks with a walk to Green Park, and on the way back I shall treat you to an ice at Gunter's. Not a word of politics the entire time! Go and put on your bonnet — and wash that ink off your face!"

"Yes, my lord. At once, my lord," Pippa said tartly, and whisked off to obey.

Changing into walking shoes, she donned her straw-colored, plumed bonnet and the matching *gros de Naples* spencer which went with almost everything. Lord Selworth awaited her downstairs in the front hall. He turned from studying with disfavor a portrait of George Debenham's great-grandparents.

"Deuced odd clothes people used to wear." He regarded Pippa with a slight frown. "Will you be warm enough? The sun is shining, for a wonder, but there is a nippy breeze."

"Do you have a dawdling stroll in mind? I had hoped for a brisk, warming walk."

"How unfashionable!" he bantered. "And what a relief. Like Miss Kitty, I find a saunter far more tiring than a stride."

They went out into Charles Street. Lord Selworth did not suggest taking a maid or footman — not that Pippa had any intention of doing so, but it went to show that he considered her past the age of needing a chaperon. Past the age of romance and marriage, she thought sadly, recalling the notably youthful heroines of his novels.

"Tell me about writing your books," she said. "It must be quite different from writing a speech."

"As I discovered, to my dismay!"

"Where do you begin? Do you plan the story beforehand, or just plunge in?"

Lord Selworth was delighted to be able to talk freely about his literary achievements, and scrupulous to avoid all mention of the naughty parts. He kept Pippa amused and fascinated all the way around Green Park and back to Berkley Square, where he turned towards Gunter's.

"Should we not come back later with Millicent and Kitty?" Pippa suggested. "They would consider it a great treat."

"As you do not?" he queried mournfully.

"Of course I do!"

"I shall bring them some other time. This is *our* morning. My heart is set upon a raspberry cream ice, and you shall order whatever elaborate and expensive concoction you please to compensate for the shock I gave you earlier."

"I had forgotten it."

"Then I beg your pardon for reminding you."

"Unnecessary, since you offer amends. Tell me," she teased, "in other circumstances would you balk at standing the nonsense for whatever elaborate and expensive confection I might choose?"

"To say no were ungallant, yet to say yes is to court bankruptcy, at Gunter's prices! Besides which, I should have to do the same for your sister and mine."

Pippa laughed. "Then this would be no special treat. However, a raspberry cream ice sounds perfect to me."

The ices, served with crisp wafers, were delicious. Lord Selworth insisted on ordering a pot of tea as well. Pippa accepted graciously, though her thrifty soul cavilled at the extra expense when they were scarcely two minutes' walk from the Debenhams' house.

Returning to the house, they found the others wondering where Pippa had disappeared to.

"Not that I was upon the fret, my love," said Mrs. Lisle, drawing Pippa aside, "but I wish you will leave a note or inform one of the staff if you go out unexpectedly."

"I am sorry, Mama. I did not think."

"And you ought to take Nan or one of the footmen."

"I know I must not go out alone in London. I was with Lord Selworth."

Mrs. Lisle glanced at the other end of the drawing room, where the viscount was teasing the girls with a panegyrical description of Gunter's ices. "The more reason for taking a servant."

"Lord Selworth behaved with perfect propriety."

"I should expect nothing less of him, but propriety is in the eye of the beholder. I know you believe yourself too old to need a chaperon, dearest, but that is utter nonsense. Anyone seeing you escorted only by a personable young man would have good reason to be shocked."

"I shall not do it again, Mama," Pippa promised. He was most unlikely ever to invite her again. "I fear I had had something of a shock myself and was not thinking straight." Looking to make sure Millicent was still beyond earshot, she continued softly, "He has guessed."

"That you are Prometheus? Oh, my love, what a horrid shock indeed! Perhaps I was wrong to propose this masquerade . . . yet you are still on friendly terms with Lord Selworth. Never say he is willing to accept assistance from a female?"

"So he claims, though he may yet change his mind. Maybe he said so only to comfort me, and he will find some excuse to cry off. He has scarcely had time enough to consider the possible consequences."

"There need be none if he can hold his tongue," Mrs. Lisle pointed out, "and if you are more careful. You left his papers out on the desk."

"Oh no, did I? My mind was more disordered than I had supposed."

"And his, too. I put the speech in the drawer, but you have the key. You had best lock it before luncheon."

"I shall go up at once. Did Millicent see it?"

"Saw, but did not read. She made some comment about how you are forever scribbling. Do take care, my love."

"I shall, Mama."

Pippa kissed her mother's cheek and ran upstairs to lock the drawer and put off her bonnet.

Sitting at the dressing table to tidy her hair, she stared at herself in the looking glass. He had said he liked her hair, unrelentingly straight as it was. He said she looked distinguished, elegant, intelligent. That was before he guessed she was Prometheus. When had he called her "my dear girl," before or after? Her head had been in such a whirl, she could not remember.

It must have been before. Though the phrase had no great significance, a gentleman surely would not use it to one he had accepted as his mentor. She would always be Athena to him now, never Aphrodite.

Not that she had ever dreamt of aspiring to

the beauty of the Goddess of Love, she thought with a sigh, regarding her cheeks, still pale despite the brisk walk. It was definitely after she fainted that he had compared her to a wilted lily, an unstarched neckcloth, a rice pudding! Admittedly Lord Selworth was given to exotic metaphor, yet surely even he would not so disparage a lady in whom he had the least romantic interest.

Still, he had described her usual paleness as pearly, Pippa recalled, a little cheered.

More important, he respected her intelligence and had not promptly refused her continued help, as she had feared. And she still had his friendship. Their walk and the visit to Gunter's testified to that.

She had much to be thankful for. Doing her best to persuade herself she was satisfied, Pippa went down to luncheon.

"You will be quite the prettiest girl at Almack's, I vow," said Pippa, fastening the last hooks in her sister's gown. "Turn around now and let me look."

Kitty twirled and curtsied, the primrose satin slip and silver Urling's net overdress swirling about her ankles. "I am in a dreadful quake," she said with no visible diminution in her usual placidity. "Suppose I say something shockingly bucolic and give the Patronesses a disgust of me?"

"Anything you say, Mr. Chubb will turn off

as wit or wisdom. Keep him at your side whenever you are not dancing. It should not prove
difficult."

"He is a dear, is he not? I cannot think why
he is so speechless in general, for he always has
plenty to say to me. Not nonsensical compliments, either, but sensible talk about things
which matter."

"Do you favor him, Kitty? He would be an
excellent *parti.*"

"Oh, I don't mean to favor anyone for ages
yet. I am enjoying myself far too much. To tell
the truth," she admitted, laughing, "I find the
nonsensical compliments most agreeable!"

"I am not at all surprised. What girl would
not delight in collecting such a court of admiring beaux as you have?"

Kitty flung her arms about her sister. "It is all
thanks to you, darling Pippa."

"Not to mention Mama! Careful. Do not
crush your gown, dearest. You must have noticed how I profit by your court. As soon as
your admirers notice that we are on excellent
terms, they spare no effort to stay in my good
books. I do not expect to sit out a single dance
tonight."

"Of course not, but it is nothing to do with
their admiring *me*, goosecap. Come, let me help
you put on your dress."

Pippa's gown for the all-important assembly
was of emerald crepe, scalloped to expose a
sarcenet slip the pale green of new leaves, the

same color as the brief bodice. The hems of over- and under-skirts were ornamented with silk vine leaves in the contrasting shade. Bina had wanted to lend her emeralds to go with it, but Pippa regretfully refused — clothes were one thing, jewelry another. She wore her gold locket with a twist of Papa's hair, the twin of Kitty's.

Going downstairs, Pippa wished Lord Selworth was to dine with them. He had been bidden to dinner at Holland House, an invitation he could not refuse, for Lady Holland was one of the two great Whig hostesses of the day and her husband was a leader of the party.

Lord Selworth had promised to meet the Debenhams and the Lisles at Almack's. However, Holland House was a few miles out of town, in Kensington. If he were to become involved in political discussions, he could very well arrive too late in King Street. The Lady Patronesses were as adamant about closing the doors at eleven o'clock as they were about gentlemen having to wear knee breeches.

Though Pippa had gained vastly in confidence since the first ball of the Season, Lord Selworth's presence was a prop on which she had come to depend. She did not want to face the most select circles of the Ton without him nearby.

13

"Five to eleven," Bina muttered in Pippa's ear as the figures of a country dance brought them together. "I shall give him a fine trimming if he misses Millie's first appearance at Almack's."

"She is doing very well without him," Pippa defended the viscount, glancing over at Millicent, who was chattering away to her partner while they danced up the next set.

"It is a matter of principle. It is his duty to support his sister," Bina insisted, pronouncing the last word over her shoulder as she tripped away to meet her partner.

Then it was Pippa's turn to take George Debenham's hand and follow. She liked dancing with her friend's husband. His saturnine manner belied a very real kindness, generosity, and patience, and she appreciated his decidedly dry wit.

"Bina fears Lord Selworth is not going to turn up in time," she told him. "She is preparing to read him a dreadful scold."

He laughed. "One of Albinia's scolds would not cow a scullery maid, far less her brother, but he will not have to suffer it. I saw him come in a few minutes ago. He is with Mrs. Lisle."

"How fortunate!" Pippa suppressed an

urgent desire to turn her head and peer back in the most ill-bred fashion at the spot where her mother sat, on the far side of the room.

Mr. Debenham apparently read her mind. "You would have to grow several inches to see them," he said with a smile. "I assure you it is really he. And he looks none the worse for having dined at Holland House."

"Why should he?" Pippa enquired, intrigued.

"One hears stories — but I have never been invited to that hotbed of Whiggery. You must ask Selworth."

"I shall."

At last the dance ended, with a fine flourish from Gow's Band in the balcony. By the time Pippa and Mr. Debenham made their way to Mrs. Lisle, Millicent and Kitty had already rejoined her. Lord Selworth stood talking to them, a slim, elegant figure in black coat, white cravat and waistcoat, and black knee breeches and stockings. Pippa thought he looked pleased and excited, his blue eyes alight with jubilation, not at all as if dinner with the Hollands had caused him any distress.

He had promised to stand up first with his younger sister, then with Kitty. "And may I hope for the honor of the dance after that with you, Miss Lisle?" he requested, adding in a lower voice, "I must talk to you."

Pippa pretended to consult her card, though she had taken care not to engage herself much in advance so as to be free in case Lord

Selworth asked her. "I believe I might squeeze you in, sir," she said, writing down his name.

"Don't mention squeezing, I beg of you!" With that mystifying plea, he allowed Millie to drag him away.

When the time came for their dance, Lord Selworth asked Pippa if she would object to sitting it out. "A country dance makes sustained conversation impossible, at least, for anyone but Millicent," he said, watching his prattling sister go off on Mr. Chubb's arm, "and I have a great deal to tell you while it is fresh in my mind."

"I want to hear all about the Hollands' dinner party. Besides, I shall be glad of a rest. My last partner stepped on my toes twice."

"Splendid!"

"Sir!" Pippa exclaimed in mock affront.

He grinned. "My apologies to your toes, and my sympathies. Mrs. Lisle, may we join you, ma'am? I have one or two messages for you from colleagues of your late husband." He handed Pippa to a chair next but one to her mother and seated himself between them. "First, ladies," he said portentously, "my news: the Lord High Chancellor has set a date for my speech!"

"Already?" said Pippa. "When?"

"Three weeks from tomorrow. That is time enough, is it not?"

"Oh yes, plenty. I was afraid you were going

to say tomorrow. As Lord Eldon is a dyed-in-the-Woolsack Tory, he might have tried to catch you unprepared."

"He might, though I doubt he expects my speech to have much effect. True, I am a dark horse, but he has hedged his bets by —" Taking in the ladies' blank expressions, Lord Selworth paused.

"A dark horse?" asked Mrs. Lisle, bemused.

"I beg your pardon, ma'am, a metaphor from the Turf — horse racing. Not that I would have you suppose I make a habit of throwing away my blunt on the races, but I picked up some of the lingo when I was looking for cattle at Tattersall's. A dark horse is one about which little is known."

"Like your ability as an orator," Pippa said. "Hedging one's bets is wagering both for and against, to avoid losing badly, is it not? I have seen it used metaphorically."

"Are you accusing me of unoriginality, Miss Lisle?"

"Never! On the contrary, Lord Selworth, you know I have been at some pains to restrain your excessive originality. What has the Chancellor done?"

"Put me last on his schedule for the day, after a debate on whether or not to raise the duty on tea by a farthing."

"A subject so profoundly uninteresting to the wealthy Lords," said Pippa, "that everyone will have fallen asleep or gone home by the time you stand up."

"Precisely."

"What a shame!" said Mrs. Lisle sympathetically. "Nonetheless, you must both do your best. Make it rousing enough and some of them will wake up and take note."

"We shall try, ma'am, I promise you, shall we not, Miss Lisle? Now, let me see, Mr. Thomas Creevey, Mr. Henry Grey Bennet, and Mr. Henry Brougham asked me to convey their respects. Oh, and Sir Francis Burdett." He passed on brief messages from those gentlemen encountered at the Hollands'. "I took the liberty of telling them you are residing at my sister's. Creevey will call without delay, and the other three as soon as their duties in the Commons allow."

"Mr. Bennet is a true reformer, is he not, in spite of being a son of Lord Tankerville?" Pippa asked.

"I'd go so far as to call him a Radical. It is a pity he is not heir to the earldom. I made the acquaintance of all sorts of interesting people at Holland House, and the conversation was fascinating." Lord Selworth described the people he had met and repeated some of the talk. "But I cannot do it justice. I wish you had been there."

"So do I," said Pippa, "except that Mr. Debenham expressed surprise on seeing you none the worse for the experience. Nor have you explained your abhorrence of the word 'squeeze.' "

"Squeeze!" He laughed. "Lady Holland is noted for always inviting more people than will comfortably fit at her table. I am told she once ordered Luttrell to make room for some late arrival, whereupon he replied, 'It certainly must be made, because it doesn't exist!' "

"If you were jammed elbow to elbow, Lord Selworth," said Mrs. Lisle, "I hope you had enough to eat, for the refreshments here are shocking. Nothing but bread and butter and cake, and the cake I had was quite stale."

"There was plenty of food, ma'am, though eating was not easy! Lady Holland is a splendid hostess, in spite of a tendency to be imperious. She doesn't take snuff at a witty retort, however. When she commanded Sydney Smith to ring the bell for her, he asked if she wanted him to sweep the floor, too, yet afterwards she was perfectly affable to him. And though she likes to rule the conversation, the result is so excellent one cannot object."

So different, Pippa thought, from the tittle-tattle which passed as conversation elsewhere. With the Season scarcely under way, she was already growing tired of gossip, scandal, fashion, and sport. Although this Season was by no means the nightmare her first had been, she would just have soon have been back at Sweetbriar Cottage — if it were not for Lord Selworth and his need for help with his speech.

213

"Even if I end up addressing an empty House at midnight," he said softly, turning from Mrs. Lisle to Pippa with a smile, as Kitty and Millicent and their partners approached, "I know it will be a good speech, because I have Prometheus to help me."

By the time Pippa saw Lord Selworth next afternoon, his mood of elation had worn off and he was less sanguine. After making his bow to Bina and Mrs. Lisle and briefly greeting some other callers, he came straight to Pippa.

"Is there any point in working so hard," he grumbled in a disgruntled undertone, slumping beside her on a sofa in the drawing room, "when I may have no audience? I tried to put pen to paper this morning and not a thought came into my head."

"You were dancing until three," she pointed out. "Mama has forbidden us to rise before noon when we are out so late, which is why she told you not to call this morning. I am sure you are no less in need of sleep because you are a gentleman."

"Very likely," he said ruefully. "I shall lose my mind, and the roses in my cheeks."

"Mama threatened Kitty and Millicent with losing their roses," said Pippa, chuckling, "and me with losing my mind. I cannot spare it, for I do not mean to let you give up. Papa made many a speech which was little heeded, but he always put just as much effort into the next."

"I stand rebuked." He sighed. "You are right,

of course. Politics requires perseverance above all else, particularly in a member of the Opposition."

"And a minority within the Opposition. Let us take a holiday today, though. Three weeks is more than enough time to finish. We shall do better tomorrow after you have slept your fill."

"An excellent idea. I don't wish to overwork Prometheus and lose 'his' assistance."

Millicent came up then, having just bid some visiting young ladies farewell. She was obviously bursting with news.

"Wynn, did you know," she began in a conspiratorial whisper, "Lady Gwendolyn just told me, when I mentioned that you dined at Holland House yesterday, and I promise I shan't repeat it in company because it is just like Lady Jersey only worse and Bina was so angry when I talked about Lady Jersey, so even though Lady Holland is not a Patroness, I don't mean to tell anyone but you and Pippa. Kitty was with me, so she heard."

"Heard what?" her brother demanded impatiently. "What is this about Lady Jersey?"

"Oh, you were not there, were you? Lord Jersey, too, really, only he was not yet earl, I think." Millicent frowned in doubt, then her face cleared. "Anyway it is always the female who is blamed. They ran away together, and so did Lord and Lady Holland, only she was already married to *someone else!* She is *divorced!*"

"Good Lord, Millie, this is ancient history. Bina is quite correct. You are going to land in the suds — land us all in the suds — if you start to rake up old scandals about important people. Leave it to the tabbies who have nothing better to do and don't care whom they offend."

"Lady Gwendolyn told us," Millicent said with an injured pout. "I *said* I shall not say a word to anyone but you."

"See that you don't," commanded Lord Selworth, "for I won't put up with a scandal-monger in the family."

Thus castigated by her adored brother, Millicent was for once downcast, but only momentarily. A new group of callers was announced, and she went off to greet them with a flood of blithe chatter.

"Seed sown upon stony ground, I fear," Lord Selworth said wryly.

"She will not repeat the story of Lady Holland," Pippa said, "but there is no guessing what gossip she may pick up next, and without a specific prohibition . . . She does not deliberately disobey, you know. When she opens her mouth, she truly seems to have little control over what comes out, as if there is some sort of filter missing in her brain. Fortunately she is most good-natured, never actuated by spite, and she is more interested in the latest modes than anything else."

"Thank heaven for small mercies. If she favored political gossip, I'd be sitting constantly upon thorns!"

Wynn found himself too busy to worry about Millicent's rattling tongue. He worked on his speech with Pippa. He attended debates in the House of Lords, both to learn what was going on and to listen to how his peers framed their speeches — many of them deadly dull as well as misguided, he decided. He hobnobbed with Radical and Reformist members of the House of Commons, which gave him new ideas. Pippa had to be ruthless to make him stick to the points they had decided on for his own speech.

Missing the frequent exercise of a country life, he made sure to ride every day and often walked with Pippa and the girls in the parks. A friend introduced him to Gentleman Jackson, in whose boxing saloon Wynn began to study the noble art of pugilism, one of the few subjects in which Pippa expressed no interest whatsoever. Indeed, she positively forbade him to mention it!

The ballrooms of Mayfair and St. James's also provided a good deal of exercise. Though Millicent was well and truly launched, no longer in need of her brother's support, Wynn continued to escort his sisters and the Lisles to dances, routs, Venetian breakfasts, soirées, musicales, plays, and the Opera. Card parties he considered above and beyond the call of duty.

Cards were for amusing the children in the long, dark evenings of a country winter. Bad enough that politeness occasionally forced him to play at Boodle's.

He found himself dining more rarely in Charles Street, more frequently with his new political cronies, at Boodle's or Brooks's or private houses. At the latter, women were usually present, though less often heard. Wynn wished he had Pippa beside him, with her firm grasp of principles and her cleverness with words.

Life without her would be flat indeed. He was tempted to propose to her at once, but the prospect of adding the complications of a betrothal to his already overfull days deterred him.

After he had given his maiden speech, he would have time to do the thing properly. That day was almost upon him.

"Tomorrow, ain't it?" asked Gil Chubb on Tuesday morning at breakfast, spearing a piece of sausage. "The great day?"

"Thursday, you clunch."

"Ah, lucky I asked. I'll be there in the gallery, all right and tight."

"You may be the only person there," Wynn said gloomily, "or the only one awake, assuming you manage to stay awake."

"I'll keep pinching myself," Gil promised. "Wouldn't miss it for anything, but I'm glad I shan't have to miss Almack's tomorrow. Lady Jersey gave Miss Kitty leave to waltz last week, and she promised to save me a waltz. She always stands up with me at every ball, you know. Deuced kind of her when there's so many clamoring for the honour."

"She is popular, but her lack of fortune is bound to knock out lots of your competitors as suitors," Wynn encouraged him. "Ah, here's the post."

"My lord." Clark proffered a silver salver with two piles of letters and cards. Wynn scooped up the nearest and leafed through as Gil accepted his pile.

"A letter from Mama and one from my bailiff. Might be trouble, I'll read 'em later. Invitations — one, two, three — Lord, at least half a dozen. Hallo, what's this?"

The folded sheet bore the impressive imprint of the Lord High Chancellor of England. Wynn carefully slit the seal, with a twinge of misgiving. It must be confirmation of the date and time, but he had not expected . . .

"Devil take it, they've postponed it! Another three weeks," he groaned, jumping up and taking a rapid turn about the room to relieve his feelings. "Another three weeks on tenterhooks, and the damned speech growing stale."

"Stale?" said Gil uncomprehendingly. "Do sit down, there's a good chap. You'll ruin my digestion, and your own."

Wynn subsided into his chair. "I had just got to the point where I could deliver it practically verbatim. Miss Lisle says if one practices too much it begins to sound mechanical. Blast Eldon!"

"Daresay Miss Lisle will know what to do."

"Yes." Wynn jumped up again. "I'm off to Charles Street to tell her."

"Hold hard, old fellow! Too early by half."

Consulting the clock, Wynn said, "Half an hour. By the time I've finished dressing and walked over to Charles Street —"

"Finish your breakfast first," Gil urged. "Can't make good decisions on an empty belly."

That reminded Wynn of Pippa's advice to get enough sleep. He gobbled down sausages and muffins before setting off for his sister's house.

As always, he asked for Bina. She had pointed out long since that for a highly eligible viscount to constantly seek out an obscure spinster was bound to arouse undesirable speculation, not to mention jealousy. Fortunately he had the excuse of Pippa's being his sister's guest, but that façade must be maintained.

At balls he was careful always to dance with Millicent first, and with Kitty whenever he could pry her away from her admirers. He took Bina or Mrs. Lisle in to supper as often as he did Pippa. The servants knew, of course, that he spent a good deal of time closeted with Pippa, but he hoped they believed it was because she was frequently the only one at home when he called.

"Is my sister in?" he said, he and the first

footman having reached a mutual accommodation in the matter of euphemisms.

"The ladies have gone out, my lord."

"*All* of them?"

"*All* of them, my lord," Reuben confirmed.

Today of all days! Wynn groaned silently. "Do you know where they went?"

"To a ladies' luncheon, I understand, my lord. The younger ladies are to practice for their Presentation to the Queen, God bless her."

"*All* of them?" He had thought the Misses Lisle were not to be presented.

"All the young ladies present, I should say, my lord. Mrs. Debenham took Miss Warren. Mrs. Lisle and the Misses Lisle went to the shops, I believe. Miss Catherine spoke of bugle beads and Miss Lisle of books."

"Books?"

"I rather think Miss mentioned Hatchard's Booksellers, my lord. Or was it Hookham's Library?"

Wynn had a disorientating sense of *déjà vu:* the confusion with the footman, followed by the news that Miss Lisle was at Hookham's — he doubted she had blunt enough to patronize a bookseller. The difference was, Gil Chubb was not with him this time. He set off for Bond Street.

The circulating library was full of patrons reading newspapers and periodicals at the long tables or browsing the bookshelves. Scanning the hushed room, Wynn damned the bonnets which hid the ladies' hair and faces from the side and rear. Yet when he caught sight of Pippa, moving away from him between two rows of shelves, he recognized her figure instantly. He hurried after her.

"Miss Lisle!" he hissed.

She swung round, her hand to her heart. "Lord Selworth, how you startled me! What is wrong?" she whispered with a frown after one look at him.

"Dash it all, does my face inform the world I'm in the briars?"

"Not the world, I daresay, but me. However, it does not go into particulars."

"Eldon has postponed my speech. For three weeks!"

"What a nuisance."

"Nuisance! It —"

"It is annoying, to be sure, but there is no need to fly off the hook," she said soothingly. "Three weeks? I should have thought the Chancellor might find an earlier time, if he tried."

"But what shall we do? I cannot —"

"Really, Lord Selworth, this is not the place to discuss it."

"Then come back to Charles Street. Allow me to escort you. You are not here alone, are you?" Wynn asked disapprovingly.

Her lips quirked and she spoke soothingly again. "Mama and Kitty are somewhere about.

I expect they have found what they want, but I have not. There is no need for haste. We have three weeks in hand."

"I didn't mean to rush you," Wynn said, abashed, noting for the first time the five volumes cradled in her arm. "Let me carry those for you. How many more are you looking for?"

"Oh, half a dozen or so," she said, laughing as she handed him the stack. "I believe people buy books by the yard to fill their library shelves, but *borrowing* by quantities is an altogether new notion!"

"All my own," he said with a grin. "Do you think it will become the rage?"

Her calm reception of his news had entirely allayed his agitation. He should have trusted her to know how to deal with the delay.

The speech they had toiled over was neither abandoned, forcing Wynn to learn a new one, nor kept as it stood, losing its freshness. Instead, they made a few major changes and several smaller ones. As the new date approached, Wynn decided it was better than ever, and once again he was confident of his ability to deliver it without too many references to his notes.

Then another letter arrived from the Lord Chancellor.

"Dammit!" he yelled. "Three weeks' postponement again. What is the man about?"

"Three weeks again? Sounds fishy to me," agreed Gil, neatly dissecting a succulent kipper.

Wynn forsook his kipper and rushed around

to Charles Street. The ladies had not come down yet. When he said he would wait, Wynn was ushered into the dining room, where he found George Debenham at breakfast.

Though not involved in politics — except at elections — or government, Debenham had Tory sympathies. He was a member of White's, and his family's considerable influence in their constituency always supported the Tory candidate. Laboring under a strong sense of ill-usage, Wynn poured out the story of his shabby treatment at the hands of the arch-Tory Lord Eldon.

"I had heard there was to be another delay," Debenham admitted.

"What? It's bandied about at White's?"

"One hears rumors. Look, I'll be frank with you. I gather Liverpool and the others have learnt you are hand-and-glove with Prometheus. Don't look daggers at me. I have not breathed a word to a soul, upon my honor! It pains me to divulge to you," Debenham continued, at his most sardonic, "that the Government is shaking in its shoes for fear of the power of Prometheus' rhetoric."

14

"They don't know who Prometheus is?" Pippa asked apprehensively, clasping her hands tight in her lap to stop her fingers twisting.

Lord Selworth shook his head. "No sign of that. You ought to be flattered, you have the Government's collective teeth chattering with terror."

"But who told them? You are sure it was not Mr. Debenham?"

"I have his word as a gentleman. It's possible — in fact I strongly suspect — he has guessed you are Prometheus, but I trust his discretion absolutely."

"As I trust Bina's — I am certain she knows — to say nothing of Mama's and Kitty's. But who, then? Not Mr. Chubb!"

"No." Lord Selworth turned to the window and gazed unseeing at the gray drizzle which dripped relentlessly on the back garden. In a voice as leaden as the rain, he said, "Millicent."

"Millie? I am quite sure Bina did not tell her. It would have been sheer folly, if you will excuse my speaking so of your sister."

"It could be no one else. She must have overheard something."

"Perhaps." Pippa thought hard. "When she

told us about Lady Holland, do you recall? When she came up to us, I believe you were saying something about not losing Prometheus' help through overwork. No doubt there were other times, too."

"I'll kill her," Lord Selworth said through gritted teeth.

"I hardly think that would be advisable! Being hanged for murder is not the way to win influence for your opinions."

He turned, with a wry smile. "True. I had best limit retribution to cutting out her tongue while administering a thorough tongue-lashing."

"Scolding will not help. Very likely she would not recollect having said anything. I daresay it just slipped out in a flood of words without her even noticing She would not realize the significance and did not know it was a secret. It is our fault for being so careless as to let her find out."

"My dear girl, you are far too lenient! Consider the damage she has done! Suppose Eldon never lets me speak?"

"Is that not impossible? You are by right a member of the House of Lords."

"I'm not sure," he said with a frown. "Even if he cannot stop me joining in a debate, he can continue indefinitely to postpone my maiden speech — my best hope to make my mark — which amounts to preventing it. No, Millie has a great deal to answer for."

"At least she does not know, or has not told, that I am Prometheus. If you rake up the subject, she will have it on her mind and may put overheard oddments together to work that out next."

"I surrender! Millie shall keep her life and her tongue. When you argue against me, instead of for me, I perfectly understand the Government's misgivings."

"Well, I do not." Pippa shook her head doubtfully. "It is prodigious hard to credit that all those powerful lords are afraid of what I might say!"

"You don't look dangerous," said Lord Selworth, contemplating her with a curious glint in his eye, "but if I could have you beside me in the House, to put the words in my mouth, I'd gladly make do with the extempore speech of a debate. Failing that, what are we to do?"

"You must give me time to think. We shall contrive," said Pippa, with more confidence than she felt.

Pippa spent most of the day reading over all the notes she had made in the course of the past few weeks, hoping for inspiration. None came. Simply rewriting the speech to concentrate on different topics would not help. It was not any specific opinion the Tory Lords objected to, but Lord Selworth's entire philosophy — and that of his mentor.

That evening she assured him that she had the seed of an idea, but did not want to discuss it until it had time to germinate. Since he had not the least notion how to proceed, he was forced to be content.

When Pippa retired to bed, she lay long awake with thoughts running aimlessly around in her head. There *must* be some way to outmaneuver Eldon, Liverpool, Castlereagh, and the rest. Lord Selworth trusted her. She could not bear to let him down. How despairing he had been that morning, before she promised to find a solution!

Drowsily, she recalled their conversation. He had called her "my dear girl" again — but only in exasperation at her defence of Millicent. He had looked at her with what might conceivably have been an appreciative light in his eye — but all he said was that she did not look dangerous. Then he had said he wanted her beside him — but only in the House of Lords, during a debate, when the Chancellor could not stop him speaking.

It was no use. She could not persuade herself he admired anything but her mind. On that unhappy thought, at last she fell asleep . . .

. . . And half-awoke at dawn with the germ of an idea. A debate, when the Chancellor could not stop him speaking, that was the key.

She did not wake again until Nan came in with the morning chocolate and drew back the curtains on a sunny day. The sunshine made

Pippa feel cheerful even before she remembered that she had come up with the beginnings of an answer to Lord Selworth's difficulties.

Yesterday the heavens wept for him, today they smiled. "The pathetic fallacy," she said aloud.

"What is that?" asked Kitty, sitting up and sipping her chocolate.

"Imputing human emotions to inanimate objects. The sky is blue in sympathy with my cheerful mood."

Kitty laughed. "More likely you are cheerful because the sky is blue. Yesterday's rain was horridly depressing. I had rather have a brief downpour than drizzle. In Town, at least. Drizzle is better for crops, if it does not go on too long. A storm tends to beat them down."

"Do you miss the country?"

"Oh yes. The Season is fun, but I could not bear to spend every spring in London. When I think what I am missing, the wildflowers, the lambs and calves and chicks . . . I hope my chicks are all right without me."

"I am sure Sukey is taking excellent care of them."

"Mr. Chubb has discovered a place where I might buy the chicks of a new breed of fowl from Cochin China, and Musk Ducks from Africa. But there is no point getting them now. I should want to be at home to make sure they settle well and to find out how best to help them thrive."

"Perhaps you can send for some next year," Pippa said absently. *Debate,* she thought, as Kitty obligingly fell silent, recognizing her sister's cogitative expression.

Debates concentrated on a single subject. She and Lord Selworth must find a subject which was to be debated in the not too far distant future. It must be something about which he had strong feelings, yet which would not threaten the status quo in such a way as to make the Government take fright. Their aim was to prove his ability as an orator, not to reform the country radically in one fell swoop.

That could come later, gradually, once he had the respect of his peers.

Two problems remained to be solved before Pippa could settle down to writing a new speech. First, she must find a suitable debate. Second, she must persuade Lord Selworth to limit himself to a single topic. The second, she suspected, might be the more difficult.

She half-expected him to be awaiting her at table when she went down, as he had the day before. However, discretion had apparently mastered impatience — he had, after all, no open invitation to breakfast at his sister's house.

Mr. Debenham, with a satirical air, handed Pippa the *Morning Chronicle,* as was his habit. Lord Selworth was probably right, she realized.

His brother-in-law had surely worked out by now that she was Prometheus. Fortunately Millicent had no interest whatsoever in periodicals without fashion plates. Since she had no idea that the *Chronicle* was full of Parliamentary news, she did not wonder why Pippa read it.

After a thorough search of every page, Pippa was no nearer choosing a suitable subject. She had hoped to present the viscount with a *fait accompli,* or at least a specific proposal to show him what she meant.

"But everything was either inconsequential," she told him when he called that afternoon, "like the farthing duty on tea, which they still have not settled, or too consequential, like the Seditious Meetings Act and the suspension of *Habeas corpus.*"

"I could talk forever on *Habeas corpus,*" Lord Selworth grumbled. "Why not?"

"Because a great many other people will talk about it, too. If you have prepared a speech, you are likely to find half of what you have to say already said. What we want is something few members of the Lords have thought about seriously or in depth. We must keep looking. Something is bound to come up soon."

"I hope so! I should hate the Tories to prevail to the extent of shutting me out of an entire session."

"You have only been a peer for a few months," Pippa consoled him. "Some only appear in Parliament for state occasions."

"They say Lord Melbourne has only made one speech in his entire life," Lord Selworth agreed. "His wife is a more active Whig than he is. I'd best go and talk to someone else now. If you and I are seen *tête-à-tête* too often now it's known that I'm consulting Prometheus, someone may add two and two."

Pippa had to agree. After all, there was no chance anyone would come to the conclusion that the eligible Lord Selworth was courting so undistinguished a female.

The drawing room was somewhat thin of company. The morning sun had given way to wind and rain, inducing many ladies to curtail their usual routine of calls for fear of damage to slippers and bonnets. However, the flock of young gentlemen around Kitty and Millicent was undiminished. Millicent was silent at present, listening with the rest to an ode a youthful poet had written to a curl on Kitty's brow.

Mr. Chubb came over to Pippa when he saw Lord Selworth leave her. "Such balderdash!" he snorted. "A crow's wing on a snowy field! Crows are vermin, and what's a wing doing in the middle of a field, anyway, without the rest of the bird? I wish I could write such stuff," he added wistfully.

"You would not if you heard Kitty and Millicent giggling about Mr. Darlington's poems when he is gone."

"Truly?" His round face brightened, then fell

again. "But I daresay she laughs at me, too, though I know you are too kind to tell me so."

"If she did, I would not tell you, to be sure, but she does not, and I would not lie to you. Only this morning she was talking of your discovery of a place selling rare poultry and her regret that she could not buy any this year as she is not at home to tend them. She hopes to try next spring."

"I shall send her some," Mr. Chubb said eagerly, "or better still, bring her the chicks myself, to be sure they are well cared for on the road." Again despondency overcame him. "But by next spring she will be long married, to someone else."

Pippa wished she was able to assure him that he had an excellent chance of winning Kitty's hand. She thought the two extremely well suited, and she liked Gilbert Chubb very well now that he had overcome his bashfulness with her. But Kitty showed no disposition to favor him — or anyone else, for that matter. She had already turned down two suitors. As far as Pippa could see, her sister's heart was whole.

Kitty apparently knew none of the doubts and fears which kept Pippa awake at night, nor the rush of light-headed joy she felt whenever Wynn Selworth came into a room — the joy which must be hidden, the light-headedness which must be overcome before she was able to concentrate on ideas and words. How Kitty would stare if she knew her intellectual sister quivered inside when her hand accidentally brushed Wynn Selworth's, went weak at the knees when she placed her hand on his arm, melted from top to toe at his smile.

Somehow she had hidden her love from Kitty, and from Lord Selworth. If he knew, he would surely relinquish his mentor rather than risk encouraging by his constant presence the passion to which he was indifferent.

Sometimes Pippa wondered whether Mama or Bina had guessed. If so, unable to encourage her to hope, they were too kind to add to her heartache by pointing out the unlikelihood of his ever returning her feelings.

Mr. Chubb had a better chance with Kitty, Pippa thought. "Kitty's affections are as yet unengaged," she said, "and you and she have a good deal in common. You must not give up."

"I shan't," he promised.

By the fourth day of searching the newspapers in vain, Pippa was ready to give up. It seemed the Lords had nothing quite suitable on their agenda this session. Lord Selworth would just have to wait and hope that Lord Eldon might relent.

She persevered, however, and the very next day was rewarded by finding precisely what she was looking for.

"Climbing boys?" said Lord Selworth dubiously.

"The children chimney sweeps send up

chimneys. There is a society trying to abolish the practice, and they are to present a petition to Parliament. It is perfect, Lord Selworth! The petition will arouse interest, but it is not a matter which will make the Government fear you are striking at the very roots of society."

"I don't know much about climbing boys."

"They are shockingly badly treated, and quite unnecessarily, for a machine has been invented — a sort of elongated brush — which does the job just as thoroughly. The sweeps prefer to use little boys because it is easier and less labor for themselves. All they need do is stick pins in the child's feet, or light a straw fire, to force them to climb."

"Good Lord! Do they really?" exclaimed the viscount, shocked.

"You see? Few people know what happens, because naturally they leave the house when the sweep comes to do his messy business."

"Yes, but bad as it is, even you can't make a whole speech out of pins and a small fire."

"Of course not," Pippa agreed. "We need to find out more, only I am not sure how. The master sweeps certainly will not tell us anything useful."

"I'll go and talk to the society who are getting up the petition," Lord Selworth proposed. "They must know the worst or they wouldn't be up in arms."

"Oh yes, why did I not think of that?"

"Are you sure you didn't?" he asked suspiciously. "You are not just trying to cheer me up by allowing me a small contribution to your plan?"

"Heavens no. I honestly never considered consulting the society, perhaps because I have always had to work from published reports. I shall go with you."

"No."

"Why not?" Pippa demanded indignantly. "Because it is your idea?"

"Don't be a widgeon. For the same reason you have always worked from published reports, only more so. If I go and make enquiries with a view to airing the matter in Parliament, and you go with me, you might as well stand on the rooftops and proclaim yourself Prometheus. Well, nearly."

"Oh. I daresay it would be rash," she conceded.

"You could go on your own account," Lord Selworth offered, "as a philanthropist considering signing the petition, but wanting to know more first. They might tell you things they hesitated to tell me."

"I cannot think what, but thank you for allowing me a part in the venture!"

He gave her a straight look. "If I had forbidden your approaching them, would you have heeded the prohibition?"

"Not unless I saw good reason for it," Pippa said promptly, "and no good reason to go against it."

"*Not* a compliant female," he said, his tone reproachful, with a sigh and a shake of the head.

Pippa was glad to see a twinkle in his eye. If she had had the least chance of winning his affections, proving herself far from submissive was likely to dish it. As it was, she said pertly, "No compliant female could possibly have directed your efforts these past two months. I should like to call upon the Society for the Abolition of Climbing Boys, or whatever they call themselves, but I do not know their direction."

"They cannot circulate a petition without coming out into the open. I'll find 'em. And I'll let you know when I do."

"Noble of you!" Pippa exclaimed, and he laughed.

When she danced with him that evening, he had not yet tracked down the society, but when they met next day he passed her a slip of paper with their direction.

"I have something else for you," he said. "Come for a drive in the Park."

"You said we should not be seen together," Pippa demurred.

"Not too often, I said. I drove Millicent yesterday, Bina the day before, and your mama the day before that — there's no getting near your sister. Be compliant for once: go put on your bonnet."

Pippa complied, her curiosity aroused. What did he have to give her that he chose not to give openly, in company? Not a betrothal ring, alas. In such an unlikely event he must have spoken first to Mama, and Mama would certainly have informed her of such a momentous occurrence.

Instead, she informed Mrs. Lisle that she was going out with Lord Selworth, and went upstairs to fetch bonnet and gloves.

The viscount's curricle was waiting at the door. He handed Pippa up, took the reins from his groom, and joined her. The groom scrambled up to his perch behind as the horses, a stalwart pair of blacks to match the carriage, set off along Charles Street.

Pippa with difficulty restrained herself from asking about her mysterious gift. Conscious of the groom's ears close behind, she made an innocuous remark about the weather. This led — the servant's presence soon forgotten — to a discussion of the prospects for a good harvest, leading to the relief of hunger across the country and its effects on politics.

The afternoon was warm for May, with a thin haze of cloud obscuring the sky but letting the sun shine through. In the narrow streets, the heat reflected uncomfortably from cobbles and brick walls, but they soon reached the Chesterfield Gate and entered Hyde Park.

The grass was bright with buttercups, daisies, and dandelions, reminding Pippa of the wide variety of wildflowers now blooming in the country. The woods would be carpeted with bluebells, the hillsides with cowslips, the water meadows with lady's smock. Much as she enjoyed them when at home, she reflected, she did not miss them as Kitty did. To her, the fascination of politics made up for spending spring in Town.

Pulling up just inside the gates, Lord Selworth told the groom to wait nearby for their return. Then he headed south, but he turned off towards the Serpentine before they reached Rotten Row.

Though there were a good many people about, it was too early for the crowds of fashionable carriages, riders, and pedestrians who would flock to the Park later for the daily Grand Promenade. When the curricle pulled up in the shade of a tall elm, they were quite private.

Lord Selworth reached under the seat and pulled out a rectangular parcel wrapped in brown paper and tied with string. "Here," he said, thrusting it into Pippa's hands, and at once looking away with an air of unconcern, apparently watching a pair of riders cantering across the grass.

Books? The size and weight were right, though several layers of paper obscured details of the shape. Pippa struggled with the knotted string, in vain. In vain she felt in her reticule for scissors. "Have you a pocketknife, Lord Selworth?"

"What? Oh, sorry." For some reason he flushed as he handed her his penknife.

Comprehension dawning, Pippa abandoned any attempt to save useful lengths of string. She sliced through it, unfolded the paper, and found three calf-bound, gold-lettered volumes. "*The Masked Marauder*! Oh, splendid!"

"I thought you might like a copy of your own," said Lord Selworth, looking pleased at her pleasure.

"Thank you, Mr. Valentine Dred. I shall treasure it. I did not know it was out already."

"In the bookshops tomorrow, the libraries the day after. The publisher says a great many copies were sold beforehand," he said modestly. "You had best keep yours well hidden, as I have inscribed each volume to you."

"Assuming it is similar to your previous works, I should in any case hide it away. It is not at all proper for Kitty or Millicent to read."

Almost reluctantly, Pippa opened the first volume to the title page, wishing his inscription might say: "To darling Pippa, with all my love, Wynn." Naturally it did not. But nor was it a formal "To Miss Lisle, from your obedient servant, Selworth."

For my dear Prometheus, she read, *this, with humble gratitude and devoted admiration, Valentine.*

Pippa laughed. "I shall keep them *very* well hidden," she promised. Devoted admiration? For Prometheus, of course.

Whatever Pippa's views on the propriety of

Kitty and Millicent reading *The Masked Marauder*, within the week all Society was talking about it. Demure damsels whispered and giggled behind their fans; mature matrons told each other, "My dear, I positively blushed when . . . ;" Corinthians and Tulips alike vowed to each other they had laughed till they cried; serious gentlemen condemned the book as trivial, indecent nonsense, but it was to be noted that not one had failed to peruse all three volumes.

And all Society asked with a single voice, "Who wrote it? Who is Valentine Dred?"

15

"Who is Valentine Dred?" asked Millicent, as she and Kitty strolled down Piccadilly, their abigail a pace behind.

It was certainly a rhetorical question, for not only did she not expect an answer, she failed to pause to allow her friend to provide one had she been able.

"No one talks of anything else, I vow," she continued without taking a breath. "It is becoming a shocking bore. Who do you think he can be, Kitty? At least, Valentine is generally a man's name, is it not? But as it is only a penname — everyone seems to agree it is a penname — it could just as well be a woman. Do you think it might be Lady Caroline Lamb? She wrote *Glenarvon* last year, after all."

"I have not read *Glenarvon*," Kitty deftly inserted into the stream, practice having made her expert, "nor met Lady Caroline, but I have heard that she has no sense of humor."

"Then it cannot be her, for everyone is laughing over *The Masked Marauder*. I wish Bina and your mama had not forbidden us to read it," Millicent mourned. "The Pendrell girls have read it. Vanessa says it is very shocking, to be sure, but funny and thrilling, too. The hero is quite the most dashing gentleman you can conceive, and the heroine's plight most pitiable."

"I do not believe I should care to be married to too dashing a gentleman. Suppose he were to make a habit of dashing off whenever one needed him?"

"You are laughing at me again," Millicent said resignedly. "It is true that in real life a dashing husband may not be altogether comfortable, but it is only a book after all. I think it very hard that we may not read it when the whole world talks of nothing else."

"Not having read it does not stop *you* talking of it, Millie dear," said Kitty, laughing aloud. "We have heard so much about it, we scarcely need to read it ourselves. Here is the haberdasher's I told you about. Let us hope they can match your ribbon."

Millicent dropped the subject of *The Masked Marauder* for quite half an hour. Unfortunately, they then happened to encounter two young gentlemen of their acquaintance who had just been to Hatchard's to purchase a copy — without luck, as the entire stock was sold out.

On parting from the disconsolate pair, Kitty said to Millicent, "I never thought to see Mr. Carlin or Sir Anthony looking to purchase a whole book! The perusal of a single page in a newspaper is a great labor to them."

"Oh, but a novel is quite different. Only think, Kitty, what a great labor it must be to *write* a whole book! My wrist positively aches at the very thought, I declare. Yet Pippa is always scribbling away with never a complaint of fatigue. I wonder what it is she writes, that she always hides it when one enters the room." Her mouth dropped open as a notion struck her momentarily dumb. "Kitty, do you suppose *Pippa* is Valentine Dred?"

"Good gracious, no!" cried Kitty in horror.

"Well then, what is it she writes so busily? I am sure it cannot be letters, for there are pages and pages and it would cost a fortune to post them all. You must know, Kitty. You are her sister. If it is not a book, what is it?"

"I cannot tell you, Millie, so be a dear and do not press me. I repeat, Pippa is *not* Valentine Dred. Oh, Millie, do but look at the signs in the window of this shop! 'Guineas taken with delight; Shillings quite welcome; Halfpence will not be refused.' "

" 'Half sovereigns taken with avidity,' " Millie read, " 'Crowns hailed with pleasure; Farthings rather than nothing.' It quite makes one want to go in and buy something, only I cannot see anything I need. That beaded reticule is quite pretty, but I have spent nearly all my pin money for the week."

Fashion regained its usual preeminence in her chatter. Kitty was able to persuade herself that the nonsensical notion of Pippa having written naughty romances had flown from her companion's head as swiftly as it had entered.

Meanwhile, Wynn and Miss Lisle had each called upon the leaders of the society circulating the petition against the employment of climbing boys to clean chimneys. By prior arrangement, they met in Charles Street in the ladies' sitting room to discuss their findings.

Before he knocked on the open door, Wynn paused on the threshold. His beloved sat at the writing table, one slender, shapely hand reaching out to dip her quill in the inkpot, her delicate profile framed against the window. In the north light her pale skin was translucent, her dark, smooth hair sleek. Wynn had a sudden, almost irresistible desire to pull out all her hairpins and see her cloaked in those silken tresses.

Had he really once told Gil Chubb she was plain?

As if she felt his gaze, she turned, her face lighting in a smile which at once gave way to anguish. "Oh, it is perfectly horrible!" she cried, casting down her pen.

"I ought not to have let you go," Wynn said grimly, striding forward to take her hands in his. Not pretty? She was beautiful in her passion! Finding his mind drifting to how her face would look under the influence of a different sort of passion, he sternly called himself to order. "I had not imagined such painful stories, I confess."

"How could anyone imagine such inhumanity? Those little boys driven up chimneys, often so narrow they can barely pass, sometimes hot enough to burn, at best scraping and bruising themselves, and suffocated by falling soot. And then, if they come down alive — which they do not always — forced to carry heavy bags of soot, and beaten; never washed and frequently not fed . . ."

"Small wonder many turn to begging and some to stealing, but that some people believe the solution is to send them to Sunday school is incredible!"

"Is it not? If they do not die of burns, or suffocation, or beatings, they may cough and choke and wheeze as they please provided their morals are good, and live on stunted and deformed."

"To die later of chimney-sweeps' cancer."

"Such *little* boys, Wynn," she said, tears in her eyes, "as young as four!"

He yearned to kiss away the tears. For the first time, she had called him Wynn, but he must not read too much into the mark of intimacy. It had probably slipped out unintentionally. After all, she constantly heard his sisters calling him by his Christian name.

Letting go of her hands, he sat down. "The official minimum age is eight, but as long as the law is not enforced, destitute parents will sell younger children to the master sweeps for a guinea or two."

"Some sweeps send their own children up the

chimneys," Pippa said with incredulous abhorrence.

"And some buy boys kidnapped for the purpose. Did Mr. Montgomery tell you about the child rescued by a Yorkshire family?"

"The Stricklands? Yes." She gestured at the papers on the desk. "I have been trying to work out the best way to make that story the centerpiece of your speech. Surely any responsible, loving parent hearing it must instantly wish to free all climbing boys, if only for fear of their own sons suffering a like fate! But I have not enough information. I should like to question the Stricklands, to meet the child if possible, only Mama would never let me travel so far. Lord Selworth, do you suppose you . . . ?"

"I do." To see the hope in her hazel eyes turn to warm approval, Wynn would have traveled a great deal farther than to Yorkshire — if it were not that he must leave her behind. "Montgomery gave me their direction in case I wished to correspond, but you are right, a personal interview will be much more useful."

"I believe so."

"What we want is details, is it not, to flesh out the story. How they happened to rescue him, what made them suspect he came from an affluent home, anything he recalls of his abduction?"

"Exactly. Doubtless you will have a better idea of just what to ask once you have spoken to them."

"I shall leave in the morning." *Will you miss me?*

"I wish I might go, too. How long do you think you will be away?"

"Two or three days each way. Say three: Kymford is not far off the Great North Road, so I may as well spend a night at home in each direction. It will not delay me much."

"Oh yes, you should take the opportunity to see your family. Two, perhaps three days in Yorkshire. Ten days in all, or less, not so *very* long." Pippa's sigh, though slight, did not go unnoticed, but she returned at once to business. "While you are gone I shall put my notes in order — you brought yours?"

"Yes, here, I copied them from my pocket-book for you." Wynn retrieved the papers from his pocket and handed them over.

"Thank you. I should be able to bring the speech into some sort of shape, ready to insert the child's story. I do believe this will be a truly splendid speech. I only wish such horrors did not exist for you to speak about."

"We are doing what we can to put a stop to them," Wynn consoled her, "but if brooding over the misery throws you into the dismals, you must let the speech wait until I come back to cheer you up. Promise?"

"I promise not to fall into a decline," she said with a faint smile.

It was two days after Lord Selworth's departure that Pippa first noticed the cold looks. Mrs. Drummond Burrell, haughtiest of Almack's patronesses and usually distantly condescending towards the Lisles, actually turned her back when they entered a room.

Then, in the course of a single evening, Pippa was invited to dance by three gentlemen of decidedly rakish reputation who had never before noticed her existence. All three made sly remarks she could only interpret as improper. One actually suggested that they should retire together to a small salon near the ballroom where he knew they would not be disturbed. When Pippa frostily refused, he muttered something about "whited sepulchres," but to her relief he did not persist.

Rather than repeat the unpleasant experience, she told her mama she was a little tired and would sit out the rest of the evening. She need not have troubled. Not one of Kitty's court, her usual partners, asked her to stand up.

In fact, their numbers were considerably diminished, and Kitty herself sat out three sets for the first time since their arrival in Town.

The next morning, Bina asked Pippa to join her in her sitting room. When Pippa arrived, her friend thrust a pile of notes into her hands. "Read these."

Every one was from a hostess requesting that Mrs. Debenham not bring the Lisles with her to her entertainment.

"What is going on?" Bina asked, troubled.

"I have not the least notion." Pippa described the insulting behaviour of her partners last night. "Surely discovery of my political interests would not lead to that particular form of disrespect," she said helplessly. "I cannot imagine what I have done to earn it."

"Nothing!" Bina was furious. "Some scandalmonger has invented a story about you for want of anything better to do. Now that Princess Charlotte is safely married, people can no longer employ themselves in wondering whether she will shy off at the eleventh hour! Believe me, if you are not welcome at these parties, you may be sure *I* shall not attend."

"But you must, Bina. It is not fair that Millicent's Season should be ruined because someone is slandering me. Poor Kitty! Perhaps if I go home to Buckinghamshire, people will forget and accept her again."

"No, I shall not let you run away, if only for Wynn's sake. It might be just as well, though," Bina said thoughtfully, "if I continue to take Millie about so as to have the opportunity to try and find out what is being said. One cannot fight a rumor one has not heard. For a start, we shall call on every notable gossip in Town."

But one notable gossip called on the Lisles while Bina and Millicent were out. Lady Jersey, an elegant and influential lady of about thirty years, came straight to the point.

"I fear you are sailing in troubled waters,

ma'am," she said bluntly to Mrs. Lisle. "I regret to say that, in view of Jersey's association with your late husband, I have been deputed by my fellow-Patronesses to request that you no longer attend Almack's."

Kitty gasped. Aching for her, Pippa took her hand.

"Why?" asked Mrs. Lisle, matching Lady Jersey's bluntness.

Her ladyship's delicate eyebrows rose. "Surely you can guess."

"Indeed I cannot! To my knowledge, neither I nor my daughters has done anything to deserve the way we are being treated."

"Can it be, ma'am, you are unaware of your elder daughter's authorship?"

Pippa felt cold inside. Was it indeed her writing which had brought down disgrace upon her family? She had expected to be laughed at if it became known, not spurned.

Kitty was frowning. Mrs. Lisle, visibly disturbed, demanded, "Authorship? What exactly is Philippa accused of writing, Lady Jersey?"

"Why, *The Masked Marauder*, of course," said the countess with a tinkling laugh. "A delicious book, certainly, but far too titillating for its author to lay any claim to the innocence Society demands of young ladies."

Stunned, Pippa burst out, "But I am not its author! I assure you, ma'am, I did not write *The Masked Marauder*, nor anything remotely similar."

"My daughter is not a novelist," Mrs. Lisle supported her. "She could not possibly have concealed it from me in our small cottage. I beg of you, ma'am, do what you can to contradict this calumny. It is utterly without foundation."

Lady Jersey looked from Mrs. Lisle to Pippa and back, her gaze shrewd and not unkindly. "Well, well, I believe you, and I will do what I can."

"Thank you, Lady Jersey!"

"However, I must warn you that many will refuse to credit the word of Miss Lisle and her family — it is only what you might be expected to say, after all. I fear the book's popularity makes the *on-dit* too toothsome a morsel to be easily abandoned. Your best hope is that the real author will come forward."

"He surely cannot like to see someone else credited with his work," said Kitty hopefully.

"So we will hope, Miss Catherine. In the meantime, I must advise you all not to appear at Almack's. I should hate to see you suffer the same sort of reception as Lord Byron's last year."

With that bitter remark, Lady Jersey took her leave.

"What happened to Lord Byron?" Kitty enquired.

"Ask Albinia," her mother advised absently. "I am very much afraid Lady Jersey is correct, and no denials from us will bear any weight."

"Mama, if I went home —" Pippa said.

"Certainly not! Your papa would never permit you to concede defeat. I shall go up to the sitting room at once and write to Lady Stanborough and one or two others of those I have come to regard — perhaps mistakenly — as friends." She went out.

"I am sorry, Kitty," Pippa said miserably.

Kitty flung her arms around her and gave her a hug. "Pippa darling, it is not *your* fault. I have a very good notion whose fault it is, only I am not perfectly sure what to do about it."

Pippa scarcely heard her. It was Lord Selworth's fault, of course, for writing those shocking books. Why could he not have been satisfied with stories which were thrilling and funny, without also making them *titillating?*

Lady Jersey thought only exposure of the real author would save the Lisles' reputation. Pippa could expose him, but — if she was believed — his political career would be nipped in the bud. Even if she could bring herself to do that to him, what of all the good he might be expected to do in the future to right the miseries of the world?

"I have the headache, Kitty. I believe I shall go and lie down for a little while."

"Let me make you a tisane!"

"No, it is not bad," said Pippa, wanting nothing so much as to be alone with her megrims. "You had best stay here in case anyone is brave enough to call. Send for me or

Mama if any gentleman comes."

Left alone, Kitty crossed to the window and stood, half-hidden by the brocade curtains, gazing down into the street. Normally at this time of day the phaetons, curricles, and gigs of her admirers would be thronging there, joined by the barouches and landaus of visiting ladies.

It was some slight comfort that Millicent also would undoubtedly suffer from the dearth. How could she do this to Pippa?

A barouche approached along Charles Street, a gentleman riding alongside. Kitty recognized the Pendrells. Her heart leapt: at least some friends did not believe the slander, and would not let the censure of the rest of the Ton influence their conduct!

The barouche rolled on without slowing, the Misses Pendrell pointing out the Debenhams' house to the two unknown young ladies in the carriage with them. Vanessa Pendrell said something to her brother, and he laughed.

Chagrined, Kitty turned from the window and dropped onto a nearby sofa. They were all the same. She did not care if she never again saw any of the so-called gentlemen who claimed to adore her. All she wanted was to go home to Buckinghamshire and live the rest of her life peacefully in the cottage with Mama and Pippa — but what about Pippa?

Pippa must be vindicated, if only Kitty could work out how to do it.

"Mr. Chubb, miss."

Startled, Kitty jumped up.

"Didn't mean to take you by surprise, Miss Kitty," Mr. Chubb apologized, bowing.

"Do you not know that we are in disgrace?" she demanded bitterly.

"Yes. That is, heard stories. Wouldn't have credited them anyway, of course, but as it happens I know the truth."

"It hardly matters, sir. We are proclaimed outcasts by Society, and if you go against Society's — You *what?*"

"As if anything Society dictates could make me stay away from you!" said Mr. Chubb with scorn, adding eagerly, "You do believe me, don't you?"

"Yes, yes, but what do you mean, you know the truth? You know Millicent dreamt up the whole thing out of thin air?"

Mr. Chubb looked bewildered. "Miss Warren? What has she to say to the matter?"

"That is the trouble. She has something to say to every m-matter!" To her own astonishment and dismay, Kitty burst into tears. "I n-never cry!" she sobbed.

After a moment of startled alarm, Mr. Chubb sat down on the sofa beside her, thrust his handkerchief into her hand, and patted her shoulder soothingly. "There there," he murmured. "I daresay it will all turn out to be a tempest in a teapot, though how even the smallest tempest can blow up in a teapot I have always failed to comprehend."

Kitty gave a watery giggle, blew her nose heartily, looked up at his sympathetic, concerned face, and came to a decision. "You are quite the nicest, kindest, most sensible gentleman I know," she said encouragingly.

Mr. Chubb turned pink. "D-dashed kind in you to say so," he stuttered, "but the others, the rest of your beaux, you know, I'm sure it's just a temporary misunderstanding. What is it Miss Warren's been saying to distress you?"

"I am certain it is her doing," said Kitty, with an internal sigh.

Was she going to have to do the proposing? Give the poor, diffident dear a bit more time to come to terms with the fact that she was available to him, she decided. Besides, she did not want him to imagine she was pursuing him because of the defection of the rest of her suitors. If she was, it was only in a roundabout way, his loyalty being the deciding factor when she was already predisposed in his favour.

"Miss Warren has been spreading the *on-dit* about Miss Lisle being Valentine Dred?" he asked in surprise. "What makes you think so?"

"She put two and two together and came up with five. She knows Pippa does a lot of writing. I *told* her it is nothing to do with novels, and I hoped she had forgot the notion. I ought to have made sure she was convinced."

"Now don't start blaming yourself, Kit . . . Miss Kitty. Whatever Miss Warren believes," Mr. Chubb said severely, "it was very unkind

— indeed, downright wrong — to talk of it."

Kitty shook her head. "Millicent is very good-natured. I am sure she did not realize the damage it would do. In fact, I doubt she intended to mention her guess at all, but she talks such a great deal things slip out inadvertently. I should not like to carry tales to her brother or sister, yet unless the source of the story is known, who will believe our denials? I cannot bear to see Pippa pilloried. What should I do?"

"I've no qualms about telling Wynn his sister started it. Ought to know. Pity he's out of town."

"It might not help anyway. Lady Jersey said our best hope is that the real author reveal himself. By the way, do you know what happened to Lord Byron at Almack's last year?"

"What?" Mr. Chubb appeared to be wrestling with a knotty problem. "George Gordon? What I heard was that his behavior was so shocking his wife deserted him and he was ostracized. Lady Jersey and some others gave a party for him to try to bring him back into Society, but everyone left the room when he arrived."

"Poor man!" Kitty glanced around the empty drawing room. "I can imagine how he felt."

"Yes, well, he really is a pretty shocking fellow, you know. Don't ask," he added hastily. "Not the sort of thing to tell a young lady. Besides, your case is quite different. Miss Lisle *didn't* write *The Masked Marauder*. I know who did."

"You do?" Kitty cried. "Then you can tell people and they will know it was not Pippa."

"That's the trouble." Mr. Chubb looked so harassed and miserable Kitty's heart went out to him. "You know I'd do almost anything for you, but this would be betraying a friend's trust."

"The author is a friend of yours? Can you not persuade him to come forward?"

"I'd do my best, believe me, only he's out of town at present."

Kitty stared at him. "Not *Lord Selworth?*"

Mr. Chubb nodded unhappily. "If people knew, they would never take him seriously as a politician."

"I shall not tell." Her promise was reluctant, but she suspected Pippa would not wish to save herself by ruining Lord Selworth's career, which she was trying so hard to get off to a good start.

Kitty chewed her lip, recollecting the warmth in the viscount's eyes when his gaze fell upon her sister. Pippa would not sacrifice Lord Selworth to save herself, but he . . . ? "I think he ought to be told as soon as possible what has happened. He will be horrified to hear Pippa is being vilified, and I am sure he will not wish to let it continue a moment longer than it need. Do you know where he went?"

"To Yorkshire. He said he was going to put

up at the Black Swan in York."

"Could you . . . Oh, Mr. Chubb, it is a great deal to ask, but could you possibly go after him?"

"I'll leave at once," said her cavalier gallantly, rising to his feet.

"No, wait a moment, let me think. You are sure his career would be badly damaged if he was known to be the author of *The Masked Marauder*?"

"Positive."

"Then it would not be fair to ask him to give himself away if other means might suffice. Let us wait until tomorrow and see whether Lady Jersey and my mother and Mrs. Debenham can quash the rumors. Perhaps the morning will bring new invitations."

"All right," said the obliging Mr. Chubb. "Send me word after you know what's in the morning post, and I'll leave right away."

"In the meantime, pray do not tell anyone I asked you to go, or about Millie or anything."

"Shouldn't dream of it."

"Bless you!" said Kitty fondly.

16

"Pippa, I am so dreadfully sorry!" wailed Millicent, rushing into the drawing room. "Bina says it is all my fault, but indeed I told people you are *not* Valentine Dred, not that you are, and only my most particular friends, laughing at myself, you see, for making such a harebrained guess just because you are always scribbling away. Forgive me, pray say you forgive me, or I declare I shall go into a decline and —"

"Of course I forgive you, Millie," said Pippa in bewilderment.

She had come downstairs a few minutes earlier, Nan having woken her from a semidrowse to tell her Reuben said Miss Catherine was alone with Mr. Chubb. The abigail had not wanted to "peach" on Miss to her mama.

"You may be sure I have rung a thorough peal over Millie's head," said Bina grimly, following her sister into the room at a more decorous pace. "But I thought it best she should not try to explain the mistake to people for fear of confusing matters still further."

"If anyone is confused, I am," Pippa declared, her arm about a weeping Millicent.

Bina sank into a chair, untying the ribbons of her bonnet. "As soon as we returned to the car-

260

riage after discovering — oh, but you do not yet know the cause of our difficulties."

"Yes, we do," said Kitty. Mr. Chubb had quietly departed, Pippa noted with a pang. No doubt he had only now learnt what was being said about her. He was just another rat deserting a sinking ship.

"Then you will have gathered," said Bina, waving at her watering-pot sister, "that this little bagpipe is responsible. When we heard of the wretched *on-dit,* Millicent confessed to me that she had suspected Pippa of writing *The Masked Marauder.*"

"I'm *sorry!*" sobbed Millie.

"But when Kitty set her straight she told her friends it was not true. Since she had never confided her suspicion in the first place, I suppose it is possible some of them genuinely misunderstood, though one cannot but wonder whether malice . . . Less fortunate girls are bound to be jealous when Kitty is so very popular."

"Was," Kitty corrected her sadly.

"Mr. Chubb was your only caller?"

"No," Pippa said, "Lady Jersey came to inform us that we are no longer welcome at Almack's. I do think she believed us. At least, she promised to contradict the rumors."

"She may," Bina said pessimistically, "but her denials may be as useless as mine. Though no one was impolite enough to say to my face that they did not believe me, I could see they thought I felt obliged to defend my guests."

"But we are not Lady Jersey's guests," Pippa pointed out. "Why should not people believe her?"

"For a start, the other Patronesses might well suppose she was trying to exculpate herself for persuading them to grant you vouchers. Then, others — especially those who *wish* to credit your guilt — could simply say you have pulled the wool over her eyes, and mine."

There seemed no answer to that. Mrs. Lisle came down with the several notes she had written, and Bina agreed that sending them could do no harm. She held out little hope of their having much effect, however. Very few people, she pointed out, were brave enough to stand up against the weight of the entire Ton's condemnation.

Bina was in two minds whether to cry off the dinner party she and George were engaged to attend that evening. Her husband persuaded her nothing was to be gained by lowering the flag, so she went off, promising to continue her efforts in the Lisles' behalf. Mrs. Lisle, Kitty, and Millicent spent a dreary evening sewing gowns which might never be needed. Pippa immersed herself in the chimney-sweep speech, which might prove equally futile should Lord Selworth's Gothic proclivities become widely known.

For herself, she would gladly keep his secret and retire to Sweetbriar Cottage, to write her articles for Mr. Cobbett and perhaps to help the viscount a little with future speeches. She could always hope he might occasionally feel the need to consult her in person.

But Kitty deserved better. If she wanted one of the craven wretches who had so meekly deserted her at the dictate of Society, she must have the chance to win him.

So Lord Selworth had to be persuaded to confess his authorship to the world.

Yet, which was more important, Kitty's happiness or the services Lord Selworth might render to the oppressed poor? Not to mention *his* happiness. That night, Pippa tossed and turned for hours, unable to make up her mind. She needed to discuss it with him. She had come to depend on debating issues with him, she realized, on sharing ideas and insights and reaching a deeper understanding together.

He would return to Town in a few days, but by then the Fashionable World might have grown so accustomed to shunning the Lisles that no rehabilitation was possible. If only he had not gone to Yorkshire just now!

The morning brought no new counsel but several more withdrawn invitations. The afternoon brought not a single caller. Pippa had hoped Mr. Chubb's apparent desertion yesterday was due to embarrassment over the to-do with Millicent, but it seemed her first guess was right. He wanted no part of the Lisles' downfall.

Kitty valiantly showed no dismay at the defection of her last remaining suitor.

Bina returned from another round of calls no more optimistic than the day before. "No one was actually rude," she said to Pippa in her private sitting room. "George's parents have consequence enough to prevent that. But I was met everywhere with indulgent disbelief. I am so very sorry, Pippa. I confess, I do not know what else can be done until Wynn comes back."

Pippa recalled Bina's claim to have guessed a secret of her brother's. "You know, do you not?" she asked. "You know Wynn — Lord Selworth — is . . ." She hesitated. Suppose Bina knew some other secret?

"He's Valentine Dred, yes. Absurd name! He used to tell me stories just like the novels, only without the naughty bits which are causing all the trouble. He was the best big brother anyone could possibly have, especially when our father died and Mama remarried. I simply cannot betray him, Pippa, not even for your sake. Can you forgive me?" she pleaded.

"Of course." Pippa hugged her friend. "I find I cannot betray him myself, so how should you?"

Bina took both her hands and looked at her seriously. "I have sometimes wondered . . . No, this is not the time. I know Wynn will do the honorable thing, but it must be his decision. We shall have to wait until he returns."

"I am just afraid people will grow so used to

shunning us that their attitudes will become carved in stone. Not that I care, but for Kitty . . . ! I wish I could go after him and tell him what has happened," Pippa cried, not because she had worked out a useful plan; she simply longed to see him and to lay her dilemma before him. She came down to earth. "However, hiring a post chaise is far too expensive, and on the stage I could not stop to make enquiries."

"As though I should let you! You must take the landau, and one of the maids, with John Coachman to drive you, if you truly believe chasing after Wynn will help."

Pippa tried to think. The prospect of taking action — any action — was tempting. If she found Lord Selworth still in York, he could hurry back to London. If she found him already on the way, he could postpone his visit to his family at Kymford and at least arrive back in Town a little sooner.

Very likely it would make no difference, but she had to try. "I shall go," she said resolutely.

Wynn was rather pleased with himself. As he tooled the curricle down Hampstead Hill, he wondered whether he would have time to tell Pippa all about little Henry before dinner.

No, alas. The sun was setting over the smoky city, and as he reached the foot of the hill, church clocks struck eight. In Charles Street they would be sitting down to dine. He was too late to join them, even had he not been grimed with a long day's road dirt.

Fortunately today was Wednesday, so he knew where to find them this evening. He would drive straight to Albany, have a wash and a bite to eat, don knee breeches, and repair to Almack's. There he could at least tell Pippa he had thoroughly fulfilled her request for all possible details of the child's abduction and subsequent fate.

A note awaited from the Chancellor. His speech had been entered into the House of Lords' calendar. Wynn nearly rushed straight round to Charles Street, but contrived to restrain himself.

Some two hours later, clean, fed, and a trifle puzzled to have learned that Gil Chubb had left town in haste and without explanation, Wynn presented himself at the King Street rooms. His reception puzzled him still more.

Mrs. Drummond Burrell and Countess Lieven, on duty in the anteroom, greeted him graciously enough, but with odd looks. As he moved on, he was conscious of their putting their heads together and whispering behind his back. One or two gentlemen spoke to him overheartily, asking if he had been out of town. Entering the ballroom, he felt himself the cynosure of every eye, the subject of a hundred low-voiced murmurs.

Had he forgotten his stockings, to display hairy shins to the world? No, all present and correct. His neckcloth? He raised a nervous hand, felt the starched folds where they ought to be. To comb his hair? His hair went its own way, always, but was scarcely noticeable among the Windswept and Brutus coiffures of Dandy and Corinthian.

Whatever was wrong, it did not stop the determined advance upon him of a horde of hopeful matrons with marriageable daughters in tow.

Lady Jersey nipped in front and appropriated his arm. "They see you for once unprotected by your sisters," she said tartly, leading him to a pair of chairs in a semisequestered nook.

"Albinia is not here, ma'am?" he asked, disappointed. "They usually arrive early."

"I understand Mrs. Debenham and Miss Warren will not be coming tonight." Lady Jersey gave him a curious look. "Out of sympathy for the Lisles."

Wynn rose in alarm. "They are ill?"

"No, no." The countess tugged him back down by the sleeve. "You have just returned to Town, I collect?"

"An hour since. What has happened? What is amiss?"

"The gabble-grinders have been tearing Miss Lisle to shreds. I have an open mind on the subject, but there is no denying nine-tenths of the world believes she wrote *The Masked Marauder*."

"*What?*" Wynn laughed wildly. "I must be

dreaming. Philippa Lisle as Valentine Dred?"

"That is the *on-dit*." Lady Jersey's inquisitive eyes gleamed. "Naturally, certain of the qualities which have made the book such a success are enough to damn a young lady author, to destroy her reputation forever."

On the instant, Wynn's slightly hysterical amusement turned to cold fury. "Miss Lisle damned on a rumor? 'Fore gad, ma'am," he snarled, "someone shall suffer for this."

"Hush, everyone is staring."

"Let them stare," said Wynn in a ringing voice, standing again and facing the room, "for they are staring at the real Valentine Dred!"

Everyone within earshot fell silent, and those who were not already agape turned to stare. Then they put their heads together, shook them skeptically, muttered, and snickered.

Lady Jersey stood up and put her hand on Wynn's arm. "Come now, Lord Selworth, you are only giving food for further scandal. Everyone knows you are close to the Lisles, that they are your sister's guests. Of course you are honor-bound to do what you can to defend Miss Lisle's reputation."

She had given Wynn time to think. "It should not be necessary to defend her, ma'am," he said reasonably, "if only people would give the matter a little thought."

"Indeed?"

"Consider: The first of Valentine Dred's romances was published eight years ago, when I was still up at Oxford. Miss Lisle is Albinia's age. Eight years ago she was a schoolroom miss of sixteen! Can anyone seriously credit that a mere chit of sixteen, living secluded in a country village, could write such a book?"

Much struck, Lady Jersey nodded. "Which one was that?" she asked.

"*The Heart and the Dagger.*" Wynn grinned. "I hope my titles improved with practice."

"I remember it well. You are right. None but a complete nodcock could believe a schoolroom chit wrote that gory farce. Much more like the work of an undergraduate — the stories, if not the titles, have certainly improved with practice. So you are the author!"

"I am," said Wynn wryly, recalling the pains he had taken to protect his anonymity.

With a raised hand and an imperious gaze, Lady Jersey collected several of her cronies. The work of reestablishing Pippa's good name began.

By the end of the evening, Wynn felt he had convinced enough people that he was Valentine Dred to be sure the news would quickly spread. The few who held out were those who preferred a juicy bit of scandal to the truth, at any cost. The new Viscount Selworth's authorship did not make half so piquant a story as a young lady's disgrace.

Piquant enough, though, to wreck his Parliamentary hopes. Lady Castlereagh had made that quite plain.

Tapping his arm with her fan, the plump, dowdy wife of the Foreign Secretary said amiably, "So you are the naughty man we have all been racking our brains to discover! Castlereagh will be excessively relieved to hear it. He and Lord Liverpool have been quite concerned about you, I collect, and all for nothing!"

Wynn returned to Albany torn between elation at having saved his beloved from public ignominy, and depression at having ruined his prospects of public service.

After spending all day on the road and half the night at Almack's, Wynn slept late the next morning. Having forgotten to tell Clark to wake him, he was annoyed with himself, for he had intended to go early to Charles Street to tell the Lisles the end of their ostracism was in sight.

He ate a quick breakfast and hurried round to his sister's house.

Opening the door to him, the first footman exclaimed, "My lord!" and peered past him into the street. The result of his peering appeared to disappoint him.

Puzzled, Wynn glanced back. A knife-grinder was receding down the street, and a groom held a pair of horses outside one of the houses opposite. What had the footman hoped or expected to see?

"The ladies at home, Reuben?"

"In the drawing room, my lord."

Wynn took the stairs two at a time. As he entered the room, Bina, Millicent, Kitty, even Mrs. Lisle surged to their feet and advanced upon him, all talking at once. The only word he could make out was Pippa's name. They, too, seemed to be looking behind him and to be disappointed by what they did not see.

Indeed, Mrs. Lisle was half-distraught, an alarming sight in a lady usually so serene.

Holding up his hands to still the clamor, he went to her and urged her to sit down on the nearest sofa. He seated himself beside her, took both her hands in his, and said soothingly, "You may be easy, ma'am. I have already refuted the rumors about Miss Lisle, at Almack's last night, and all is in train to set matters to rights. I'm heartily sorry she, and you, landed in the suds on my account."

"On your account?" said Millicent. "But —"

"*I* am Valentine Dred," said Wynn, "as half the *haut ton* knows by now, and the other half will by nightfall."

"You! But —"

"Does Pippa know?" asked Mrs. Lisle eagerly.

"Yes."

"Then at least that explains it!"

"Where is she, ma'am? I must make my apologies to — Explains what?"

"Why she went off to find you, hoping you might be able to alleviate our troubles."

"She what?" Wynn cried, springing to his feet. "When? How?"

"It is my fault," Bina said penitently, "at least in part. She spoke of going by stagecoach to search for you. I could not let her do that, so I offered the landau and John Coachman and a maid. I wish I had not, for she might have realized the impossibility and stayed at home to wait for you."

"But you are back, Lord Selworth," said Kitty, "and Pippa is not. You must have missed each other on the road."

Bina frowned. "She was going to enquire for you along the way, though, Wynn. She must surely have been told you were on your way south, yet you arrived last night in time to go to Almack's and she has not come home."

"Where can she be?" moaned Mrs. Lisle. "How could she go off alone like that?"

"My dear ma'am, she has the Debenhams' coachman and a maid with her." Wynn forced himself to sound calm. "I'm sure she is quite safe and will turn up at any moment, but if she is not here very shortly I shall go and look for her. When did she leave?"

"The day before yesterday," Kitty told him. She took a deep breath, apparently steeling herself to continue: "And the day before that, Mr. —" She stopped, staring at the door. "Pippa!"

Wynn swung round. There she stood, tired, tousled, begrimed, and absolutely the most beautiful sight he had ever seen.

And behind her stood Gilbert Chubb.

"Pippa, my dearest!" Mrs. Lisle rushed to

272

embrace her errant daughter. "Thank heaven you are safe. Where have you been? What happened?"

Pippa kissed her. "Pray let me sit down, Mama. I am quite exhausted. Though Mr. Chubb's gig is excellently sprung" — she smiled over her shoulder at Gil, firing a dart of pure jealousy through Wynn's chest — "a gig is not the vehicle I should choose for a long journey!"

She sank into a chair. Gil, exposed to everyone's gaze, bleated, "Accident!"

"What do you mean, accident?" Wynn demanded. "Where do you come into this?"

Gil turned bright red and threw a pleading glance at Kitty.

"I asked Mr. Chubb to try to find you," she said defiantly. "He told me the author was a friend of his, and I guessed it must be you. I could not bear Pippa to be under a cloud a day longer than need be."

Mrs. Lisle gave her a penetrating look.

"Wynn has already told people he wrote that book, Pippa," Millie said. "He went to Almack's last night and —"

While his sister chattered, Wynn met Pippa's eyes, full of gratitude and regret. "It was the only way," he said softly, knowing she understood what it cost him to protect her.

"But what is this about an accident, my love?" Mrs. Lisle interrupted Millicent, "and why have you been traveling with Mr. Chubb?"

"The landau went into a ditch in the dusk in a narrow lane, after we turned off the Great North Road to go to Kymford."

"That's where we missed each other," Wynn said. "I didn't stop at Kymford on the return journey. I was in a hurry to get back. You were not hurt?"

"Not at all. The wheel of the landau broke, I fear, Bina, and we were some distance from a village where it could be repaired. I cannot tell you how delighted I was when Mr. Chubb turned up and offered to drive me back to London!"

"Couldn't leave you beside the road," Gil exclaimed.

"I am not sure where Kymford is," said Mrs. Lisle. "How long were the two of you traveling together?"

"Since Tuesday evening, Mama. We owe Mr. Chubb for two nights' lodging on the way."

"Oh dear!" Her mother shook her head in dismay. "As I feared. You are hopelessly compromised, Pippa dearest. Mr. Chubb, I know I can rely upon you to do the gentlemanly thing. Come, Kitty."

Somehow, without being quite aware how it had happened, Wynn found himself swept out of the drawing room with the others, leaving Gil and Pippa alone there.

"I shall order refreshments," said Bina. "Wynn, will you take tea or would you prefer Madeira? Or shall I send for champagne, Mrs. Lisle?"

274

His best friend was proposing marriage to his love, and his sister offered him tea or Madeira! Champagne? Pah! "Hemlock," he growled inaudibly.

Turning on his heel, he sprang down the stairs and strode away from the house, his heart in his boots, bleeding with every step.

17

Pippa gaped after her mother, too taken aback to believe she had heard correctly. But there she was, alone in the drawing room with Mr. Chubb.

Who stood with his mouth agape, looking utterly terrified.

"It is quite all right, sir," Pippa said kindly. "I shall not accept, you know."

Hope flared in his eyes. "You won't?"

"No. I do not intend ever to marry. I shall keep Mama company when Kitty is married."

"M-miss Kitty m-married?"

"She is bound to be, you know. Her suitors will flock back now that Lord Selworth has exonerated me. Kitty is not the sort to hold a grudge."

"Not at all," spluttered Mr. Chubb. "Sweetest temper, kindest, most —"

"Exactly," Pippa cut short his paean, "and very pretty, too, so she is certain to marry, even though she has no portion."

"Money! Who cares about money?"

"Well, if one has none . . ."

"Got plenty. M'father's no Chronos — that the fellow I mean?"

"Chronos was a Titan who swallowed his children. I expect you mean Croesus," Pippa

276

suggested, fighting to keep a straight face. "The richest man in the world."

"That's the chap. M'father ain't one, but he's not short of the blunt and he's no nipfarthing. When I marry —"

"Mr. Chubb, you do not need to tell me all this. I promise you, I do not expect an offer."

"B-but Mrs. Lisle relies on me," he said, distressed and uncertain. "Said so."

"Very well, then, make your proposal, and I promise you I shall refuse you."

Awkwardly, Gil Chubb went down on one knee before her. "Miss Lisle," he said earnestly, "it would be a great honor if you would give me your hand. And I mean it, even if I know you won't."

"I am honored by your offer, sir," Pippa said, as gentle as she could be when she wanted to burst into tears, "but I cannot marry where my heart is not given. And nor should you."

"No." He sighed, then heaved himself to his feet with a thoughtful look. "Dashed if you ain't right, ma'am. Dashed if I won't try my luck."

"I cannot say whether Kitty will have you," Pippa warned, "but I shall send her to you." She sped from the room.

A couple of sniffs restored her control of her emotions. She went up to the sitting room, where she found her mother, Bina, and Millicent, but no Kitty.

Millie rushed to meet her. "Are you betrothed? I am so glad everything has worked out so well. I think it is excessively romantic, Mr. Chubb coming to the rescue when you were stranded, but Kitty is quite overset for fear you are forced into a distasteful marriage, though I am sure the heir to a baron must be considered an excellent match and Mr. Chubb is not so very ill-favoured, only a little shy, so I daresay you may be as happy with him as with —"

"I am *not* betrothed, Millie," Pippa said firmly.

"But you are compromised! Mrs. Lisle said so."

"I do not care if I am, but Mama gave us no opportunity to explain. We stayed at small, out-of-the-way inns, where I had a chambermaid sleep in my chamber each night, and we kept off the turnpike, so no one saw us together. I see no need to marry Mr. Chubb. Mama, what were you thinking of to put me in such a position?"

"I had my reasons, dearest." Mrs. Lisle was her usual serene self once more. "I did not for a moment suppose you would accept Mr. Chubb, though I fear Kitty was not so certain."

"Where is she? I told Mr. Chubb I would fetch her to him."

Her mama and Bina exchanged a congratulatory glance. "Locked in your chamber, weeping her heart out," said Bina. "If I am not mistaken, the position your mother put you in forced her to examine her own feelings."

"Mama! I have had reason before now to accuse you of being hardened in deceit, have I not?" Pippa protested, half-cross and half-laughing. "I shall go and tell her he is waiting for her."

Kitty felt as if the world had crashed about her ears. Pippa was to marry Gil Chubb! And all because he had so gallantly agreed to go off on a wild-goose chase, at Kitty's request, to spare her and her family a day or two of infamy.

He was not as dashing as Lieutenant Pendrell, not as romantic as Lord Fenimore, not as handsome as Mr. Carson, as witty as Lord Bellamy, as smart as Lord Edward Stanborough, nor as good a dancer as Mr. George Tarrington. But Kitty could not imagine spending the rest of her life with any of those attractive and eligible gentlemen — even if they had not abandoned her in the time of trouble.

Gil was kind and constant. He was clever and knowledgeable about the things which interested Kitty. Above all, she was always comfortable with him.

And he was to marry Pippa! Tears flowed afresh.

"Kitty, I must speak to you," came her sister's urgent voice through the door.

"C-coming." Kitty blotted her eyes, blew her nose, and tried to prepare herself to offer sincere-sounding felicitations. It was not

279

Pippa's fault she had stolen Gil away. She did not even know Kitty loved him, for she had been at pains to show no preference amongst her suitors.

She unlocked the door, opened it, and was enveloped in a hug before she had time to attempt a smile.

"I am *not* going to marry Mr. Chubb," Pippa said at once. "He is waiting for you in the drawing room, and Mama says you may see him alone — if you wish."

"I wish!" The world sparkling about her, Kitty floated down the stairs, her heart as light as her feet.

Mr. Chubb was standing by the window, fiddling aimlessly with the catch. He turned as Kitty entered the room.

"You came!" he said in some surprise.

"Of course."

He came towards her. "You have been crying," he accused her. "Did your mama make you come down? Is my suit so distasteful? I wouldn't for anything make you cry."

"I was crying because I thought you were going to marry Pippa," she said with a tremulous smile.

His face lit. "Then you won't refuse me?"

"You have not asked me yet," Kitty pointed out demurely.

But the diffident Mr. Chubb enfolded her in a passionate embrace, and it was some time before he actually got around to offering his hand and his heart.

Which Kitty gladly accepted, giving her own in return.

Wynn felt as if the world had crashed about his ears. He had given up his career to save Pippa from ignominy, and she was to wed his best friend!

Of course, had he known in advance that she was lost to him, for her sake he would still have broadcast his authorship. But how was he to face the future without even the prospect of a useful career in Parliament to console him?

Retreat to Kymford to tend his acres was all that was left to him, he supposed. He wouldn't have minded with Pippa at his side. They could have discussed politics at least. She would have helped him decide which Parliamentary debates he should go up to Town for, to add his twopennyworth for whatever good it could do. She might have let him help her with her articles. But all that was over.

Betrothed to Gil — Wynn recalled all the bustle and turmoil attendant upon Bina's betrothal — why should Pippa even go on helping him with his speech, when it had more prospect of being laughed out of the House than of doing any good?

If only he had not been in Yorkshire just when she needed him most! She had been right to send him, though. Speaking to the child himself, and to the compassionate family who had rescued him, had ignited a fire in Wynn to fight for the thousands of little boys who had not escaped.

Dammit, he *would* fight! Between what he had learnt in Yorkshire and what work Pippa had already completed, he would cobble together a speech good enough for the few listeners who were likely to turn up. If all he achieved was to awaken one or two consciences, so be it.

His agitated strides had taken him across Berkley Square and down Bruton Street to Bond Street. He turned south towards Albany.

Bond Street was the wrong place for a notorious gentleman in a hurry to seek the solace of solitude and hard work. Every three paces he was stopped by strolling friends and acquaintances. Carriages halted in the street to allow their occupants to call to him. Shoppers dashed out of shops at the sight of him passing the windows.

The same question was on every tongue: "Is it true you are Valentine Dred?"

"I was."

Dowagers scolded indulgently. Matrons decried his announced intention to write no more. Damsels blushed and giggled. And gentlemen quizzed him, laughing.

As Wynn had expected, he would never again be taken seriously. Somehow he managed to reach Burlington Gardens without losing his temper. Turning off Bond Street, he almost ran to the shelter of his lodgings.

Gil Chubb was not there. A last, unacknowledged seed of hope — that in spite of being compromised Pippa would refuse him — shrivelled. Rejected, he would surely have come home. Accepted, he had stayed in Charles Street to celebrate and make plans.

Wynn sat down at the table in the window, pulling from his pockets the sheaf of Yorkshire notes he had taken to give Pippa. "Damn!" he muttered. He had forgotten he hadn't got her notes for the speech. How long would it be before he could bear to face her and ask for them? He'd send a message through Gil, he decided, if he could ever bear to speak to his friend again.

Running footsteps sounded on the stairs and Gil burst into the room. "Congratulate me!" he cried jubilantly. "She loves me!"

The shrivelled seed died. "I thought you loved Kitty," Wynn said sourly.

Gil blinked. "I do. She is the dearest, sweetest girl in the world!"

"Then why should I congratulate you for being engaged to marry Miss Lisle?"

"You shouldn't. I'm not. We aren't. She won't. It's not Miss Lisle I'm going to marry — it's Miss Kitty."

Somewhere within the seemingly dead seed, life must have lurked, for in a fraction of a second it sprouted, budded, put forth leaves, and burst into bloom. "Not Pippa?"

"Not Pippa," Gil confirmed. "Had to propose to her. Honor of a gentleman, don't you know. Mrs. Lisle said I ought. But Miss Lisle said she don't mind being compromised, ain't planning to marry anyway. She sent Kitty down to me, and I had the whole thing all settled in a trice," he said proudly.

"Congratulations, old fellow!" Wynn said with fervor, jumping up to give him a hearty handshake. "I'm sure Lord and Lady Chubb will be delighted."

"D'you think so?"

"I do. Miss Kitty is amiable, and pretty, and enters fully into all your country concerns. I have never seen two people so well suited."

"Well, I have. You and Miss Lisle. Going to propose to her now?"

Wynn hesitated. "Not yet, I think," he said reluctantly, remembering again the fuss and bother when Bina was betrothed to Debenham. "I have too much on my mind at present — we both do. There is this business of making sure everyone knows she is not Valentine Dred, and dealing with everyone knowing I *am*, and my speech is only ten days away."

Only ten days! With all her own troubles, Pippa might not have been able to put her mind to the troubles of sweeps' boys. If he was going to make the speech at all, he might as well make it as good as possible.

Swinging round, Wynn swept up his papers and stuffed them back into his pocket. "I'm off!" he announced unnecessarily, bolting through the door and down the stairs.

A few minutes later, the first footman opened the Debenhams' door to him for the second time that day.

"Miss . . . m'sister in, Reuben?"

"Mrs. Debenham is in her sitting room, I believe, my lord." The footman looked even more impassive than usual, so much so that Wynn fleetingly wondered what the servants were making of the recent goings-on.

He hurried upstairs. Having asked for Bina, he supposed he had best, for the sake of appearances, at least stick his head into her sitting room to say hello. He knocked on her door.

"Who is it?"

"Wynn."

"Oh, good. Come in. I was just going to write you a note."

"Saying what?" Wynn advanced into the room, where Bina sat at her bureau. "I know Gil and Kitty are engaged."

Bina beamed at him. "Is it not splendid? They are perfect for each other. That was one thing I had to say, though I was sure Mr. Chubb must have told you by now."

"What else?" Wynn asked, a trifle impatiently. He wanted to go to Pippa, and he was just afraid that if he lingered his sister might want to know why he had rushed off in such a hurry when Gil was about to offer for Pippa.

"Well, I have already given the order — request, rather, for one cannot precisely order such a thing — but it can easily be rescinded if you do not like it."

"You sound like Millicent. Cut line, Bina!"

"Millicent is another . . . Do sit down, Wynn, instead of hovering over me like a buzzard."

"What order?" he demanded, sitting.

"Request. No, suggestion. I suggested to my housekeeper that she should delicately pass the word to the staff that it would be no bad thing if they should gossip to other people's servants about you having written *The Masked Marauder.*"

Wynn sighed. "I daresay it's as good as any way to spread the word fast. Your butler and footmen frequent the Running Footman, no doubt, as it is just up the road."

"Yes, and George's valet, too. All the best people's menservants go there, I collect. And the worst scandalmongers seem to place the most credence in what they learn from their servants. You are not angry?"

"No." He shook his head. "If the Ton is busy ripping my dignity to shreds, why shouldn't the servants have their share? What were you going to say about Millie?"

"I thought it might help if she confessed — to a select few — that she started the *on-dit* about Pippa."

"She *what?*" Springing to his feet and starting for the door, Wynn shouted, "I'll wring her neck!"

"Wynn, come back! I phrased that badly. Do come back and calm down. It was all a mistake." Bina explained what their sister had done. "It would not surprise me if someone deliberately twisted her words, someone envious of Kitty's success perhaps."

"If I ever find out who —"

"Unlikely. In any case, now that she is to marry Mr. Chubb, her other suitors will have attention to spare for her rivals, so the jealous cats will have no reason to try to drag her family's name in the mud. So, do you think it will serve to have Millicent explain the origin of the rumors?"

"No, best not. It would undoubtedly embarrass her, which would be fitting punishment, but it would also draw further attention to Pippa's . . . Miss Lisle's writing. Someone might guess the truth."

"You are quite right, best not to have Millie publish to the world that she suspected Pippa because she is forever scribbling."

"Where is she?" Wynn asked, reminded of his speech.

"Wait a minute. Two more points."

"You said you were writing me a note, not a four-page screed."

"Two more points," Bina said firmly. "First, you and I will drive with Pippa and Mrs. Lisle in the Park this afternoon."

"We haven't the time to spare, Miss Lisle and I. My speech is in not much more than a week!"

"You will have to make the time, and for more than that. If we are to reestablish Pippa, she must be seen about as much as possible for the next week or so at least."

Wynn groaned. "If you say so."

"And what is more, you must be nearby, to deflect any attacks. Starting with the *soirée* I am giving tomorrow. It is very short notice, to be sure, but that means if people do not come — and some are certain not to — I can tell Pippa they must be already engaged elsewhere, so she will not be hurt."

"Bless you, Bina." Wynn kissed his sister's smooth brow. "I shall be there. But that makes it the more urgent to get to work. Where is she?"

"Up in the ladies' sitting room, with her mama, writing invitations. Millicent and Kitty are in the drawing room at the same task, as am I now, since I do not have to write to you. I am inviting practically everyone I have ever met, so as to be sure of a good crowd. It will be an informal betrothal party for Kitty and Mr. Chubb. We shall hold a formal one for family and close friends as soon as Lord and Lady Chubb can come up to Town."

"Kitty is not family," Wynn pointed out, purely in the spirit of accuracy, since he had no objection whatsoever to the Debenhams giving a party for her.

"Almost," said Bina cryptically.

As he left, Wynn wondered just what the

deuce she had meant by that.

Pippa was progressing with utmost sloth through her share of the invitations to be written. She kept catching herself gazing out of the window.

Not that there was anything of particular interest out there, just the usual view of the mews, and the backs of the houses in Hill Street, and roofs and chimneypots beyond. She would have had to stand up to look down to the patch of garden below, but in any case she did not see what lay before her eyes. Her mind was elsewhere.

Delighted as she was for Kitty and Mr. Chubb, she could not help wondering whether Mama had also intended her ploy to bring Pippa and Lord Selworth together. If so, it was a dismal failure. He had not even waited to discover the outcome of his friend's proposal to her. Obviously he did not care in the least whom she married.

His noble gesture in relinquishing his political prospects to save her from disgrace was not a sign of his feelings for her, but purely impersonal gallantry. For just a moment, when Millie told her he had revealed his alter ego at Almack's, she had fancied he must have done it for love.

Sheer folly, she sighed, dipping her pen and returning to the list of names and addresses, only to find her attention wandering again a moment later. Would he give up his speech, robbing her of those precious hours together?

Came a tap on the door, and Mrs. Lisle, seated at the large table, called, "Come in."

Lord Selworth entered, looking distinctly harassed. "Mrs. Lisle, Miss Lisle." He bowed slightly. "Will you excuse me, ma'am, if I beg Miss Lisle to give me her assistance at once? Time grows short."

"Of course, Lord Selworth," Mrs. Lisle said cordially, with a smile. "Just allow me to thank you for your promptness in disabusing the Ton of their mistaken apprehensions."

"It was nothing, ma'am. Honor demanded it. A gentleman could do no less."

Not even a generous gesture, Pippa thought. Merely a moral obligation.

"Still, we are vastly grateful," her mother maintained. "Pippa, you had best give me your list. I have nearly finished mine."

"I have not got very far," Pippa said guiltily.

"No matter, my love. You have more important things to do."

With the smile that turned Pippa to jelly, Lord Selworth took her list from her hand and passed it to her mother. Taking some papers from his pocket, he set them before her on the writing table.

Anxious to avoid talking about anything remotely personal, Pippa said eagerly, "Your Yorkshire notes? You mean to proceed with the speech?"

"Yes. I've decided anything I can do to alleviate the lot of those miserable children is worth a try. At worst, no one will come to listen, or only those who come to scoff."

"They may go to scoff, but surely when they hear the horrors you have to tell, they will stay to weep?" Seeing his doubts in his face, Pippa hurried on. "I shall study your notes later. Tell me what you learnt from the Stricklands."

"It seems they were visiting neighbors when a tiny boy, about four years old, came crashing down the chimney and was seriously bruised. They took him home, the master sweep being glad to rid himself of a bungling encumbrance. When he was cleaned up, he turned out to be a handsome little fellow — I met him, by the way, and can vouch for his looks. Whether the Stricklands would have taken such an interest in an ill-favored child, I cannot tell."

"Perhaps not," Pippa said soberly, "but let us allow them the benefit of the doubt. What is his name?"

"Henry. He's well-spoken, too, clearly from a prosperous family, as the Stricklands guessed when he saw a silver fork and cried out in delight that his papa had such forks. Other things also were 'just like Papa's.' He knows the Lord's Prayer and will not get into bed without repeating it, but unfortunately he is too young to know his surname — or was when he was stolen away."

"He was abducted, then?"

291

Lord Selworth nodded. "The Stricklands pieced the story together. His mother died and his father went abroad, 'across the sea,' leaving him with his uncle, of whom he was very fond. He was picking flowers in Uncle George's garden one day. A woman came by, asked if he liked riding, took him up on her horse, and carried him off."

Pippa shuddered. "So easily! Enough to give any parent nightmares. And the House of Lords is made up of parents. The Stricklands could not find his family?"

"He comes from southern England, to judge by his accent. He says he and the woman sailed to Yorkshire by ship."

"I daresay he thought he was going to join his papa."

"Very likely," Lord Selworth agreed. "According to the master sweep, it was in Yorkshire that the woman sold him the child. The Stricklands advertised in southern newspapers, without success."

"I am very sorry for the poor little boy, but, you know, from the point of view of your speech, it is better that he will never see his family again. Or rather, that they will never see him. Too happy an ending would lessen the impact on all those noble fathers and grandfathers. What is to become of Henry?"

"A friend of the Stricklands will adopt him and educate him," said Lord Selworth with satisfaction.

"I am so glad, but I believe we shall leave his fate up in the air. Let us hope his story helps to alleviate the lot of all those other unhappy mites. It will fit perfectly into what I have already prepared."

"You have contrived to work on my speech in spite of . . . your recent difficulties?"

"Oh yes," Pippa said dryly, "I have had all the time in the world with no parties to go to, scarcely daring to leave the house for fear of being snubbed. It is not a pleasant sensation." She shivered. "I must confess, grateful as I am to Bina, I positively dread tomorrow's *soirée*."

18

Pippa dressed with the utmost care next evening. She wore her emerald green crepe, remade to open down the front over a white satin under-dress, the set-on ivy leaves replaced with white silk roses. Instead of the fashionably brief pale green bodice, it now had a white one with a rather higher neckline, trimmed with emerald ribbons. For tonight, modesty was the watch-word, but it must not be so blatant it became an obvious attempt to belie the immodesty attrib-uted to her.

Fastening her locket about her neck, Pippa prayed that all the efforts to restore her to favor would not be in vain. The stitchery; the writing of invitations and running of footmen to deliver them; the magnificent refreshments provided by Gunter's at a moment's notice; George Debenham's noble sacrifice of the best wines in his cellar; all would go for naught if the Ton re-fused to accept her innocence.

Mama and Kitty would be devastated. Per-haps Lord Chubb would make his son break off the engagement. The Lisles would have to re-treat to the country to lick their wounds in ob-scurity, leaving the Debenhams no choice but to repudiate their guests in order to regain their own position.

As Pippa descended the stairs with Kitty and Millicent, Lord Selworth and Mr. Chubb were admitted to the house. Mr. Chubb had flowers for Kitty, the viscount two nosegays, for Pippa and his younger sister.

"You look particularly lovely this evening," he said to Pippa, presenting a posy of white rosebuds.

She scarcely heard him. Her looks were irrelevant tonight. "Thank you," she said automatically, then voiced the only thought her mind was at present capable of accommodating: "What if no one comes?"

But everyone came. Had everyone come at once, Mrs. George Debenham's party would have been not a "dreadful squeeze," an accolade, but an unbearable crush. However, most people had prior engagements, so they came before, or after, or in between.

Those who apologised for giving credence to false rumor could be counted on the fingers of one hand. Some, like Mrs. Drummond Burrell, brazened it out as if they had never given the Lisles the cut direct. Some, like the Pendrells, were shamefaced and would not quite meet Pippa's eye. Some, like Lady Stanborough, were overeffusive when they complimented Mrs. Lisle on her younger daughter's splendid match.

To Pippa's relief, though few guests were so embarrassed as to avoid her altogether, Kitty was the focus of attention. Less satisfactory was the attention Lord Selworth received.

He stayed near her all evening, ready to spring to her defence if necessary, so she could not but notice the way the gentlemen chaffed him about his books. In spite of his prophecies of disaster, she had hoped he might still be taken seriously as a politician. Dismayed, she realized it was now highly unlikely his unconventional views would receive a respectful hearing.

As he said, all they could do was to make his speech as brilliant as possible, regardless of the probable outcome.

Delighted as he was to see his love no longer an outcast, Wynn wished her sister's disappointed suitors would leave her alone. Whether they wanted to make reparation for having snubbed the family, or, no longer blinded by Kitty's more obvious attractions, they had discovered Pippa's quiet charm, they flocked about her.

"She was engaged in advance for every single dance last night," Wynn grumbled to Gil one morning.

"Eh? What's that?" Gil went around in a revoltingly blissful daze these days.

"I said, Miss Lisle didn't stand up with me even once last night."

"You should ask her the day before. Or better still, pop the question. There's nothing like it, old chap, simply nothing like it. You can dance with her all night and no one gets in a pother."

Wynn grunted. He was not ready yet to propose. In fact, though he loved her more each day, he was less ready than ever, in spite of his jealousy of her new admirers.

They were part of the problem. Whereas before he had at least been able to tell himself that he had little competition, now he had a lot. This one was richer than Wynn, that one handsomer, one of higher rank, another the very image of elegance, another the height of *savoir faire*.

What Wynn had hoped to offer Pippa was the opportunity to support and share in a political career devoted to the principles they held in common. He might as well ask her to buy a gold mine in Peru as beg her to enter upon a betrothal without knowing whether he had a career before him or not.

Suppose no one came to hear him? Or suppose the peers were kind enough to attend despite his notoriety as a trifling creator of frivolous fictions — and he made a mull of her brilliant speech?

In spite of her new popularity, Pippa found time to work hard with him on the speech, and that it was brilliant he had no doubt. She played every note of pathos, every sharp of terror, every flat of despair, with a sure ear, never overornamenting the tune as he was still wont to do.

If Wynn did it justice, the House of Lords ought to end up weeping bucketfuls. He was just afraid that, while they might howl into their handkerchiefs, it would be with laughter, not tears.

He pushed away his breakfast half-finished and turned once more to conning his speech.

The day after tomorrow . . .

The petition to abolish the employment of climbing boys was presented to the House of Commons that afternoon. Despite its thousands of signatures, it aroused little interest among gentlemen more concerned with putting down the uprisings of desperate men across the country. The harvest promised well, but would it be enough to make up for last year's deficit? Would the mills start rolling again in time to prevent revolution?

The torment of several hundred, even thousands, of small boys was of little importance in comparison with the torment of a nation.

The Commons found time, however, to crowd into the Upper House that evening to listen to the maiden speech of a new member of that august body. Viscount Selworth was an author of novels; more, an author of Gothic romances which were ribald as well as funny and thrilling, said those who had read them. His speech should be worth hearing.

The noble lords were apparently of the same opinion, for every seat on the red leather benches was filled. To Wynn, rising to his feet upon the invitation of the Lord Chancellor, the room was a sea of heads, an ocean of pale faces all agog.

He took a deep breath and launched his words, Pippa's words, upon that sea, fragile lifeboats to save yet more fragile children from drowning in misery.

"My lords, gentlemen, . . ."

Thanks to Pippa, he had no need to resort to his notes, yet he had not studied so much as to render the matter stale. He spoke with fire and passion, the horrors of a climbing boy's life vivid in his mind as the periods rolled from his tongue. Lords and Commons alike, they hung upon his words. A collective gasp went up when he spoke of little Henry, torn from the wealthy family he would see no more.

Not so short as to seem unimportant, not so long as to bore the audience — and then, closing with a final plea to end the unnecessary suffering, it was over. With a slight bow, Wynn dropped exhausted to his seat.

The Whig lords crowded round, shaking his hand, slapping him on the back, congratulating him, lauding his eloquence. As they eventually began to drift away, some of the Tory lords took their place. Even the Prime Minister and the Lord High Chancellor approached Wynn to present their stiff, cool compliments.

"How soon can a bill be presented?" Wynn asked eagerly.

"Oh, as to that," said Liverpool, "the agenda is already overfull, is it not, Eldon?"

The Chancellor agreed. "No knowing when we shall be able to prorogue," he said testily.

"After all," put in Lord Lauderdale, "affecting as was your tale of the child Henry, there are only one or two cases of the sort. I for one am not acquainted with anyone who has had a child abducted, are you, my lords?"

The rest of the noble gentlemen nearby shook their heads.

"As for the rest," Lauderdale continued, "they are guttersnipes who if they were not engaged in an honest trade would be out on the streets a-begging — or picking our pockets!"

Amid laughter, the group broke up.

Furious, Wynn strode out to the lobby. Half an hour had passed since his speech ended, and the Commons had long since returned to their chamber. No doubt by now they had forgotten all about him.

A page boy stopped him. "Lord Selworth? Mr. Bennet, m'lord, he told me to beg you to wait a while till he can have a word with your lordship. The gallery's that way, my lord, if you was to wish to go up."

Wynn hesitated. He was in no mood to be polite, nor to lounge about waiting. He wanted to hurry back to Charles Street to acquaint Pippa with his success and his failure. On the other hand, he did not want the Radical Commoners to think him too top-lofty to care for their opinions of the speech.

He turned to head for the stairs to the gallery, just as the doors of the Commons chamber opened and Henry Grey Bennet came out. With him were Brougham and Burdett and two or three others.

Bennet saw Wynn. "Selworth! Well met. I was just coming to look for you. Any luck with the Lords?"

"None," Wynn fumed. "Oh, they liked the speech."

"Damn good speech," put in Brougham. "I'd be hard put to it to do better myself, and I'm not sure I wouldn't bet on you against Orator Hunt, if you weren't on the same side, more or less."

"Thank you," Wynn said, "but what's the use of speaking well if you can't persuade anyone to take action? They don't care a rap for the agonies of mere guttersnipes."

"They may not," said Burdett, "but we do. And what's more, you have talked enough Members into caring to pass a vote to set up a Select Committee to study the question. Congratulations!"

As the others added their congratulations, Wynn's spirits soared.

"It's a small first step," Bennet warned, "but I'm to be chairman of the committee, and I'll see its findings don't gather dust in a corner. Come, let's go and drink to your achievement and the abolition of climbing boys! Tell me, is it true you had Prometheus' help in drafting the speech? There are others who could do with his help."

Parrying questions about Prometheus, Wynn accompanied his friends to the Blue Boar to celebrate.

Pippa was on tenterhooks. She knew exactly how long Wynn took to deliver his oration. He ought to have finished an hour ago, but he did not come.

She made allowances for a late start. Perhaps it would take him a while to escape afterwards if everyone wanted to talk to him, to congratulate him. He did not come.

As time passed, she grew more and more certain that the speech had been an abject failure. Wynn was reluctant to face her and tell her he had made a mull of it. Or he had delivered it perfectly, but what had seemed so clever in the sitting room in Charles Street turned out to be hopelessly inappropriate for the House of Lords. He did not want to tell her she had wrecked his chances.

It was time to change for dinner, and still he did not come. Pippa was in two minds: Should she go and hide in her chamber lest he arrive with a tale of disaster? Could she bear to be in the middle of dressing and thus unavailable if he turned up in need of comfort?

Her mother chased her upstairs. "My love, your sitting and moping will not alter matters for better or worse," she pointed out. "I daresay he will come in time for dinner. Your papa was wont to say nothing gave him such an appetite as making a speech."

As soon as she was upstairs, Pippa knew she wanted to be downstairs. Not waiting for Nan's help, she flung on the first evening gown which came to hand, though she had decided days ago that the azure crepe, made over from one of Bina's, did not become her. She unpinned her hair, swiftly ran a comb through it, and hurriedly pinned it up again.

"That is a mess," said Kitty. "It is going to fall down any moment. Let me do it for you."

"No, it does not matter. We are staying at home this evening and not expecting visitors."

"Except Gil and Lord Selworth," Kitty reminded her unnecessarily as she departed.

If he came. Where was he?

Pippa went down to the drawing room. At least she would not have to go out and dance, nor even stay in and try to help entertain guests. Mama and Bina had decided a quiet evening at home was a good idea after all the gallivanting of the past ten days, besides giving Lord Selworth a chance to tell them all about his speech.

If he came. Pippa went over to the window and looked out, just in time to see Gil Chubb arriving. Alone.

She heard Gil's knock on the door, his voice as he spoke to the butler, his feet on the stairs.

Turning from the window, she was moving towards the door when he came in.

He glanced swiftly around the room. Seeing no one else there, he said, "Congratulations, Miss Lisle!"

"Congrat— ? It went well?"

"Brilliantly. Almost had me in tears. I was up in the gallery, of course. Could have heard a pin drop while Wynn was talking — well, almost." He frowned dubiously. "Don't know if you could have heard a pin drop while he was actually talking."

"But they listened? Were many there?"

"Place was full to bursting. All the Commons came in, too. A good half of 'em, anyway. You should have seen 'em crowding round him afterwards — the Lords — patting his back and shaking his hand. A grand success." Puzzled, he added, "He hasn't come to tell you?"

"No," said Pippa bluntly. "You have not seen him since?"

"Missed him somehow at Westminster Hall, what with all the people swarming about. He'll be here any minute, I expect."

Kitty came in then and distracted Gil's attention. Pippa went on hoping Lord Selworth would arrive at any moment right until they all went in to dinner.

Then she began to grow angry.

Rearranging the food on her plate to pretend she was eating, she let Millie's chatter wash over her unheard as she racked her brains to think why he should stay away. Only one answer came to mind. Now that his speech had proved a triumph, he did not want to acknowledge her part in writing it. He wanted all the glory for himself.

Pippa neither expected nor desired any public glory. She did not want Lord Selworth's gratitude — she had worked for herself and for the climbing boys as much as for him. But she did want to know he appreciated her help and recognized its value. Here, where all but Millicent knew she was Prometheus, he would have to share the honors.

So he did not come.

At long last dinner ended. The ladies arose to leave George Debenham and Gil Chubb to an undoubtedly brief session with their port. Pippa was telling the truth when she murmured to her mother that she had the headache.

"Go to bed, my love, and I shall bring a tisane."

"It is not bad enough to need rest, only quiet. I shall go up to the sitting room."

Mama nodded understandingly. "I am certain there is an explanation," she said.

Indeed there was, and Pippa had guessed it. By now he had probably persuaded himself it was all his own doing. After all, when it came to politics, what had a mere female to offer?

The others went into the drawing room. Pippa continued up the stairs to the sitting room, where she slumped into an easy chair. Tears pricked her eyelids, but she refused to let them flow. Crying would only worsen her headache, and he was not worth it.

How could she have believed he was different from all the rest, that he respected her talents and was glad to see her make use of them? No doubt all along — or at least since he guessed she was Prometheus — he had told himself he was humoring her while he did all the real work. He was deluding himself, as he would discover when he tried without her, but nine hundred and ninety-nine men out of a thousand contrived to delude themselves that they were superior beings.

Only Papa was different. Even Mr. Cobbett had not liked to admit that a woman was capable of taking on the mantle of Prometheus. Only his friendship for Benjamin Lisle had persuaded him to consider Pippa's articles, though once convinced of their value he remained a staunch friend.

A letter from him, from America, had arrived yesterday, when Pippa was too busy putting the final touches to the dastardly viscount's speech to pay much attention. Now she needed something to distract her thoughts.

She went to sit at the desk, unlocked the drawer, and took out Mr. Cobbett's letter. Holding it so as to catch the fast fading light from the window, she reread it. He intended to resume publication of the *Political Register*, writing from America, and he wanted Pippa to start writing articles again. What should she write about? Her mind was still full of chimney sweeps.

Chimney sweeps and Wynn Selworth. Again she felt the prickling of tears, tears of anger, not of heartache, she told herself.

She concentrated on the view. Chimneypots silhouetted against a dusky pink sky, so many chimneypots, every one needing to be swept, every one an instrument of torture to a small, terrified child. She would start an article with that view, and lead on from climbing boys to other injustices equally capable of solution by men of goodwill.

Men like Wynn Selworth. How could someone of such generous principles prove so perfidious? And having betrayed her, would he next betray his principles?

Pippa sat musing unhappily, the twilight deepening about her. When she heard the door open behind her and a soft glow suffused the room, she assumed Mama or Bina had sent a footman up with a branch of candles.

"Thank you," she said without turning.

"Wrong way round," said a slurred voice. "I've come to thank *you*."

"Wynn!" Pippa swung round. "Lord Selworth, I mean."

"Wynn'll do nicely." He stood leaning against the doorpost, his flaxen hair in wild disarray, cravat loosened, candelabra in hand.

"I thought you were a footman," she said inanely.

"Met him on the stair. Said I'd bring you this." Beaming, Lord Selworth gestured with the candelabra. As candles wobbled and flames flickered and flared, Pippa sprang to rescue it. "Sorry. A trifle bosky — just a trifle, mind!"

"You had best sit down." She took the candelabra to the desk and set it down.

He was close behind her. "Come and sit with me," he begged, taking her hand and tugging her over to a sofa. "Got a lot to say to you. Lots and lots."

The hours of anxiety burst forth. "Then why did you not come sooner?" Pippa demanded angrily, withdrawing her hand from his clasp.

"Tried. Tried and tried and tried. Every time I got to the door, someone else came in, same thing all over again. Congrat— you know, drink to your success — my success, that is, only *your* success, too. Pro-me-the-us," he said with great care. "All his doing. Yours. Had a deuce of a time answering all their questions."

"You did not tell them who I am? Who Prometheus is?"

"Not *that* bosky. Anyway, wouldn't give you away if I was drunk as a wheelbarrow. Want to keep you. All for myself."

He recaptured her hand. However bosky he was, his smile was the same as ever, and had the same effect on Pippa.

"Wh-what do you mean?" she faltered.

Lord Selworth looked surprised. "Marry you," he said. "Marry me. Pippa, do say you'll marry me. Be a viscountess, and it's the only way I'll be sure of an endless supply of brilliant speeches. Do say you will."

It was exactly what she wanted, was it not? A gentleman who truly appreciated her abilities and was not reluctant to admit it. So why the sinking feeling, as if her heart were heavy enough to plunge all the way to the tips of her blue kid slippers? Why the catch in the throat, making it impossible to speak, to accept Lord Selworth's flattering offer?

"Dash it, I nearly forgot." He slid from the sofa and thumped to his knees before her. "I adore you, you know. Life won't be worth living if you won't marry me. I've loved you for ages and ages and ages . . ."

Gazing into his hopeful, slightly bloodshot blue eyes, Pippa knew he spoke the truth. Touching his lips with her finger to stop the string of "ages," she murmured, "Oh Wynn, I have loved you for simply ages, too," and she kissed him.

Historical Note

Henry Grey Bennett's Select Committee produced a bill to abolish the use of climbing boys, but there was no time for a hearing that session. The following year, 1818, the bill passed the Commons. In the Lords, Lord Lauderdale made a funny speech which killed it.

Though the practice gradually decreased, little boys continued to be forced up chimneys until it was at last banned in 1875.